Slick

Slick

Brenda Hampton

www.urbanbooks.net

Urban Books, LLC
97 N18th Street
Wyandanch, NY 11798

ISBN 13: 978-1-60162-707-0
ISBN 10: 1-60162-707-6

First Trade Paperback Printing November 2014
Printed in the United States of America

10 9 8 7 6 5 4 3 2 1

Distributed by Kensington Publishing Corp.
Submit Wholesale Orders to:
Kensington Publishing Corp.
C/O Penguin Group (USA) Inc.
Attention: Order Processing
405 Murray Hill Parkway
East Rutherford, NJ 07073-2316
Phone: 1-800-526-0275
Fax: 1-800-227-9604

Slick

by

Brenda Hampton

INTRODUCTION

SYLVIA

Jonathan Tyrese Taylor was what I called a true gift from God. He had it going on all the way around, and my girlfriend, Dana, couldn't ask for anything more. Thing was, she was unaware of what kind of man she had. Jonathan went over and above the call of duty for her, but the appreciation she showed him wasn't worth a damn. Every time I put my two cents in, she told me to mind my own business. Maybe I should have, or maybe I shouldn't have, but what were best friends for? I thought I was supposed to be the one to tell her when things weren't right, or when I thought she was making a big mistake. Hell, she told me when I was, but when it came to Dana, her business was her business. I tried not to interfere, but I just couldn't help myself. We'd been friends since the second grade at Black Jack Elementary, and I knew her better than anybody. We'd always had each other's backs, but lately I was feeling as if we were losing touch.

Married to Jonathan for almost ten years, Dana had been seeing a twenty-two-year-old nobody, Lewis Mc-Farlin, for the past three years. A secret only Dana and I shared, though we knew better. Lewis worked with me, and, yes, his smile was to die for. His skin was silky brown smooth, and his body was cut in all the right places. My coworkers said he was hooked up—body tight and ass right. From those who had the opportunity to be with him, they said a sista would die for a second date. Other than the "ohhh you make me wanna holla" sex they claimed he dished out, through my eyes, he seemed to be a true waste of time. I told Dana time and time again about all of the rumors, but she didn't seem to care. She said Lewis and she had a lot in common, so his sleeping with other women didn't bother her.

Lewis worked in the mailroom at Duncan, Taylor & Bradford, a law firm in Clayton where Jonathan and I worked together. Every day, Lewis strolled his mail cart around, smiling in our faces like everything was all good. From what Dana told me, the brotha was struggling to make ends meet. In my opinion, if he'd stop sleeping with so many females and chill out on having babies, maybe he'd keep some money in his pockets. Dana said he was always complaining about taking care of his four kids, and whenever he fell short on his child support payments, she helped him out. I told her that was bull, especially when she wasn't even working. She took money from Jonathan's account to provide for another person. That didn't make any sense at all. All of this mess drove me crazy, but there was no way in hell I was going to betray Dana and tell Jonathan what was really going down. He had to find out on his own. I thought he suspected something, but he was so wrapped up into making money that nothing else seemed to catch his attention.

Sometimes, I found myself thinking about what being with a man like Jonathan Taylor would be like. He was smart, made mega money as a lawyer, and could wear the heck out of any suit when he slid his thick, tall body into it. A deep, dark brown chocolate, all the women in our office went crazy over him. But since most of them knew my connection with Dana, they stood clear. Jonathan barely gave any of us a second look. He laughed when he heard our comments and brushed them off.

Being the true gentleman he was, when I was laid off from my previous job, he hooked up a job for me as his secretary. I didn't start giving him any attention until Dana started cheating on him. I always thought he was my kind of man, but I always knew he was hands off. Lately, though, I'd been feeling sorry for him. When he strolled in every morning, I waited to see what type of mood he was going to be in. I could always tell when things were a bit shaky at home because he immediately closed the door to his office and I wouldn't hear a peep out of him. Then Dana would start ringing the phone, asking me all kinds of questions about his demeanor.

Bottom line: someday, all of this mess was going to hit the fan. The truth would come to the light, and when it did, I hoped I was nowhere to be found. But if I was, I was going to have the pleasure of watching Dana squirm herself out of this mess. It wasn't that I was hoping to see her lose out on a good thing, but what goes around comes around. If she had to pay for what she'd done, I didn't care how much love I had for her, she deserved whatever it was that she had coming. Especially since I warned her. I tried over and over again to tell her what a good man she had. I reminded her every day how many women would love to be in her shoes. Thing was, she thought that every man was a sucker for a light-skinned, big-breasted, thin woman with long, bouncing, and behaving hair and green eyes. I admitted, over the years, some men had played the fools, but then there were those who hadn't catered to her snobby, sometimes selfish and uppity ways. Those were the brothas who liked women with a little more meat on their bones and with a better attitude. That, of course, would be the darker sistas, such as myself, who know the blacker the berry, the sweeter the juice. And once you go this black, you'll never go back. I was a living witness to that. Every man who came my way always came again.

I was sort of on lockdown right now because this fool, Marlin, tried to stalk me after I told him it was over. He was cool, but he was too cool. He was all up in my business, and whenever I had to work late, he'd be lurking at my door waiting for me. That shit drove me crazy. How about, "I'll just call you when I get home?" It didn't make sense for a fine brotha like him to be clowning like that. His dick was good, and I truly missed it, but I could for surely do without all the insecurities that came attached.

In the meantime, I was keeping my eyes on Jonathan and making sure none of these other hoochie mamas dug their claws into him. Dana knew I was looking out for what was in her best interest, because if I wasn't, I would have told him the scoop a long time ago. I hoped she appreciated a friend like me because most women would have loved to have me in their corner. If she would have taken my advice and stopped spending her money and time on that low-life fool, Lewis, she'd have been all right with me.

JONATHAN

Stress, stress, and more stress was all I'd been feeling lately. Between my job, my sixteen-year-old daughter, Britney, and my wife, I couldn't say who had been stressing me the most. Sometimes, I felt like running away from it all. I knew that would never happen because I worked too hard to get to where I was today, I loved my daughter, and my wife meant everything in the world to me. Thing was, though, sometimes, I didn't quite understand my unhappiness. I put in long hours at work so my family could have the finer things in life, but then there was no time for enjoyment. And when I thought there would be time, something always came up and I had to go handle my business.

My wife, Dana, complained constantly about not spending "quality" time together, but I gave her as much quality time as I could. If she wasn't complaining about our minimal time together, she was bitching about not having enough money to do what she desired to do. I was straight up in a no-win situation. Damned if I did, and damned if I didn't. Dana had threatened many times to leave me, but I knew better. She could never make it without me. She was too lazy to get a job, and since day one, she looked for someone who could provide for her. Who could blame her, coming from a wealthy family where daddy's little girl had everything she always wanted?

Sometimes, I could shoot myself for falling in love with her, but then there were times that I loved her to death. Like when she surprised me with candlelit dinners or she took me on surprise vacations and fucked my brains out. Just last week, she knew I had to work late and she came to my office with a little of nothing on and freaked me down. That was the Dana I loved. She was a beautiful woman, and most of the time, I was proud to have her as my wife. It was the times when she was yakking on the phone with her girlfriends, and running the streets on the weekends that drove me crazy. I asked her all the time, if she was married, then what in the hell was keeping her in the streets so much? It didn't make sense to me, but maybe since there was a ten-year difference between us, maybe she still had some things she wanted to explore.

Running the streets was over for me a long time ago. I wrapped that up after I got married to Dana. When my career took off, I had to leave the street life behind me. Normally, if I wasn't working on the weekends, I was at home chilling. I didn't really trip too much about Dana going out because I trusted her. I trusted her to come home at a decent hour, to never bring me any drama from another brotha, and to respect me for as long as we were married.

A part of me suspected that she was seeing someone else, though, but I'd never been the type of man to chase after a woman, not even my wife. What was meant for me to know I would definitely know. And since I was just speculating, I refused to go out and throw myself at other women. Now, there were some beautiful women I worked with, and they would have loved the opportunity to be with a man like me. But for now, Dana had me all to herself.

Even her friend, Sylvia, looked at me like she could tear a brotha up. From what I could tell, and according to Dana, Sylvia had so much drama in her life that it was ridiculous. Five years ago, right after her husband was killed in a car accident, she lost her job. I felt sorry for her and asked her to work for me, since my secretary was on her way out. It was a good move for me because Sylvia definitely knew her shit. She was always on time, I didn't have to ask her to do things over and over again, and whenever I asked her to work overtime she never complained. I thought she would take advantage of this situation, being like family and all, but she hadn't. She said that since I came through for her, she would continue to come through for me. That was a good thing, and my only gripe was when she was on lengthy phone calls with Dana, or when she was yelling at one of her male companions about something. Normally, I just stood in the doorway to my office and stared at her. After that, she knew what action to take and that was to put a halt to her conversation.

Sylvia was an attractive woman, so I didn't understand the brothas she chose to date. She was always asking me for advice, and I recently went with her to obtain a restraining order against a man who was stalking her. I took her home one night and there he was standing at her door, smoking a cigarette, and looking as if he'd lost his mind. When he saw me, he really started acting a fool. I calmed his ass down and told him to chill. Later, I asked Sylvia what made a brotha act that way and she said it was all about the pussy. I might have known a little about that, too, since my friends seemed to think I was whipped by Dana's pussy. But stalking a woman was truly uncalled for. No man should ever have to stoop that low, especially when there was plenty enough to go around.

And, yes, I'd had my share of pussy. It set me back a few times, but the best thing that came out of it was my daughter, Britney. She was sixteen, but going on twenty-five. I hadn't a clue what I was going to do with her because she was off into her own jacked-up world. Britney's mother, Beverly, had no control over her. She was always calling me to discipline Britney, but if she would have let Britney stay with me from the beginning, like I asked her to, things wouldn't be as bad as they were now.

Before I met Dana, Beverly and I dated for a while. I planned on marrying her, but somehow Dana just managed to steal my heart away. I could have done the right thing by marrying my baby's mama, but I just wasn't feeling Beverly enough to marry her. The only reason we somewhat got along now was because of Britney. I kept my conversations with Beverly short. We could never stay on the phone for more than five minutes without cursing each other out or blaming each other for Britney's mistakes. Bottom line was I knew Britney was probably screwed up because of all the shit Beverly and I had been through. That was why I tried to understand Britney's aggressive and bad behavior. Beverly blamed me and insisted that if I had married her, we would all be one big, happy family and everything would be cool. I rejected that notion, but since she was the kind of woman who thought she knew everything, I just let it be.

Hopefully, soon, everything would work itself out. I knew life could sometimes be difficult, but I hoped things would get better. But if it didn't, I was the kind of man who had no problem packing up my shit and moving on.

1

SYLVIA

When Jonathan came in, Jackie, Audrey, and I were sitting around running our mouths. He didn't say good morning or anything, just walked right past us, went into his office and closed the door. That only meant one thing: the brotha was in a shitty mood. All we got on a Monday morning was a whiff of his addictive cologne and a glimpse of his dark brown Brooks Brothers suit that fit his broad, thick shoulders and his fine ass to a capital T. It was a shame that we didn't even get a smile, but I was starting to get used to his behavior. Mondays and Tuesdays were pretty much the same. On Wednesdays, he was somewhat perking up. Thursdays were always up in the air. But Fridays were always good days because it was payday. Usually, I didn't give him much attention on Fridays because I was excited about finally having some money in my pockets.

When the phone rang, we all looked at each other, knowing what time it was. Dana was calling to check up on her man, so Audrey and Jackie glared at me, rolled their eyes then walked away. I sat at my desk and answered the phone.

"He ain't here yet, Dana," I said.

"Quit lying, Sylvia. You know darn well he is."

"No, seriously, he's not. But as soon as he comes in, I'll call to let you know."

"Come on, girl. Why do you be holding back on your best friend like that?"

"Because, you need to stop bringing him so much grief. Must you have his butt walking in here every Monday morning looking like he lost his dog?"

"For your information, Jonathan brings it upon himself. All I did was ask for some money, like I do every Monday morning before he goes to work. I like to plan my week out, and I can't do so if I don't have any money. I told him I'm tired of hearing his lectures about how much money I spend and he got mad."

"That's why you need your own money. That way you can spend all the money you want to on Lewis's broke ass."

"F you, okay. I don't spend my money on Lewis, so stop saying that before Jonathan hears you."

"You're right, it's not your money, but, whatever, that's your business. Anyway, I'll call you around lunch. If my timing is correct, your husband will be opening up his door in about two minutes demanding something from me. If you keep on acting a fool, I might decide to put a smile on his face for the week."

"Sorry, honey, but he was smiling his behind off last night. By noon, he'll be thinking about what I put on him and I'm sure he'll come to his senses. In the meantime, I won't be around for lunch. I'm meeting Lewis, so I'll call you later tonight."

"Good-bye, hoochie mama. And tell that nasty-dick Negro to use a condom if y'all decide to skip lunch and shoot for something else. He already spreading enough diseases and he got enough babies he can't take care of as it is."

"Sylvia, jealousy will get you nowhere. Please tell my husband I love him and I'll see him later."

"Will do, Miss Trifling. And expect for it to be real late because this pile on my desk ain't going nowhere anytime soon."

"Good-bye, Miss Hater," Dana said then hung up.

I shook my head and put the phone down. Dana was playing with fire. I loved her to death, but I was truly worried about the outcome of this mess she'd gotten herself into. She didn't even listen to me anymore, but I still had to come down hard on her because I cared.

I prepared Jonathan's calendar for the week and after twenty minutes into it, I noticed he still hadn't come out of his office. A bit worried, I straightened my navy blue short skirt and walked over to his office door. Before I knocked, I unbuttoned a few buttons on my multicolored silk blouse and rubbed my weaved-in, long hair back with my hands. As I stood trying to get myself together, Jonathan quickly swung the door open.

"I'm sorry. I . . . I was coming to see if you were okay," I stuttered.

"I'm fine," he said, putting the doorstopper underneath the door. "Come on in and have a seat."

"Before we get started, would you like some coffee?"

"Once I tell you what I need from you today, then you can get it."

I sat down and crossed my healthy legs so he could get a glimpse of them. "So, what is it that you need from me today, Jonathan?"

He let out a deep sigh and tapped his pen on the desk. "First, I need for you not to be lollygagging in front of my office with your coworkers every morning. This is a place of business, not a time to socialize with your lady friends. You get one hour for lunch, two thirty-minute breaks, and that's plenty of time for you all to chat."

"Fine, Jonathan. If you want me to sit around cooped up at that desk and not talk to anyone, then I will. This is not the first time you've complained about it; however, I really don't see what the problem is if you're not even in the office yet."

"The problem, Sylvia, is I'm working late nights because there's so much work to be done. If you get to the office before I do, take the initiative to get started on things early. The time you spend out there running your mouth, you could have had my calendar completed for the week and on my desk when I got here."

Furious, because I worked harder than anybody in this whole place did, I stood up and went to my desk to get his calendar. I walked back into his office and tossed it on his desk.

"Communication is the key, mister," I said sharply. "How do you expect me to have things right for you and you barely even say hello when you come through the door? I'm not a mind reader, Jonathan, and I'm not going to allow you to dump on me because you got problems."

"All right, calm down," he said, knowing I was upset. "I don't need you getting all emotional and loud up in here so close the door."

I closed the door and gave Jonathan a quick grin before I sat in the chair, just to let him know that everything was all good between us.

"Go ahead and smile," he said, smiling at me with his to-die-for smile.

"I am going to smile, but don't be hurting my feelings like that anymore."

"I'll do my best not to, but you really need to stop all that gossiping out there, woman. What in the hell do y'all be talking about that early in the morning anyway?"

"Do you really want to know?"

"Yes."

"Are you sure?"

"Yes, I'm sure."

"Well, I had an amazing sexual experience over the weekend and I couldn't wait to come to work and tell Audrey and Jackie about it. Audrey had oral sex for the first time and Jackie—"

Jonathan's brows rose, and he put up his hand to stop me. "All right, I got your point. But can't y'all talk about that stuff during lunch?"

"When I've had something that good, I usually don't like to wait on telling my girls about it. Ask Dana. She knew about the size of his package, two seconds after my date left."

"Come on now, Sylvia. Don't be telling my wife about another man's thang. That's kind of disrespectful, isn't it?"

"Nope. What's disrespectful is what she be telling me about you." I stood up because by the look on Jonathan's face, I was sure he wanted details.

"Where are you going?" he asked, smiling again. "We haven't finished our conversation yet."

"Yes, we have." I grinned and walked over by the coffee machine to pour his coffee. "And if you think I'm going to tell you what she said about you, you're sadly mistaken."

I bent over to pick up a paper cup I'd dropped on the floor. I knew Jonathan's eyes were glued to my curvy hips and apple-bottom booty because it was hard for any man not to notice. He got up and came over by me. He leaned against the counter and folded his arms.

"So, you're really not going to tell me what she said?"

I handed him the coffee mug. "Nope. Dana is my girl, and if I want to keep hearing about y'all's juicy sex life, I'd better keep my mouth shut."

"Juicy, huh?" He took a sip of his coffee. "On that note, I'm not going to put you on the spot, but, uh, do you have any clue where I'm supposed to meet Britney for lunch today?"

"Yes, Jonathan," I said, walking over to his desk and picking up his calendar. "If you would look at this darn thing, you're meeting her at Applebee's on Clayton Road around eleven-thirty."

"Thanks, Sylvia. Now get out of my office so I can get some work done today. And close my door behind you."

I put Jonathan's calendar back on his desk and smiled at him on my way out. Before I closed the door, he stopped me.

"Hey, Sylvia."

"What's up?"

"Aside from the juicy sex . . . is Dana at least happy?"

I nodded. "Yeah, she is. I know sometimes it doesn't seem like it, but really, she is."

He grinned and I closed the door.

I walked over to my desk and plopped down in my chair. I thought hard about Dana. Honestly, I really wasn't sure if she was happy. And Jonathan, it seemed as if he lived for her happiness. According to him, it was all about her and that was what frustrated me more than anything.

I was typing up a thank-you letter for Jonathan when Audrey and Jackie were heading my way. Thinking about what Jonathan said earlier, I tried to keep our conversation short. But when Jackie gave me the scoop about Lewis screwing around with this new chick in accounting, I couldn't help myself.

"Girl, quit lying," I whispered to Jackie. "He was just with a friend of mine last weekend."

"Sylvia, who is this friend of yours?" Jackie asked. "He's been with her for a while hasn't he?"

"I told you her name is Nora," I said, lying. "She works at the post office with my sister. And yes, they've been together for some time now."

"And you've told her about Lewis and his other women?" Audrey asked.

"Yes, I have, but she's trifling like that. She's got herself about four or five different men anyway."

"So sad," Audrey said, shaking her head.

We all looked and saw Lewis coming our way with the mail cart. Audrey and Jackie stood there lusting for his ass. Disgusted, because I knew what time it was, I rolled my eyes and told them to get away from me. They flirted with Lewis, and he had the nerve to rub hands with Jackie. She whispered something in his ear and he laughed out loud, and then headed my way with the mail.

I tapped my fingernails on the desk and waited for him to give the mail to me as he fumbled through it. "Isn't it your job to have the mail ready before you bring it to me?" I asked with attitude.

He ignored me, and then placed the mail in the mail trays on my desk. "There you go, Miss Lady. And I'll be up again around three this afternoon with the rest of it. Naw, I take that back," he said, looking up as if he were in deep thought. "I'll probably be fucking your friend around that time so I'll ask Jeff to bring the mail to you."

I shooed him away. "Lewis, get away from my desk. I hope your dick run away from you one day, then what are you gonna do? Who or what are you going to get to provide for you then?"

"Don't be so angry, baby. In due time, you'll get some of this. Just be patient, all right?"

"Nigga, get your—"

I paused when Jonathan opened the door and walked out with his briefcase in his hand. He closed the door behind him and stood in front of my desk, next to Lewis.

"Hey, man," he said, shaking Lewis's hand. "How's everything in the mailroom going?"

"Just fine, Mr. Taylor," Lewis said with a fake-ass smile. "Couldn't be better."

"Well, that's good. But we need to talk about how we can get you out of the mailroom and into a better position."

"Hey, that sounds like a great idea to me. I mean, I'm digging the mailroom, but it sure would be nice to have one of these offices, Mr. T."

"One day at a time, Lewis. But, uh, why don't you make an appointment with Sylvia to come by and talk to me. I'd like to know a little bit more about your experience and we can go from there."

"Will do, sir, and thanks."

"Anytime," Jonathan said, patting him on the back. Jonathan put his briefcase on my desk and looked at me. "I'm meeting Britney for lunch, then I have to go to court for the Dickerson case. If I'm not back by five, lock my door. I have a long night ahead of me so I don't expect for you to stay."

"Are you sure? I mean, I'll at least stay until six," I said. "If you're not back by then, then I'll leave."

"Five o'clock is fine, Sylvia. Thanks, but I don't want to keep tying up your nights."

"Take your time. If you're not back by six, I promise you I'll leave. Anyway, I need to catch up on my filing."

He removed his briefcase from my desk. "Woman, I don't know what I'd do without you. If Dana calls, tell her she can reach me by cell phone."

"Will do," I said, watching as Jonathan walked off.

Lewis stood there looking at me like he wanted something.

"Can I help you?" I asked in a nasty tone.

"Yes, you can. Mr. T told me to make an appointment to see him."

"And I'm telling you that Mr. Taylor's appointment book is full. Stop by sometime next year; he might have an opening then."

Lewis snickered, leaned down, and put his face in front of mine. He then licked his lips. "Umm, I can taste you now. If you'd like, we can go ahead and get this over with tonight. That way I can stop by tomorrow and you'll figure out a way to pencil me in."

Before I knew it, I placed my hand on Lewis's face and pushed it back. "Lewis, I'm warning you. Gone now, before you get your feelings hurt."

When Lewis saw his supervisor coming, he backed off. He told me to have a good day and went on about his business. Steaming, I grabbed the phone to call Dana and curse her out again for even messing with somebody so foolish. When she defended him and said that "he just be playing" I hung up on her.

I spent the next several hours getting things organized for Jonathan. His files were in order, his calendar had been printed off for the next couple of weeks, all of his letters had been typed, and even his office was spotless. Since I didn't have anything else to do for the night, I stayed until he got there, which wasn't until almost seven o'clock. He was surprised to see me, and the look of tiredness was written all over his face.

"What are you still doing here?" he asked then loosened his tie. He sat in a chair next to mine.

"Hey, I do not want to hear your mouth tomorrow morning so I'm handling my business tonight."

He laughed. "Well good, and it's about time." He closed his eyes and leaned back in the chair.

I couldn't help myself from being so attracted to him. I wanted to take off his clothes, massage his body down, rub his black wavy hair, and help him release some of the tension I knew he was feeling. As my mind floated into the gutter, he opened his eyes and stood up.

"Did Dana call?" he asked.

"Yeah, she called about an hour ago. She said you didn't answer your cell phone so . . ."

"I was in court," he said, walking into his office. I stood up and followed him.

"Listen, I'm getting ready to take off. Before I go, do you need anything?"

"Naw, I'm cool. And thanks for cleaning up my office. It looks really nice in here."

"You know I got your back, Mr. Boss Man. Have a good night and I'll see you in the morning."

"Be careful, Sylvia," he said, reaching for his phone.

I shut down my computer, grabbed my purse, and jetted. As I waited for the elevator, when it opened, Dana got off with a long trench coat on, some high-heeled shoes, and she had a picnic basket in her hand. I already knew what time it was, and I stood there shaking my head.

"Girl, you really need to stop," I said.

"Stop what, Sylvia?" She smiled.

"Didn't you already serve up Lewis today?"

"If you must know, I cancelled. Okay?"

"Dana, please. If anybody cancelled it was him."

"So, wha . . . what difference does it make? My husband is here, isn't he?"

"Yeah. He's in his office on the phone. He's had a long day and he looks awfully tired."

"Well, we'll just have to see about that," she said, walking off. "I'll call you later. If not later, I'll call you tomorrow."

"Good night, Dana," I said, pushing the down button on the elevator again.

I was in my car in the parking garage, thinking about how I was losing respect for my friend. Not only that, but I was seriously falling for her husband. She didn't deserve to have him, and I was the only person who could see that. If he didn't even suspect she was up to no good he was blind. A huge part of me wanted to tell him, but I couldn't. If I the least bit interfered, I knew I would lose the both of them and that was something I wasn't prepared to do.

2

JONATHAN

When Dana came in, I was at my desk massaging my temples and thinking about Britney walking out on me at lunch today. Dana, being as seductive as she was, sat on my desk and opened her coat. I took a look at her naked body, and feeling the way I was, I couldn't even get excited. I closed her coat and tightened the belt around it. Then I wrapped my arms around her and laid my head against her chest.

"Not right now, baby, all right?" I said, feeling drained.

She rubbed my head. "What's wrong?"

"It's Britney."

Dana released a deep sigh. "What now? Is this still about her going to summer school?"

"She isn't even going to summer school. When I asked why, she said that she had plans to go to Florida this summer and summer school would interfere."

"Duh, but the last time I checked, she was going to fail the tenth grade if she didn't go."

"I know, Dana, but I'll call Beverly tomorrow to find out what's going on."

Dana moved my head and slid off my desk. She folded her arms, while she looked out of the window. "I really think you should call Beverly tonight. If not, this mess is going to linger on for another day, and personally, I'm getting kind of tired of seeing you so down because of Britney."

"She's my daughter, Dana. I can't help for feeling the way I do. If anything, you know I want things to be right."

Dana turned to face me. "Baby, but that's what you want. Britney plays mind games all the time and she knows how to work on you. I wish you'd wake up and put her in her place for one time in your life."

"Yeah, there are a lot of things I need to wake up to." I stood up and put on my jacket. "I just don't have time to deal with them right now."

"A lot of things like what?" Dana asked. She walked up to me and put my arms around her.

"A lot of things like where were you this past weekend? Sylvia told me she had company and you told me that you were with Sylvia until two o'clock in the morning."

"Well, honey, Sylvia lied to you. We had dinner, after that we went to a bar for a drink, then to the casino. As for her having company, maybe she did have company later that night."

"Maybe so," I said, taking my arms from around her. "But she never mentioned being with you."

Dana stood with her mouth wide open. "Jonathan, I don't know where all of this is coming from, but are you saying that you don't believe me?"

"All I'm saying is I'm not a fool, Dana. Some shit with you hasn't been adding up lately. Actually, it hasn't been adding up for quite some time."

"Fine," she hissed, and then walked toward the door. "Thanks a lot for trusting me, and if you're that insecure about our marriage then end it." She grabbed the picnic basket off my desk and left.

Never going after her when she was angry, I sat on the edge of my desk and rubbed my chin. Maybe I was being too hard on her, but I couldn't control these feelings I had inside of me about her not being honest. When I thought about it more, maybe it was the pressure I was feeling from Britney's rejection and from working so many hours at work. My mind was on overload, but I, at least, was glad I had a hard worker like Sylvia to help pick up some of the slack.

Trying to give Dana time to cool off, I stayed at the office until midnight. Sylvia took care of the tedious tasks for me, but there were still plenty of things left for me to do. Since tomorrow was Secretary's Day, I made myself a note to order her some flowers.

On the drive home, I called home to see if Dana was still awake. When she didn't answer, I figured she must have fallen asleep. Thinking deeply about her, as I drove to our beautiful home in Lake St. Louis, I pulled my Lexus into the garage next to her Jaguar and rushed into the house. I stopped in the kitchen to see if Dana had cooked anything. I noticed she hadn't, so I grabbed a bagel and put it in my mouth. As I walked through the living room eating it, I saw her lying on the couch sound asleep. An empty bottle of Chardonnay was next to her on the floor and magazines were spread out on the table. After I finished my bagel, I picked up the bottle and put it on the table. Then I kneeled down in front of her. I moved her sandy-brown long hair away from her face and kissed her cheek. She opened her pretty hazel-green eyes and stared at me. When a tear slipped from the corner of her eye, I wiped it and held her face in my hand.

"I'm sorry for not trusting you," I said. "I didn't mean to come off like I did, but please understand what I'm going through."

She nodded and pulled me in close to kiss her. I removed my jacket and stood up to take off my pants. Anxious to feel me, she helped me remove them, and then she unbuttoned my shirt. After she took off her silk nightie, our naked bodies hit the plush carpet. I closed my eyes, knowing that my wife never had a problem with

satisfying me. She licked her tongue up and down my
chest, sucked my nipples and swallowed every inch of
my dick into her mouth. Always in control, she straddled
me backward and pounded down hard on me as I had
the pleasure of watching her pretty ass work me so well.
When she leaned forward, I massaged her ass cheeks
apart and watched my goodness break into her pussy that
was locked on me. At that moment, I felt as if I didn't
have a worry in the world. I turned Dana sideways and
stretched one of her legs high upon my broad shoulders.
Before going inside again, I tickled her insides and
sucked her healthy breasts in my mouth. Wanting me,
she inserted me, and rolled my jewels around in her
warm hands. I was on cloud nine, as we fucked our way
into the bedroom and finished up beside the bed. Dana
lay flat on her stomach with her legs spread wide apart.
Exhausted, I lay in between them. I moved her hair away
from her neck and kissed it.

"Umm," she moaned. "I was waiting a long time for
that."

"I know. I could tell by how gushy and wet you felt," I
said, giving her ass a smack then stood up.

She rolled over. "Where are you going?"

"To take a shower tonight, so I don't have to do it in the
morning. I need to get up early for work."

"I have a better idea," she said also standing up. "How
about you not go to work tomorrow so we can spend the
entire day together messing around."

"I wish I could, baby, but I have so much that I have to
do. Maybe next week, okay?"

Dana shrugged then lay across the bed. "Yeah, maybe
so."

I gathered my things for my shower and stood in the
doorway looking at Dana who seemed to be disappointed.
Feeling bad, I walked over to her and lay in bed with her.

"Would you like to join me in the shower?"

"No, maybe next time."

I left her alone and didn't push. After my shower, I saw that she had fallen asleep. I kissed her forehead and got some rest before my busy day tomorrow.

When I came through the door, as usual, Sylvia, Jackie, and Audrey were standing by Sylvia's cubicle running their mouths. I gave them a hard stare, didn't speak, then went into my office and closed the door. Knowing that Sylvia would be knocking soon to apologize, I sat at my desk counting the seconds down before she knocked. Sure enough, there was a knock and her head came peeking through the door.

"Are you up for coffee or orange juice this morning?" she said, smiling.

"Neither."

"A doughnut or bagel?"

"Nope."

"Tylenol or Excedrin?"

"Tylenol because you are a pain in the ass, aren't you?"

"And so are you." She came into my office and closed the door behind her. "So," she said, sitting down and crossing her legs. "After I left last night, did you enjoy yourself?"

"As a matter of fact, I did."

"Good. But you and Dana should be careful messing around like that in here. Somebody is bound to catch y'all in action."

I looked at her breasts that stared me in the face, and then looked at the birthmark on her upper thigh I'd noticed many times before, since she always wore short miniskirts to work. "Sylvia, why are you constantly outside of my office running your mouth when I've asked you to chill?"

"That's not what you were thinking about asking me," she said.

"How do you know what I was thinking about asking you?"

"Because I know you, Mr. Jonathan Taylor. So, out with it; wha . . . what's on your mind?"

"Okay, Miss Mind Reader, I have several other questions for you."

She bounced her crossed leg on top of the other and bit into her nail. "I'm waiting."

"What did you do Saturday night? Who were you with, and why do you come to work dressed like that?"

Sylvia looked at herself, pulled her skirt down and glared at me. "I already told you what I was into Saturday night. And if you must know, I dress like this because I like the clothes I wear, and because my boss can't seem to keep his eyes off me when I wear them."

I laughed and pointed to my chest. "So, you dress like that for me?"

"Yep," she said, laughing her damn self. "It's the least I can do. You need some type of enjoyment being cooped up in this place all the time, don't you?"

"That's why I have a wife, Sylvia."

"But, she's not here all the time. So, in the meantime, feel free to undress me with your eyes anytime. Trust me, I enjoy every bit of it."

"Okay, if you insist. You are crazy; do you know that?"

"I know, but I love to see my boss laughing, especially if I can make him forget about being mad at me for running my mouth to my coworkers all the time."

"Yeah, you're right. I almost forgot about that. One of these days, I'm going to fire you for that mess. In the meantime, though, I need my coffee, a bagel with strawberry cream cheese, two Tylenol, the paperwork on the Johnson case, and before you leave today, I need those fifteen letters I put on your desk last night typed. If you get finished early," I said, reaching for a pile of papers on my desk that needed to be filed, "you can file these away for me."

Sylvia stood up and put her hands on her hips. "The coffee, I got your back. The bagel and Tylenol, you can get that yourself, and as for the letters, I'll have them to you within the hour. After that, I'm going to Audrey's office for the rest of the day to loiter there since you won't let me do it here."

"Well, loiter on, sista, but make sure I get my things."

"Will do," she said already pouring my coffee. She came over to my desk and put my mug on top of it.

Before taking a sip, I looked up at her. "Sylvia, you didn't see Dana this past weekend, did you?"

She sucked her teeth and released a deep breath. "Jonathan, look. We hung out for a while, but I also had other things to tend to. Please don't start questioning me about our whereabouts, okay?"

"You're right and I'm sorry. Just ignore me, okay?"

"It's hard to ignore you but I will try," she said on her way to the door. "In the meantime, if you need me, I'll be at my desk."

Sylvia closed the door, and five minutes later, she came back with my bagel and Tylenol. I thanked her for being so good to me and tried to focus on getting something accomplished for the day.

Unable to focus, and thinking about my amazing night with Dana, I called home to check on her. When she didn't answer, I called her cell phone only to get voicemail. I left a message and told her to get back with me soon.

By four o'clock, I still hadn't heard from Dana. I couldn't concentrate on anything, and by the time I came out of my meeting, which wasn't until 5:30 p.m., she still hadn't called. I put the phone down and walked outside of my office to ask Sylvia if she somehow missed Dana's call.

"No, Jonathan," she said with a serious attitude, and shoving her paper around on her desk. "I've been trying to reach her myself."

"Are you sure she hasn't called? I mean, you did say that you were going away from your desk for a while."

"Look," she said in a higher pitch. "Ju . . . just in case you haven't noticed, I haven't been anywhere but right here. I didn't even have time for lunch today so stop asking me if I've heard from your wife. I'm not her keeper."

I was in shock by Sylvia's tone, and I stood for a moment gazing at her for yelling. I decided to suck it up for now, but as I turned away to go back into my office, she placed her hands over her face and began to cry.

"Sylvia?" I said, walking over to her. "Hey, I was only kidding when I mentioned you being away from your desk all day."

She pulled some tissue from the box and wiped her tears. "It's not that, Jonathan," she sniffled. "It's that . . . Never mind."

"What? You know that you can talk to me about anything." I leaned against her desk, trying to let her know that I was there for her too. She took a deep breath and wouldn't say a word. "Okay, do we need to go into my office and talk about what's bothering you?"

She nodded and followed me into my office. I closed the door and pulled the chair back for her to sit. Before I could even take a seat, she tore into me.

She pointed her finger at me. "As much as I do for you, Jonathan Tyrese Taylor, if you ever forget about me like you did today, I will never in my entire lifetime go over and above for you again."

Wrinkles lined my forehead. I had no idea what she was talking about. "Wha . . . what do you mean by forgetting about you, Sylvia?"

"I mean, every secretary in this office got flowers today. Candy, a card, or something from their bosses, and for you not to even think about me was really hurtful."

I shamefully dropped my head and rubbed my face. "I am so, so sorry. I made myself a note yesterday about ordering your flowers, but it totally slipped my mind. Please forgive me," I said, getting up and walking over to her. I kneeled down beside her and placed my hand on top of hers. "Please know that I appreciate everything you do for me. You are everything I can ask for. Without you filling in when you did, I would be truly lost. If you let me, I'll make it up to you."

Sylvia glared at me with a blank stare and didn't crack a smile. "Don't you ever hurt me like this again. If you do not appreciate me, I will leave, Jonathan, I mean it."

"Again, I'm sorry. I'm entitled to some mistakes, aren't I?"

When my door came open, we turned our heads. Dana came in and looked at me kneeled down beside Sylvia, and I still held her hand.

"Did I interrupt something?" she asked, closing the door behind her. I stood up and walked up to give her a kiss. She turned her head to avoid it. "Like I said, Jonathan and Sylvia, did I interrupt something?"

"No, you didn't." Sylvia shot up from the chair. "Thanks for the pep talk, Jonathan, but I'm going home." She walked past Dana without saying a word. Dana called her name, but Sylvia ignored her, gathered her belongings and left.

"What's with her?" Dana asked and followed behind me as I sat in my chair. She eased on top of my lap.

I puckered for a kiss, and then put my arms around her. After she kissed me, I told her what Sylvia's and my dispute was about.

Dana cocked her head back, appearing to be in disbelief. "She's mad at you over some gotdamn flowers? The
nerve of her after all we've done for her."

"Dana, I'm not going to defend myself this time. I was
wrong, baby. Sylvia is the best secretary I've had, and for
me to forget about her wasn't even cool."

"Please. Sylvia is looking for some attention and if she
thinks that she's going to get it from my husband, she is
out of her mind. It's bad enough she be wearing all that
revealing and provocative stuff around you, but trying to
get you to feel sorry for her is taking things too far."

"Baby, calm down. Let me deal with this, okay?"

"Just like you deal with Britney and Beverly, right? I
bet you haven't even called to straighten things out like
you said you would, have you?"

I rubbed my forehead because I was starting to get a
headache. "Damn, I forgot about calling Beverly. I had a
busy day, and I've been trying to reach you all day. Where
were you?"

"I was out," she said, standing up.

"Out where?"

"You know, the usual: browsing the malls, going grocery
shopping, getting my nails done, whatever."

I looked at Dana's nails and could immediately tell they
hadn't been recently done. "The usual, huh?" I got up and
stood in front of her. "Usually, you have your phone on so
I can reach you. Lately, though, I know you've been lying
to me, Dana." I grabbed her hand and put it in her face.
"Whoever recently did your nails, they did a shitty-ass
job. And as for Saturday night, like today, again, you were
missing in action." I let her hand go and removed my
jacket from the chair. "Whoever he is, Mrs. Wifey, you'd
better damn be sure he's worth losing me."

I walked out and left Dana behind.

On the way home, I called Beverly and told her I'd stop by on Friday night so we could talk about what to do with Britney. And when Crissy, Mr. Duncan's daughter, rang in, I told Beverly I'd call her back. Crissy asked if she could stop by the office tomorrow and talk to me about her father. Mr. Duncan, my partner, had been out of the office for months, trying to fight his battle with prostate cancer. I told her to come by as early as possible so we could talk.

When I got home, as usual, and as I had expected, no dinner had been cooked. Little food was in the refrigerator, and if I looked hard enough, I could see dust particles floating around the rooms.

Trying to relax myself, I took a lengthy hot bath and changed into my burgundy silk pajama pants. By then, Dana had already made it home and was in the hearth room with her legs crossed, while paging through the newspaper. I pretended as if she wasn't even there, grabbed a beer from the refrigerator, and went into the bedroom.

Before falling asleep, I called May's Florist and paid for them to deliver Sylvia ten dozen yellow roses by tomorrow morning. The florist put me on hold to make sure they had enough in stock, and after she told me they did, I ordered ten more dozen for every day up until Tuesday of next week. I asked for different colors, and when she provided me with a total, I was shocked. Knowing that Sylvia was worth it, I didn't trip, but the florist offered me a discount for ordering so many. I thanked her. Afterward, I closed my eyes, thinking about what Sylvia would do, and wondered what tomorrow would bring.

3

SYLVIA

As I was coming through the door with my groceries, the phone was ringing off the hook. I put my groceries on the kitchen counter and hurried to answer it. It was Dana. By the sound of her voice, she wasn't too thrilled to talk to me.

"Sylvia Marie McMillan, I don't care how hard you may try, but you will not get my husband to lay you!"

"And Dana Yvette Taylor, I don't know how naïve you are, but one of these days, he will!" I hung up.

I ignored Dana's phone calls until I finished putting up my groceries. After that, I called her back to see if she was ready to talk to me like she had some sense.

"So, Miss Thang," I said. "Are you ready to talk about what you walked in on today?"

"Jonathan already told me. And I think you really need to grow up and stop trying to get him to notice you."

"Dana, don't make me go off on you, all right? I'm in no mood to argue with you tonight, especially after what kind of day I've had."

"So, you didn't get any flowers. Get over it! Jonathan has missed our wedding anniversary before, he's missed my birthday before, and, sometimes, I do get passed over on Valentine's Day. For you to be crying over something like Secretary's Day is ridiculous."

"Well, I'm sorry that you allow your man to miss important days like those, but I will not allow him to forget about me when I bust my butt for him every day of the week. Maybe even more than you do and you're his wife."

"Whatever, Sylvia. No matter what, you really need to back off. I don't ever want to walk in on him holding your hand and comforting you again. My feelings were truly hurt, and just so you know, I don't like it one bit."

"I don't expect for you to like it, but you know better than anybody that Jonathan is a caring man. He realized his mistake and made me feel better once he apologized. I know how much I joke around with you about being with him, and even if you're worried about me snatching him up, don't be. He's the type of man who will never let that happen."

"And you're the kind of woman who's hoping something will evolve from your friendship with him."

"Dana, you know that since Derrick's been gone I haven't found happiness with anyone. Fortunately, Jonathan has been there for me. He makes me laugh, he talks to me when I'm feeling down, and anything I need he'll do for me. Sometimes I can't help myself from being attracted to him, but our friendship means a lot to me. I've been frustrated with you for a very long time for cheating on him. He deserves so much better, and more than anything, I hate to be caught in the middle."

"Then step out of the middle. Quit your job and find somewhere else to work. Bottom line is I'm not going to stop seeing Lewis because there are things Lewis gives me that Jonathan does not."

"Like what, Dana, a disease? What in the hell does Lewis give you that Jonathan can't? Tell me because I'm lost."

"It's none of your business."

"It is my business when you lie on me and tell your husband that you're with me and you're not. I wish you would stop including me in your mess and find somebody else to use."

"I don't be using you. I hate the way our friendship is diminishing, but you need to mind your own business. This bitterness between us didn't start until you started dipping into my Kool-Aid."

"I'm going to continue to dip because not only do I care, but because I don't want to see Jonathan get his feelings hurt. As for you, your mind is so twisted that you can't even think straight. Dick got you all fucked up, and if you want it to mess up your life, you go right ahead."

"Good-bye, Sylvia. Are we still on for lunch tomorrow or what? If we are, I don't want to spend our entire lunch talking about my amazing life."

"I'll see you at noon, and if you're late, I'm leaving."

After we ended our call, I stayed up until two o'clock in the morning watching TV and playing Uno with myself. It wasn't that I couldn't ask someone to come over and entertain me, but the men I had in my life were pathetic. Marlin was on hold because of the restraining order, Cory was a one, two, three o'clock in the morning brotha, and I was getting sick of that shit, and Bryan was in a half-ass commitment with another woman and lying about it. I was so much better off without any of them, but when my needs had to be met, I for surely knew who to call. That was Jonathan. All he'd have to do was remind me how gorgeous I was, encourage me to stop settling for less, and remind me to never play second best to another woman. After talking to him, I'd usually call Lorenzo with the big dick over, let him shake a sista down, and send him out the door with a smile on his face.

Since I stayed up so early in the morning, I was running extremely late for work. I didn't roll over until 7:30 a.m.

By the time I showered, got dressed, and drove to work in Clayton, it was almost nine o'clock.

Jonathan leaned against his doorway with his arms folded and looked spectacular with his suspenders on, a white crisp, clean shirt, and some gray pinstriped slacks that hung over his square-toed leather shoes. I rushed toward him because I could tell he was waiting for me.

"I'm coming," I said, taking my purse off my shoulder and walking abruptly to my desk. As I neared my desk, I noticed him smiling. I looked inside my cubicle, and it was filled with yellow long-stem roses in beautiful crystal vases. I screamed, and then covered my mouth because it was so loud. Jonathan said good morning to me, then went into his office and closed the door.

Truly overjoyed, I sniffed several of the roses and sat down in my chair. Audrey and Jackie came over and gazed at the roses.

"Who in the hell did you screw last night, Bill Gates?" Audrey laughed.

"Girl, please. These are from Jonathan."

Jackie's eyes widened and Audrey's mouth dropped. "Don't tell me you and him . . ." Jackie said.

"No, Jackie. Yesterday, he forgot about Secretary's Day and he made it up to me today."

"Shit, I wish he'd make it up to me," Audrey said. "With something else, of course."

"Don't we all," Jackie agreed. "Sylvia, you are so lucky. If he were my boss, it would be on! I know his wife is a good friend of yours, but how do you keep yourself from going in there and ripping off his clothes?"

"Trust me, it's hard, but y'all know Jonathan don't mess around like that. If he did, we'd all be running around here with wet panties on. If y'all looking for action like that, I suggest y'all find Lewis. He's sharing with everybody these days."

Audrey cleared her throat and looked at Jackie. "He sure is, isn't he, Miss 'I'm not even feeling him like that' knowing damn well she was."

"Jackie, no," I said in awe. "You didn't, did you?"

She rolled her eyes at Audrey then looked at me. "I was curious, okay?"

"Curiosity killed the cat, and a dick like that can damn sure kill the woman. What in the hell were you thinking?" I questioned.

She threw her hand back at me. "Girl, I don't know. I got caught up, I guess. Caught up in that sizzling, hot sex he be dishing out."

I folded my arms and pursed my lips. "Don't tell me because I don't even want to know."

"Yes, you do, Sylvia."

"No, I don't."

"Yes, you do," Jackie said, again. "Doesn't she, Audrey? She'd wanna know about this, wouldn't she?"

"Yeah, you would," Audrey said, looking at me as if it were interesting.

"Fine, go ahead and tell me." I laughed.

Audrey and Jackie moved in closer to me, and just when Jackie started to tell me about the strawberry gel he slurped up between her legs, Jonathan opened the door and cleared his throat. They spoke to him and quickly walked away.

"Sylvia," he said in a stern tone. "Where's the file on the Anderson case?"

I walked to the file cabinet to get it. "Thanks for the flowers, Jonathan. One dozen would have been enough for me to forgive you."

He took the file from my hand then went back into his office and closed the door.

Since today was Wednesday, normally he'd be in a better mood. I could tell things were getting a bit more complicated between him and Dana because his bad days were starting to outnumber his good days.

As I was typing and trying to think of something I could do to repay him for the flowers, I looked up and saw Crissy coming my way. She was one white girl I hated to see coming. Prissy Crissy was what I called her because she acted as if her shit didn't stink. She was always looking down on people, and I assumed that she couldn't wait until her father kicked the bucket so she could take over the company.

So, there she was swinging her blond long hair from side to side, sticking out her breast implants, as if they were really hers, and moving her flat, pancake ass from side to side. By the time she reached my desk, I leaned down, picked up some paper, and pretended as if I didn't see her. She hummed so she could get my attention, and when I didn't lift my head, she slammed her briefcase on my desk.

"Shanequa," she yelled.

"Sha what?" I shot back at her, and then sat up in my chair. I didn't care if she would someday be the boss or not. I treated people the same way they treated me. "It's Sylvia, Crusty, so get it right."

"Crissy," she said. "Crissy Duncan and I'm here to see Jonathan this morning."

I looked at Jonathan's calendar and didn't see her name. "Darn, I guess you're out of luck, Crusty. Your meeting is not on his calendar, and he throws a fit when I try to squeeze people in."

"Listen, Shanana, if you'd just tell Jonathan I'm here to see him, I'd appreciate it. I already talked to him yesterday so do your damn job and get him for me, please."

"For the last time it's Syl-ve-a, bitch! Can you pronounce that? If not, I'll be willing to walk you through it again."

"You are such an evil bitch," she said, snatching her briefcase off my desk. She walked over to Jonathan's door and knocked.

"I am a bitch, Crissy. One who will mess you up if you keep coming in here disrespecting me."

Jonathan opened his door and smiled at Crissy.

"Gimmie gimmie hugs," she said, wrapping her arms around him and pressing her implants against his chest. His eyebrows rose as he looked over her shoulder and grinned at me. I rolled my eyes.

Crissy was in Jonathan's office for about two hours. When they came out he said they were going to lunch and told me he'd be back by one o'clock. I reminded him about my lunch plans with Dana and told him I'd see him when I got back.

When Dana came in, I put the finishing touches on a letter I'd typed for Jonathan. She was on her cell phone, but when she saw all the flowers at my desk, she told whoever she was talking to she'd have to call them back. Her eyes searched the flowers and she stood with much attitude.

"I know he is not responsible for all these flowers."

"Well, I sure in the hell ain't responsible, so let's go, I'm hungry."

"I can't believe him," she said, standing with her mouth open.

"Get over it, Dana."

"Get over it my tail, Sylvia! I don't like this mess at all. Is he in his office?"

"No, he's at lunch."

"With who?"

"With Prissy Crissy."

"I'll be sure to confront him about this later. A few dozen are fine, but he don't need to go all out for you like this."

"Chile, jealousy will get you nowhere. Now, my stomach is calling me all kinds of bad words for not putting nothing into it. Can we go?"

We walked toward the elevator and Dana continued to rant about the flowers. As we stood waiting for the elevator to open, Lewis came out of the men's restroom and saw us. I turned my head, but, of course, Dana had to get his attention.

"Hey," she said, twirling her fingers in the air and waving. He smiled and walked up to her. Before he said anything, he looked around to see if anyone was near. Noticing that there wasn't, he put his arms around Dana's waist and kissed her cheek.

"Say, baby," he said. "Damn, you're smelling good."

She blushed and backed away from him. "It's Issey Miyake. And thanks, but why didn't you return my phone call yesterday?"

As the elevator opened, I wanted to tell her that he hadn't returned it because he was too busy fucking Jackie. But when I turned around, Lewis had pulled Dana over to the door that led to the staircase and opened it. She looked at me and shrugged. "I'll meet you downstairs in about ten minutes."

"Twenty minutes," he said, as he continued to pull her by the arm.

"Look," I said with anger visible on my face. "When you get finished just meet me at CJ's across the street. If you show, fine. If you don't, that's not a problem either."

Disgusted, I pushed the down button on the elevator and went to CJ's by myself. I asked the waiter to seat me for two, just in case Dana decided to show. No sooner had I sat down, I noticed Jonathan and Crissy at another table having lunch. I was sure he hadn't seen me, and hoped that if he did, he wouldn't come over and ask where Dana was.

When the waiter came back, I ordered a salad and some hot wings. Twenty minutes had gone by and Dana was still a no-show. I looked at Jonathan, as he and Crissy seemed to be wrapping things up. And right when he stood up and walked toward the door to leave, then Dana came in. She looked startled to see him, and after they embraced each other, they headed my way.

"I didn't know you were in here, Sylvia," Jonathan said, pulling the chair back for Dana to sit.

"I just got here moments ago," I said. Jonathan watched as the waiter put the wings and salad on the table.

"Oh, I see your lunch buddy finally made it," the waiter said, looking at Dana. "Your friend was about to have lunch without you."

"I, uh, got caught up in traffic," Dana said. "She knew I was coming."

Jonathan glared at me for a few seconds, and then he leaned down to give Dana a kiss. She put her hand in front of his face. "We need to talk about those flowers later, okay," she said.

He ignored her, moved her hand away from his face, and kissed her cheek. "We'll talk about the flowers, baby, for sure. And as soon as we finish that conversation, we're going to talk about that cheap-ass men's cologne I smell all over you right now."

Dana cocked her head back, I covered my mouth, and Jonathan walked away. I took a sip of my iced tea and shook my head.

"Your time is running out! I hope you've planned a life absent from Jonathan."

Dana laid a napkin neatly in her lap. "Sylvia, Jonathan isn't going anywhere. Tonight, I'm going to tell him I was at the mall sampling some men's cologne for him."

"That's not going to work because the key word he said was 'cheap.' He knows damn well you ain't out sampling no cheap cologne for him. Not only that, but you look like you just got fucked. Your hair all out of place, your lipstick gone, and that outfit you have on got more wrinkles than an eighty-year-old white woman's face."

Dana let out a deep sigh. "Is it really that obvious?"

"Yes. And I'm afraid to get any closer because I'm sure after screwing Lewis that coochie is clowning."

"Girl, stop. For your information, Lewis adds extreme excitement to my life. He's not only handsome but he's creative, he's spontaneous, and he can make me come faster than any man I've ever been with."

"If I can recall, a few years back, you were saying the same thing about Jonathan. It seems to me that the problem ain't with the man; it's with you."

"Maybe, or maybe not. But I try very hard to keep my sex life spiced up with Jonathan. He's magnificent in bed, but we're always on his time. Sometimes, I can't wait for him to come home and make love to me. When he does, he's either too tired from working, or he goes right into his office and works there for the night. I get tired of putting myself out there for him. Just last week, I lit some candles in the bedroom, put on some soft music, stripped naked, and waited for him to come home. When he did, he turned on the lights, looked at me like I was out of my mind, and said his famous words: 'not tonight.'"

"He's acting that way, Dana, because he ain't no fool. Deep down he knows you've been seeing someone else. You're lucky he's still having sex with you at all. Besides, Jonathan doesn't seem like the type of man to go behind another man."

"I wish you would stop being on the outside looking in, because that's all you're doing. Nobody understands what I'm going through but me. I love Jonathan, but I'm not giving up on my relationship with Lewis until some things change."

"Well, you need to get Lewis to change. Since the last time I talked to you, he's added two new women to his collection and the strawberry gel might be running a little low."

Dana looked surprised that I knew about the strawberry gel. Also, she could tell I wasn't lying because I had a feeling as if she'd been there and done that with Lewis before. After my breaking news, there were no more comments about Lewis from her. But I found myself rushing through lunch so I could get back to the office and see if Jonathan would mention anything about Dana. I quickly downed my dessert, told Dana I would call her later, and jetted.

Surprisingly, when I got back to the office, Lewis was in Jonathan's office talking to him. I poked my head in to let Jonathan know I was back.

"Come on in, Sylvia," Jonathan said. "And close the door behind you."

I closed the door and stood behind the chair that Lewis sat in. First, Jonathan looked at Lewis, and then he addressed me. "Sylvia, my man here was just telling me about you not making an appointment for him yesterday. Now, you clearly heard me tell him to make an appointment so why would you not do it?"

"Because Lewis has an attitude problem, and I don't appreciate the way he talks to me, that's why."

"So, I guess Crissy has an attitude problem as well?"

"Yes, she does."

"Just because you seem to think certain people around here have attitudes, that doesn't mean you interfere with them seeing me. Last night, I made an important appointment with Crissy, and I'm trying to help this brotha move up the corporate ladder. So, the next time I get a complaint about *your* attitude, it's going to cost you."

I couldn't believe how Jonathan had put me on blast, and I hated to go there with him like this. "Fine, Jonathan, and help whoever you want to help, that's your business. But Crissy, Lewis, or any other fool up in here will not come to my desk and disrespect me. You don't pay me enough to put up with bullshit and I'm not going to do it." I swung around and stormed toward the door, opening it.

"Sylvia," Jonathan shouted. "Close the door. I'm not finished talking to you yet."

"Yes, you are," I said and then walked out.

Feeling as if I was ready to kill somebody, I quickly gathered a few things at my desk and left. There I was trying to protect Jonathan and he had the nerve to diss me in front of that stupid fool Lewis. And the "that's what you get, bitch" look Lewis gave me as Jonathan talked was enough to send me over the edge. It took everything I had not to blurt out him fucking around with Dana, but as usual, I refused to go there.

By the time I reached the highway, Jonathan called me on my cell phone. I turned it off and laid it back down on the seat. When I got home, I called Lorenzo so I'd have something to tear into, but unfortunately for me, the sex wasn't even worth it. I needed something better, and there was only one man who could give me what I really needed.

4

JONATHAN

Sylvia was out of her mind walking out on me today. After I wrapped up my conversation with Lewis, I called her cell phone and later tried her several times at home. Getting no response, I went into my four o'clock meeting and wasn't out until seven.

I was in no rush to go home and see Dana because I knew my argument with her was probably going to last all night. She was seriously working my nerves. There was no way for me to sweep her lies under the rug as if they didn't even exist. She put the evidence of a cheating woman out there and she seemed to be purposely doing so. She had to know her lies weren't adding up, and if she thought I believed her, she was out of her mind.

After sitting in CJ's for about an hour enjoying several drinks, Audrey came over and sat next to me at the bar.

"I hope I didn't take anybody's seat," she said with a smile.

"No, hey, it's anybody's seat who wants it."

"Good, because I'm claiming it."

I took a sip of my cognac and looked over at Audrey's tall and thin light brown legs. "So what's a nice looking woman like you doing in a place like this on a Wednesday night?"

"I was waiting on one of my girlfriends to join me, but she stood me up. And when I saw you sitting at the bar, I decided to hang around for a while. Question is, though, what's a handsome man like you doing here all alone?"

"Well, I'm just about to wrap this up." I gulped down the last of my drink.

"Do you have any plans after you wrap this up?"

"As a matter of fact, I do."

"Would you be willing to cancel your plans and meet me at my place in about an hour?"

Again, I looked at Audrey's beautiful legs, visualized them high on my shoulders, and thought about her thick, juicy lips going up and down on my dick. When I remembered Sylvia telling me about Audrey's previous sex partner, I declined, not wanting to be the morning news.

"Audrey, I'm married. Besides, you shouldn't be putting yourself out there for a married man."

"If I know he's not happy I will. And you, my dear, are far from it."

I stood up and Audrey stood up as well. I didn't bother to elaborate on her comment because she wasn't worth my time. "Where are you parked?" I asked. "It's late and I'd like to walk you to your car."

After I paid the bartender, I walked with Audrey to her car. On a piece of paper, she wrote directions to her place and her phone number. She told me if I changed my mind to stop by.

Having no desire to go home, I called Sylvia's place, again, to see if I could reach her. The number was still busy so I figured she must have taken her phone off the hook. Trying to calm things down before work tomorrow, I drove by her place to see her. Her car was parked outside, but as I walked to the door, I could see that the inside of her house was dark. I knocked for a while, and as soon as I turned to leave, an overly muscular brotha opened the door with a towel wrapped around his waist.

"May I help you?" he said in a deep, strong voice.

"Hi, is . . . is, uh, Sylvia here?"

"Yeah, she here," he said, stepping away from the door so I could come in.

I stepped in and stood by the door after he closed it. He went into Sylvia's bedroom, and moments later, she came out with a royal blue silk robe on that was cut above her knees. She tied it tightly around her waist and looked at me as I stood by the front door.

"Hey, I . . . I can come back if—"

"Jonathan, have a seat," she said, sitting on the arm of the couch.

"Are you sure? I didn't mean to interrupt."

"You didn't. We're finished and he's getting ready to go."

Moments after I took a seat, the man came out of Sylvia's room fully clothed. He stood in front of her and opened his arms. As they embraced and kissed, he massaged her ass. He then patted it and told her he'd call her tomorrow. Before he left, he said good night to me and closed the door behind him.

Sylvia returned to her spot on the arm of the couch. She crossed her legs and gathered her robe together so I couldn't see her healthy breasts.

"Do you need to go put on some clothes?" I asked.

"No. I'm comfortable. Now please tell me why you're here?"

"Because we need to talk about what happened today."

"Jonathan, before I say anything to you, please know that regardless of you being my boss, I'm going to speak my mind in my own house. After tonight you may decide to fire me, so are you sure you want to have this conversation?"

"Trust me, I can handle it. Just don't start calling me names, all right? Anything else, I'm prepared for when it comes to you."

"Good, because I'm not coming back to work until we get one thing straight."

"And what's that?"

"Don't ever put me on blast like you did today. If you have a problem with me, pull me aside and confront me. It was tacky of you to confront me with Lewis around and I kind of lost some respect for you."

"You really think you got me in check, don't you?" I said, laughing.

"No, but I know you be thinking about your mistakes after you've made them."

"Calling you into my office and confronting you about going off on people wasn't a mistake, Sylvia. And even if you don't like Crissy or Lewis, you still need to show them some respect when we're in the workplace, especially Crissy. Her father owns sixty percent of the company and you might have to answer to her one of these days."

"Before I answer to that thing, I'd work at McDonald's. Lewis and her are on my hit list. They're always telling you stuff about me, but if you only knew what I knew, mister."

"And what do you know?" I asked. "That question is, of course, pertaining to my wife."

"Uh, no," Sylvia said, getting off the couch. She walked over to the huge picture window and looked outside. "You are not going to get me caught up in the middle."

I got up and stood next to her. "Come on now, Sylvia. Who is he?"

Sylvia cocked her head back and sniffed. "Have you been drinking?"

The direction of my eyes lowered to her thick breasts, which were now clearly showing.

She tightened her robe again and nodded. "Yeah, you've been drinking. I can tell because you never looked at me like that."

I shrugged. "I've been drinking a little, but answer my question. I already know she's seeing someone, but I want to know who he is."

"Jonathan, you are so wrong coming to me with a question like that. I don't know anything. Dana doesn't tell me anything anymore. Just in case you haven't noticed, we're not as tight as we used to be."

"I've noticed and I wonder why?"

"We're just not. She's moving in one direction and I'm moving in another."

"Yeah, I bet she is." I went back over to the chair and sat down.

Sylvia stayed by the window and folded her arms. "Have you tried talking to her about your feelings?"

"Not really because I'm so angry with her that a part of me really doesn't want to know the truth."

"Well, if you need answers, you need to go home and talk to her. I don't have the answers for you."

For now, I left it there. We sat around for the next hour or so talking about work, the crazy people there, and Lorenzo. I told Sylvia he looked like the Incredible Hulk and insisted she could do a lot better. When she implied I was jealous, I denied it.

"Jealous of who?"

"Jonathan, don't play with me. You know darn well you were jealous because that brotha was fine, and because he had just finished making love to a beautiful woman such as myself."

"You're right. I want more than anything in the world to see how great you are in bed. And if that brotha beat me to it, then yes, I'm jealous."

Sylvia's brow rose. "Are you serious?"

"No, I'm not," I said, laughing. "I'm only kidding."

"See, you play too much." She stood up and opened the door. "Why don't you take your butt home before you get hurt up in here tonight?"

I looked at my watch and I couldn't believe how late it was. "I don't feel like going home. Do you mind if I crash out on your couch for the night?"

"Yes, I do mind. The last thing I need is for Dana to know that you're over here. She's already upset about the flowers and I don't want to hear about how I'm trying so desperately to steal her man."

"If she calls, just tell her you haven't seen me. You don't want me to have an accident tonight, especially since I've been drinking. Do you?"

Sylvia closed the door. "Don't be trying to play games with me, Jonathan. You are not that drunk where you can't drive home. If Dana calls, I'm giving the phone to you so you can talk."

"Fine," I said, moving over to the couch. "Can I please get some covers and a pillow?"

Sylvia walked off into the other room. When she came back with the cover and pillow, I was down to my boxers, while still on the couch.

"Here," she said, looking at me as with lust locked in her eyes.

I took the pillow and cover from her. "Are you okay?" I asked, as she was still staring.

"Yeah, uh, I'm fine. If you need me, I'll be in the other room."

Just then the phone rang. Sylvia answered and I could immediately tell it was Dana. I shook my head and whispered to Sylvia that I didn't want to talk. She told Dana she hadn't seen me, and then told her she'd call her in the morning.

"Thank you," I said after she hung up.

"Anytime." Sylvia turned down the lights and went back into her room.

Trying to get comfortable, I fluffed the flat pillow and lay on my back. I propped my feet on the arm of the couch, since I was so tall, and looked up at the ceiling fan that blew cool air on me.

After finally falling asleep, I was awakened by the sound of water running in the shower. I looked at my watch and it was only two-thirty in the morning. I knew damn well Sylvia wasn't getting ready for work already, and when she came out of the bathroom, I called her name.

"What?" she whispered.

"What are you doing?"

"Washing my ass, that's what." I laughed and she turned on the light. "Have you been asleep?"

"Yeah, I was until you started making noises."

"Sorry, but I needed a shower."

"And I need some sleep. Now, turn the light out and leave me alone."

Sylvia laughed and turned out the light. When she went back into her bedroom, I couldn't help myself from thinking about having sex with her. Knowing that she was naked underneath the towel aroused me, and finding myself a little bit jealous of her boyfriend, I knew some type of feelings were there.

Just as I started to doze off again, I was startled when Sylvia sat next to me on the couch. The room was mostly dark, and when I asked Sylvia what she was doing, she placed her fingers on my lips.

"Don't say a word, Jonathan. Tonight, I'm coming clean and I haven't a clue what this is going to do to our friendship and our work relationship. Thing is, I can't hold back any longer."

Before Sylvia could say another word, I sat up on my elbows, and then moved her hair away from her face. I placed my hand on the back of her neck and pulled her lips to mine. Feeling the nervousness in her body as we kissed, I backed away. She slid off her robe and rested her naked body on top of mine. As the kiss continued,

I rubbed my hands up and down her back, and over the mountain of her soft ass. Feeling my steel rise between her legs, she straddled herself and reached inside of my boxers to touch my goods. She rubbed my head against the slit of her pussy, but when I tried to ease inside, she stopped me. She lifted herself off me and let out a deep sigh.

"I'm sorry, Jonathan, but I . . . I can't."

Not saying another word, she walked off into her bedroom and closed the door.

Dying to finish what we'd started, I got off the couch and went to her door. I knocked a few times and when she didn't say anything, I opened it and went inside. I could see Sylvia lying in bed sideways while resting her head on a pillow. I eased up from behind her and put my arm around her waist.

"I had no idea how difficult this was for you," I whispered in her ear. "One day at a time though, Sylvia; one day at a time."

She nodded and held my hand together with hers, as we both fell asleep.

5

SYLVIA

The next morning, I was a nervous wreck. Jonathan woke up around five o'clock and headed home. He told me he wasn't coming in until eleven, and feeling the way I felt, I didn't even want to go in at all.

I couldn't believe after years of dreaming and thinking about being with him, I had the nerve to freeze up like Frosty the fucking Snowman. There I was with his dick in my hand and didn't even know what to do with it. My body trembled so badly and I knew he'd felt it. The thought of Dana finding out and my betraying her was what stopped me. Not only that, but I knew Jonathan was a hurting man. I didn't want to complicate his life any more than it already was. One day at a time, he suggested, and that was how I was going to approach this situation going forward.

I was a little late for work, and when I got there, Audrey and Jackie stood close by my desk. As I got closer, I saw them looking at all the flowers that surrounded my cubicle. There were dozens and dozens of peach ones this time and the yellow ones started to bloom. They were amazingly beautiful and all I could do was smile. A card was on my desk, and I could barely read it with Jackie and Audrey looking over my shoulder.

"Get back or I'll cut ya," I playfully hissed while holding the card close to my chest.

"Miss Thang, you need to tell us what's really going on," Jackie said. "Jonathan ain't giving you all these flowers and you ain't putting out nothing."

I ignored Jackie, opened the card and read it.

I'm not finished with you yet! was written inside of the card, and Mr. Boss Man signed it. I laughed and put the card back inside of the envelope. I wasn't quite sure what his words meant, but I put the envelope inside my purse so no one would see it.

"Sylvia," Jackie said, snapping me out of my trance. "I can't believe you've been holding back on us."

"Girl, I haven't been holding back on nothing. Jonathan is a really nice person, Jackie, and I couldn't have asked for a better boss."

"He really is a true gentleman. I came this close," Audrey said, holding her fingers closely together, "to screwing his brains out last night."

Shocked, my eyes widened. "Last night? Audrey, quit your lying, girl."

"No, I'm serious. He and I had a drink at CJ's, and by the time we left he was all over me. I made it perfectly clear to him that I do not sleep with married men. After that, he walked me to my car and left."

"Really?" I was pissed, but still a little skeptical about Audrey's claim. "It doesn't seem like Jonathan to be so forceful but—"

"Well, he was. He be putting on this act when he's at work, but don't get him alone with you. He's like a wild animal trying to break out of a cage."

Disappointed by what Audrey had said, I told her and Jackie I was on my way to the bagel shop to get a bagel. On my way downstairs, I couldn't help but to replay the entire night in my mind over and over again. I knew Jonathan was hurt, and if he was looking for any woman to give him some attention, I wasn't going to be the one. After thinking about him never giving me any attention, until reality finally hit him about Dana, I was discouraged with myself for letting things go as far as they did last night.

When I got back upstairs, many people walked slowly by my desk to look at all the flowers. I got so tired of everybody asking me about them that I posted up a huge sign that said: MY MAN LOVES ME!

It was almost ten o'clock, so I knew Jonathan was coming in soon. I was a bit nervous about seeing him, but if anything, I really wanted to know how he felt after what happened between us last night.

As I filed some papers away, the phone rang and it was Dana. I knew her call was coming soon, and when I told her I was a little busy, she wouldn't let me go.

"You've never been too busy to talk to me before, Sylvia."

"Truly, today, I am. Jonathan will be here soon and I haven't done anything this morning."

"You never do anything anyway. And if you do any work today, you need to work on throwing all those darn roses in the trashcan."

"Whew, you are on a roll this morning, aren't you?"

"You're damn right I am. Do you know that playboy husband of mine did not come home until six o'clock this morning?"

I pretended to be shocked. "For real!"

"Yes. And when he got here, he didn't say anything to me. I tried to argue with him and he completely ignored me. He showered, changed clothes, and left."

"Girl, that's a shame."

"Sylvia!"

"What!"

"Normally, you have a slew of shit to say."

"Well, today, I don't. I told you I was busy."

"Okay, fine. Then, let me speak to Jonathan."

"I already told you he wouldn't be in until eleven."

"Where is he?"

"I don't know. According to his calendar, he should be here soon."

"Girl, I swear, if he's sleeping with another woman . . ."

"What, Dana? Just what are you going to do when you've done nothing but fuck him over?"

"Stop taking his side all the time, please. I wish you would see things from my point of view."

"I've tried, Dana. Lord knows I've tried, but I will never understand how you could let a man like him slip away. Anyway," I said, as I saw Jonathan coming through the door. "I'll tell him to call you when he gets here. I gotta go because Mr. Bradford been walking around and I don't want him to see me running my mouth on the phone."

"Bye, girl. And call me later. I have something else I need to talk to you about."

"I will," I said, hanging up.

Jonathan stopped at the receptionist's desk and talked to Sandra. Feeling nervous about seeing him, I stood up and went over to the file cabinet, pretending to be busy. My back was turned, and when he snuck up from behind me, I acted surprised.

"You startled me," I said, holding my chest.

"Yeah, right, Sylvia. Has anyone called?"

"Dana. Other than her, it's been kind of quiet this morning."

"So," he said.

"So, what?"

His eyes scanned my cubicle. "Do you like the flowers?"

"Oh, yeah, thanks. I love them, but you really didn't have to."

"I know, but when I forget about you next year, I don't want you crying about it."

"You'd better not forget about me next year, and if you do, you will most definitely pay for it."

"I'm sure I will," he said, looking through some papers on my desk.

I noticed Jonathan's casual attire and checked out how amazing he looked in a peach Ralph Lauren shirt, khakis, and shiny loafers. When I asked why he was casually dressed, he said that he was leaving and would be gone for the rest of the day. When I asked where he was going, he wouldn't tell me. I followed him into his office.

"So, we got secrets now, huh?" I asked.

"No, Sylvia. I'll be out for the entire day. Take messages for me and let my callers know I won't be back until Monday."

"Monday?"

"Yes, Monday."

According to Jonathan's calendar, he had three appointments scheduled for today, and two court cases scheduled for tomorrow. "So what are you going to do about your appointments?"

"I've already taken care of them," he said, reaching for his phone. "Now, is there anything else?"

"I guess not, but I wish you would have told me so I could have prepared myself for you being out of the office."

"That's why I'm telling you now."

"Don't even go there with me, Jonathan. You know better than I do that we've always communicated better than this."

"Sylvia, look. I told you I had something to take care of. Stop pressing the issue and chill, all right?"

His tone upset me, so I raised my voice. "Excuse the hell out of me. Let me get out of your hair, since I seem to be such a pain."

"Sounds like a good idea to me," he said then dialed out on his phone.

I didn't bother to respond and just left his office. This was becoming an everyday habit. I was truly getting sick and tired of it. What was with his attitude? He knew that abruptly changing his schedule would complicate my day, and he always let me know things ahead of time so I could prepare. He'd never done this before, and I didn't like the changes I was seeing in him.

I went to the ladies' room to freshen up a bit. Audrey came in and filled my head with some more juice on Jonathan. I didn't know whether to believe her about his behavior, but by the way he was acting, it must have been true.

After I left the ladies' room, I walked down the hall and someone snatched me into the boardroom. The room was pitch-black, but I knew it was Jonathan when he covered my mouth and I got a whiff of his cologne.

"I need to go find out some things about my wife," he whispered. "Do not tell anyone what I'm doing, including her. All you know is I'm in court today, okay?"

I nodded and he removed his hand from my mouth. "When I asked you earlier, that's all you had to say, Jonathan."

"Not with my door open, Sylvia. There are so many nosy people around here, and I didn't want to take any chances with them listening in on us."

"You're right. And I hope you find out what it is that you're looking for."

"I think I already found it." He inched forward to kiss me. Foolishly, I rubbed the back of his head and indulged myself in a lengthy kiss with him. Feeling myself getting so caught up with him, I backed away.

"Jonathan, I don't think this is going to work out for me. I—"

He silenced me with another kiss, and then his hands started to roam on my hips and ass. I was scorching hot from his touch and wanted more than anything to break the brotha down right then and there. But my thoughts of Dana stopped me.

"Please," I whispered. "Stop forcing yourself on me like this, Jonathan. You know this ain't right."

"I can't help myself," he said.

When he moved in for another kiss, I turned my head. "Work it out at home first. After that, then we'll talk about us."

Jonathan turned on the lights and searched deep into my eyes. "I need you, Sylvia. Soon, Dana's going to need you, too. I hope that whatever goes down between her and me, it doesn't interfere with us."

"I hope it doesn't either, but I'll do the best I can to be there for both of you."

I opened the door and Jonathan walked out behind me. As we headed back to his office, Audrey walked past and slid something in his hand. He held it tightly, and when I asked what it was, he shrugged his shoulders.

"What do you mean by you don't know?" I asked, standing in his doorway.

"I mean, it's still in my hand and I haven't looked at it."

"Well, look at it."

"I will, but what's it to you?"

"Nothing, I guess, especially since you almost wound up at her house last night, instead of at mine. It's a good thing she doesn't mess around with married men, huh?"

"Is that what she told you?"

"Yes. She also told me you were begging for it."

"Sylvia, do I look like the kind of man who would beg for sex?"

I smiled and shook my head. "No, but just be careful, okay? One thing can always lead to another."

Jonathan packed up a few things in his office and told me he'd see me on Monday. Three whole days without seeing him, and I wasn't sure what I was going to do. My feelings for him were now beyond my control. I knew it would be a matter of time before we had sex, but I was going to fight it with every ounce of strength I had.

By the end of the day, I really didn't have much to do. I'd been to Jackie's and Audrey's desks about fifty times today, getting the scoop on Lewis, and listened to more lies about Jonathan. I wanted to tell Audrey to go to hell, but I continued to let her make a fool of herself.

Before leaving, I called Jeff from the mailroom to see if he would help me take my flowers to my car. And just when we were about to leave, the phone rang. I was going to let it go to voicemail, but something inside told me to answer. When I did, it was Britney. She was crying hysterically and was asking for Jonathan. When I told her he wasn't there, I asked where she was. After she told me, I told her I was on my way.

Jeff piled my car with the flowers, and I headed to Forest Park where Britney said she would be. I drove around for a while looking for her, and when I saw her sitting on some steps near the Art Museum, I pulled over and got out of the car. Still crying, Britney ran up and held me tightly.

"What's the matter, sweetie?" I asked, hugging her back.

"Da . . . Darron," she sobbed. "Punched me in my face today."

"He did what?" I yelled, then moved her back and looked at her face. I noticed swelling underneath her left eye. "Come on over here and sit down so you can tell me what happened."

Britney and I sat on the steps, and in so many words, she told me this damn fool punched her in the face because she refused to have sex with him. *Who in the hell was responsible for raising that idiot?* I thought.

I placed the tip of my finger on Britney's face that was swollen. "Does that hurt?"

"Yes, a little."

"Britney, why were you skipping school? You have so many good things going for you and look at how beautiful you are. Jonathan pays a lot of money for you to go to a private school, and all you can think about is skipping school and hanging out with a knuckleheaded fool."

She rolled her eyes and placed her hand on the side of her face. "I'm beginning to hate school, Sylvia. Darron and me always skip, but I never thought he would hit me over something so stupid."

I balled my fist and put it on display. "That's just the beginning. And if you ever skip school again, I'm going to hurt you myself."

Britney laughed. When her cell phone vibrated, she looked at it. "This is him calling me now."

I held out my hand. "Give it to me."

"No, Sylvia."

"I said, give me the phone!"

Britney gave the phone to me. "Hello," I said, sharply.

"Britney?"

"No."

"Let me speak to Britney."

"I don't think so. But let me warn you before you even think about putting your hands on her again. I will mess you up, Darron. If you don't believe me, hit her again. If you put your hands on her again, the last time anyone will see you will be on the news."

He hung up, and Britney reached over to hug me. She laughed again. "You are so crazy. Thank you, but you don't have to worry about me seeing him again. Nobody ever put their hands on me before, not even my daddy."

"Well, he should have. I'm not going to make excuses for you, Britney, but you need to get your act together. You don't need that cell phone, you need to stop walking around with those low-cut jeans on that show your thong, and must you get your nails and hair done every week? I work hard and I can't even afford to do that."

"Every teenager I know got a cell phone, Sylvia, and the things I wear, everybody wears them. I guess you haven't seen my tattoo yet, have you?" She turned around and showed me BABY-B tattooed right above the crack of her ass with a rose next to it.

I shook my head. "That is ridiculous. Y'all need to stop trying to compete with each other and just be yourself. If attention is what you're looking for, because that's all it is, you won't get it if you're looking like everyone else around you. Be different, original. Then you'll see how much attention you get."

"None," she said, standing up and tucking her DKNY purse underneath her arm. She put her cell phone in her pocket and pulled her skimpy T-shirt down that showed her midriff. When I noticed her navel pierced, I stood up and looked at her.

"Let's go. You need some serious guidance, and some ice for that eye before it swells even more."

Britney and I got in the car and left. Before heading to my house, we stopped at Dairy Queen and got two strawberry shortcakes with extra whipped cream topping and nuts. As we came through the door, we laughed because she dropped hers on the ground.

"Damn," she yelled, then covered her mouth.

I gave her a hard stare, and then tossed my keys on the table. "Watch it, girl. You ain't that grown yet."

"I'm sorry, but I really wanted that." She plopped down on the couch.

I turned on the TV and called my neighbor, Steven, to ask if he wouldn't mind helping me with my flowers. Shortly after, he came over to get the keys to my car. Britney and I sat on the couch eating my strawberry shortcake and watched him bring the flowers in.

"My daddy must really love you. I have never seen so many flowers."

"Neither have I. And the only people your daddy loves are you, his parents, and Dana."

"I can't stand that bitch," Britney said, covering her mouth again.

"Britney, that's my last time warning you. Young girls ain't supposed to curse like that. You are too much of a classy young lady to be using such foul language."

Britney rolled her eyes, slid down on the couch, and continued to eat the strawberry shortcake. After Steven brought in all my flowers, I thanked him and stood at the door listening to him hint about us having sex.

"Must everything you do for me always have to end up with us having sex?" I whispered.

"Not always, baby, but you know you be putting something on a brotha's mind."

I looked over at Britney who was all ears, listening to our conversation. "Maybe next time, okay?" I said, looking back at Steven.

"I'm cool with that. Just don't have me waiting so long and I'm right next door."

"I won't, Steven, if maybe next time you figure out a way not to come in two minutes, darling. And even though you're right next door, I'm a tiny bit more excited about the brothas who last a lot longer than you."

"Well, next time, you get them to help you with your shit. Don't be calling—"

His voice rose, so I slammed the door. "Tired, truly tired," I said, walking back over to the couch and sitting next to Britney. She was cracking up. When I saw that she ate the shortcake, I snatched the empty container from her.

"Greedy, child. What in the heck happen to all of my shortcake?"

"You were running your mouth too long and I was hungry."

"Well, go home and eat."

"I don't like being at home."

"Okay. You don't like being at school, you don't like being at home, and you don't like my friend Dana. Who or what do you like, Britney?"

"Dana is not your friend. And I don't like anyone but you and my daddy. I wish y'all had somehow hooked up. That way, I could have lived with y'all."

I was quiet because that was not only her wish, but my wish as well. Thinking about Jonathan, I went to the kitchen to get Britney an ice pack for her eye. While I was getting it, she came in and sat at the kitchen table.

"Sylvia?"

"What?"

"What's up with this sex thing? I mean, I'm still a virgin but I have thought about it."

"And that's all you need to do is think about it," I said, giving her the ice pack. She placed it underneath her eye. "Britney, sex is a beautiful thing. But beautiful things aren't meant to be shared with any- and everyone. As a young lady, you need to have respect for yourself. I'm not telling you not to have sex because I have a feeling that you're going to do what you want to do. I'm just saying that life is about making choices, some good and some bad, but the bad choices are the ones that hurts us every time. We both know that it is not a good choice for a girl your age to be having sex, so with that being said, just know and understand the consequences."

Britney smiled and laid the ice pack on the table. "Do you love my daddy?"

My mouth dropped open. "Wha . . . Why did you ask me that?"

"I don't know. I guess I kind of see something in you when he's around you and when you talk about him."

"Yes, Britney, I love your father," I said, standing up. "But, I'm not in love with him, if that's what you're asking."

"If you say so." She stood up and walked off to the bathroom. When the phone rang I answered it.

"What kind of friend are you?" Dana shouted.

I was silent for a second and my heart raced. "Wha—"

"Didn't I tell you I had something I wanted to talk to you about?"

I was relieved to hear that it wasn't about me and Jonathan. "Girl, I'm sorry. I completely forgot."

"Can you meet me at CJ's in about an hour?"

"No, I can't. I have company right now."

"Well, tell that Negro you got something else to do."

"I will do no such thing. If you can't talk to me over the phone then it'll just have to wait until tomorrow."

"Some damn friend you are," she said, and then hung up. Feeling bad about not meeting Dana, I called her back and told her I could meet her in a few hours. When she declined to wait, I hung up on her.

Britney wanted to stay the night, but I insisted that she call Beverly to tell her she was on her way home. When Britney refused to call, I made the call to tell Beverly. Britney pouted and fell back in the chair.

"Let's go, Britney. I have to get up early for work tomorrow."

"Why can't I stay here? You can take me home in the morning."

"Because I'm sure your mother is worried sick about you. Besides, why sleep on my uncomfortable couch when you have a lovely room at home waiting for you?"

She jumped up and folded her arms. "Whatever. Now, I have to go home and listen to my mother's mouth about my face. If I tell her what happened, she's going to be mad at me for skipping school."

"Okay, this time and this time only will I lie for you. I will tell her that the school called because you hurt yourself in gym, and since Jonathan was out of the office, I came to pick you up. I will, however, tell Jonathan the truth and you'll have to deal with him instead of her."

"Fine," she said with an attitude.

We headed to the car, and on the drive to Britney's house, she wouldn't stop questioning me about Jonathan. I didn't think my feelings for him were that obvious.

"Okay, Sylvia, if you don't want to be honest with me about your feelings for my dad, then tell me when you lost your virginity."

"I am honest with you about my feelings and I lost my virginity when I was fifteen. After that, I turned into a promiscuous little something. I was screwing any- and everybody who wanted some."

"Why? And then you have the nerve to tell me what you think I shouldn't do."

"I only told you what I thought was best. And that little promiscuous little something who was screwing around with any- and everybody was the reputation I got for giving it up to a loudmouth Negro who wasn't worth my time. After my first time, it took me a long while before I had sex again because the rumors were damaging."

Britney smiled, and when we got to her house, I went inside and lied my ass off to Beverly. I didn't feel good about doing so, but Britney was at a stage in her life where she needed someone to trust. Not only that, but she needed someone to depend on. And if Jonathan or Beverly wasn't there to make her feel at ease, I didn't mind her relying on me.

6

JONATHAN

I was on a mission to find out what was going on with Dana. More so to find out who in the hell she was screwing. There was no way for me to continue on with our marriage and things weren't right. I worked too hard to be unhappy and it was high time that my life started to make sense.

The other day when Lewis was in my office, something hit me. If it wasn't the same cheap-ass cologne on him that I smelled on Dana, it was Sylvia's hateful ways toward him that sparked my curiosity. I really wasn't sure if I was on to something, but it was a start. I figured if I worked on Sylvia a little while longer, she would tell me everything I needed to know. I hated more than anything to put her in the middle, but there was no other way to find out the truth. I was desperate. And even though I had some feelings for Sylvia, finding out what Dana was up to was more important to me.

After I left the office, I went back home and watched for Dana to leave. When she did, I followed her. She drove to her parents' house, stayed there for a while, and then she drove to West County Plaza. Spending very minimal time there, then she drove to the movie theater and watched a movie alone. By eight o'clock, she checked herself into the Holiday Inn, and just when I thought my man was about to show, she checked back out two hours later. She called me numerous times, but I refused to answer my phone. By 10:30 p.m., she was back at home, calling it a night. I decided not to go home yet and got myself a room for the night. I wanted to go see Sylvia, but I also wanted to wait until I had a little more evidence. That way she wouldn't be able to deny me the truth about Dana.

Friday morning, I checked out of the hotel around seven. Trying to give Dana some ammunition, I went home and slammed the back door as I entered the house. My shirt was unbuttoned and it looked slouchy, hanging outside of my pants, as if I'd been out doing my thing. She rushed toward me, as I rushed to the bathroom to take a shower.

"Where in the fuck have you been?" she yelled, and then smacked my face.

I grabbed her hand to stop her from doing it again. "Stop! Get a hold of yourself and back the hell away from me."

Dana's face was turning red she was so mad. "You have not called, nor have you been here for almost two days, Jonathan! For the last time, where in the fuck have you been?"

"None of your business. When you're ready to tell me who in the hell you've been screwing, then I'll tell you where I've been. Until then, don't expect me to come home because I won't." I walked into the bathroom and slammed the door.

"What in the hell do you expect me to do?" she yelled and banged on the door. "I'm tired of being alone! You are never here for me, nor have you ever been here for me!"

I ignored Dana and took a shower. When I came out with no clothes on, I saw her sitting on the bed, wiping her tears.

"Do you want a divorce?" she asked.

"Only if you do."

I went into the closet to find something to put on. Dana followed behind me and wrapped her arms around my chest. "A divorce is the last thing I want, but some things need to change around here."

I removed her arms from around me and turned to look at her. "Some things like what, Dana? You have everything that you need. I treat you like a queen and that still isn't good enough. Yes, I'm a workaholic, but you knew that before you married me. The only question I have for you is, are you seeing someone else?"

She moved her head from side to side, denying it. "No, I'm not seeing anyone else."

"Now is the perfect opportunity to come clean with me. I will not give you another chance again."

"Jonathan, for the last time, I'm not seeing anyone else. You're accusing me because you're the one seeing someone else. If you want to be with her, then just say so. Don't put all your bull and insecurities off on me."

I moved Dana aside and went into the bedroom. As I put on my clothes, she stood next to me and asked where I was headed. I told her to work, and then told her we'd continue our conversation tonight. After that, I left.

Having no intentions to go to work, I parked my car far down the street and waited for her to leave. When she did, I followed her again. This time, she stopped at the St. Louis Bread Company and had breakfast, and then she checked herself into the Holiday Inn again. Not knowing if her lover would show soon, I parked my car across the street and went inside the hotel. I asked for Dana's room number, and when the front desk clerk gave it to me, I headed up to Dana's room. Nervous, I stood by a vending machine in the hallway and watched.

As I started to feel down on myself for stalking my own damn wife, when I clearly said I never would, I decided to leave. I went to the elevator and pushed the down button. My head hung low, but when the elevator opened, I looked up and stared face to face with Lewis. His eyes grew wide and a sly smirk was on his face. I was surprised to see him with another woman on his side. He stepped off the elevator with his arm resting on her shoulders.

"Hey, Mr. T," he said, and then slapped his hand against mine.

"Wha . . . what's up, Lewis?"

"Nothing. Just enjoying my few days of vacation. But, uh, this is Alisha. Alisha, this is Mr. Taylor. He is like the Man where I work and he's the one I told you about possibly hooking a brotha up."

"Hello," she said with a smile.

"Hi, Alisha. Lewis," I said, shaking his hand. "Enjoy your vacation. Come see me when you get back to the office."

"Will do, Mr. T. Most definitely, will do."

Lewis and Alisha walked off, and before I got on the elevator, I watched as they walked right by Dana's room and went into another. Confused more than ever, I headed back to my car and left.

My mind was going a mile a minute. I couldn't think straight. The only conclusion I could come to was Dana, the woman I loved more than life itself, was having a threesome? Of course Lewis wouldn't go into her room after seeing me, but why get another room if they were all in it together? Something wasn't right, and I felt stupid for not being able to put my finger on this shit.

After having a late lunch, I chilled in my car for a while and waited for most of the cars in the parking garage to clear. By six o'clock that evening, I noticed most of the cars gone so I headed upstairs to my office. Being payday, mostly everyone had jetted. But when I heard the copy machine going in the copy room and saw the light on, I went into the copy room to see who was there. It was

Sylvia. She had her back turned and had piles of paper stacked everywhere. I stood in the doorway and checked her out from head to toe.

Her gray short fuzzy skirt that she wore gripped every bit of her ass, as well as her hips that she often swayed from side to side to get my attention.

With Sylvia's back facing the door, I saw her glance at the round clock on the wall. I assumed she was ready to go, but I didn't want her to leave just yet. The room felt kind of stuffy, and I stepped up behind her, as she reached over to the thermostat to lower the temperature. She felt me press my body against her, and without saying one word, she lifted her hand to rub the back of my head.

"I need you, Sylvia," I whispered with my lips close to her ear. "I need you now."

Without hesitating, all she said was, "Take me now."

I slowly removed the buttons on her silk blouse, one by one. I then pulled it open, massaging her breasts together and manipulating her hard nipples. She squirmed from the touch of my hands, and turned around to face me. We stared into each other's eyes, knowing that what we were about to do was wrong on so many different levels. I, however, inched Sylvia's miniskirt over the curves in her hips and eased her lace panties down to the floor. She happily stepped out of them then turned to face the copier. Afterward, she bent slightly over, and hiked her right leg on top of the copier, providing me with easier access to her pussy. I held her leg in place with one hand and unzipped my pants with the other. They dropped to my ankles, and it didn't take long for me to step out of my pants and shoes. I pressed my hardness against her round ass, but didn't enter her just yet. Wanting to taste her, I dropped to my knees and began to take light licks between her slit. Her pussy was staring me right in the face, and I couldn't help but to go deeper, causing her legs to buckle.

"Hold on, baby," I said. "I need more of this."

Sylvia nodded, but she couldn't get a hold of herself. My thick fingers kept circling her clit, and my tongue felt so good to her that she sprayed my face with her sweet juices. So eager for her, I cut her orgasm short and released my tongue from her insides, replacing it with my dick. Almost immediately, her breathing halted. She squeezed her eyes, and unsure of what she was thinking, I didn't move until she started bouncing her ass against me. The sounds of her pussy juices echoed in the tiny room, and the smell of sex scented the air, turning me on even more. I was hyped and could no longer remain quiet.

"Thi . . . this pussy is so wet and good, baby, that I can barely stand. I want this shit to last longer, so let's move over to the chair or table," I suggested.

I hated to pull out of her, but as soon as I sat in the chair, Sylvia straddled me. I gripped her ass and pulled her cheeks far apart so my thick meat could fill her to capacity. We both moaned together, giving the chair a for real workout. It squeaked, rolled around, and almost tilted over as she gave me a damn good ride. Even better than Dana's riding skills. I wanted to say that shit out loud, but I was too caught up to say anything right now. My mind, however, was racing. I kept telling myself that this was wrong, and fuck Dana. Fuck her, and damn her for betraying me. I knew she was; I just had to find out more. Right now, Sylvia was helping me cope. I closed my eyes and lowered my head to suck her firm breasts. Sylvia stopped me, though. She lifted my head, causing me to open my eyes and look into hers. A slow tear rolled down her cheek, but she continued to ride me.

"I . . . I had to do this, Jonathan," she said tearfully. "Please don't hate me for betraying Dana."

I said not one word. All I did was rise up from the chair, and secure her in my arms. I laid her on the floor and maneuvered my body in between her legs. She wrapped them around me, and I rubbed up and down them before entering her wetness again. I continued to search into her eyes, looking for answers.

"I've had a rough day, Sylvia," I finally said. "I'm hurting, baby, and I know you have the answers for me. Please, tell me. I'm begging you to tell me if Dana is cheating on me. If so, I need to know with who."

I dropped my head on her chest, shielding the hurt that was visible in my eyes. Sylvia paused for a minute, and then she pressed her hand against my chest for me to back away from her. My limp dick slid out of her. I waited for a response.

"Jonathan, I told you before that—"

"Please!" I yelled, knowing that she was about to feed me a bunch of bullshit. "It is Lewis, isn't it? Just tell me, damn it! Is it Lewis?"

Sylvia quickly stood up and pulled down her skirt. I figured she was about to leave, so I rushed up from the floor and reached out to embrace her.

"I'm begging you, Sylvia, please. Just tell me if it's Lewis. That's all I need is a yes or no."

Her mouth opened, but she hadn't said anything. Then there was a soft whisper. She whispered, "Yes," and told me that Dana had been cheating with Lewis for the past three years.

After the admission, near tears, Sylvia ran out of the room. Stunned by the longevity of Dana and Lewis's relationship, I fell back in the chair, feeling numb. I placed my hands over my face and rubbed it up and down, as I thought about all I'd done for Dana. And for her to cheat on me with a brotha like Lewis was gut-wrenching.

When Sylvia came back into the room, I was a mess. My head was on the table and all I could ask myself was why. She rubbed the waves on my head, thanked me for the flowers, and told me if I needed a friend to call her. After that, she left.

Soon after she left, I put my clothes back on and went into my office. I looked at the thirty-six messages Sylvia had taken for me today and listened to several voicemail messages from Beverly who cursed me out for not meeting with her today about Britney. I had forgotten about our meeting. My mind was focused on nothing but finding out the truth about Dana.

And now that I knew, I didn't know what to do next. Was kicking her out and divorcing her the answer? I hadn't a clue. Either way, I knew I'd have to face her about what I knew and soon.

By the time I'd gotten home, which wasn't until one o'clock in the morning, my mind was in shambles. Surprisingly, I'd thought about killing both of the motherfuckers and calling it a day. I had no idea how I would react when I saw Dana, but I prayed to the Lord for Him to give me strength. If there ever was a time in my life I needed Him to keep me on the right track, it most certainly was now. And Lewis? Out of all the men she could cheat on me with, why him? What was it about this young, punk-ass fool that attracted her? One time, maybe, but for three damn years? What a serious fool I had been.

I quietly entered the house through the back door. Finally, in the kitchen, Dana had the nerve to leave a plate of food covered with a napkin on the table. Thinking that she probably wanted to poison my ass, I took the plate and threw it in the trash. When I entered the living room, she was in her normal place, which was knocked out on the couch with an empty bottle of wine next to her. I stood for a moment, and then I took a seat in a chair across from her and stared. Her hair hung down over her face. I could barely see her eyes. She was naked and had a towel covering her body. As I looked around at our beautiful home, I wondered what in the hell was missing? Everything we wanted, we both had. And if we didn't have it, we could always get it. So, why? I couldn't stop asking myself, why did she feel as if she needed something else?

As I continued in deep thought, Dana squirmed around on the couch. When she saw me in the chair, she moved her hair away from her face and slowly sat up.

"What time is it?" She squeezed her forehead then reached for her watch on the table. After seeing what time it was, she looked at me. "How long have you been here?"

I ignored her question and continued to stare.

"Jonathan, did you hear me?"

I nodded. "Too long, Dana. I've been here for too long."

She moved the towel away from her and slowly walked over to me, placing her hand on the side of my face.

"Make love to me, tonight," she softly whispered. "Please don't tell me you're too tired or you don't feel like it, okay?"

I closed my eyes and placed my hand over hers to stop her from touching me. Trying to get my thoughts together, I finally opened my eyes to look at her. "Did you ask Lewis the same question today?"

She took a hard swallow. "I'm aware that you know. I can tell by the look in your eyes and by the sound of your voice. An . . . and all I can say is that I'm sorry. I'm sorry for hurting you and I never intended for things to go this far."

This time, I took a hard swallow as I'd finally heard it straight from her mouth. A sense of relief came over me, but the pain inside was unlike any pain that I'd felt before.

"Sorry?" I said, as a tear rolled down my face. "Is that all you can stand there and say to me?"

She kneeled down. "There's so much more, but before you go making any critical decisions, I want you to listen to me. I love you," she said, touching my hand. "But there were so many things wrong in our marriage that—"

I snatched my hand away from hers. "If there was so many things wrong, Dana, you should have confided in me! Why didn't you come to me and tell me?"

"I tried." She dropped her head and cried. "I tried so hard, but you never had time to listen to me. I asked you over and over to make time for us and you never would. I was so lonely, baby, I swear—"

"I don't want to hear it!" I said, standing up. "I want you out of this house and out of my life as soon as possible. You are not going to blame me for your fuckups, Dana, and I mean it!"

"Jonathan, please baby, listen to me." She followed me into the bedroom. "I . . . I can't make it without you. You are my life. I made a mistake and I said I'm sorry."

"It's not that simple!" I turned around, gritting my teeth. "Sorry my ass! I want a divorce and there's nothing else that needs to be said." I walked into the bathroom and slammed the door.

I could hear Dana's cries through the door, and hurting my damn self, I let some tears fall too. Our marriage meant everything to me, and knowing that we were about to lose it tore me up on the inside. In so much pain, I took off my clothes, sat on the seat in the shower, and let the warm water pour on me.

7

SYLVIA

I rushed out of the office, thinking about what I'd done. If allowing Jonathan to fuck me wasn't bad enough, confirming for him Dana and Lewis' relationship definitely was. SNAKE-ASS BITCH was written across my face, and even though my pussy felt complete satisfaction, I was a wreck.

After I went home and showered, I sat in front of the TV that had buzzed for hours. I thought about Jonathan the entire time. God was I loving this man so much. I couldn't help myself, and after what happened between us today, I loved him even more. His touch was all I'd imagined it to be, and how gentle he was, I couldn't stop thinking about him. He was deeply hurt, though, and I'd never seen him look so torn before. The look in his eyes, as he held me in his arms, I'd never forget. I could kill Dana for cheating on him. If anybody deserved to be hurt, it for surely should not have been Jonathan.

Dana called several times about us getting together over the weekend, but I wasn't sure if it was one of her attempts to use me so she could see Lewis. Either way, I put off her phone call until early Saturday morning. When I called her, Jonathan answered their home phone. I was almost at a loss for words.

"Hi, uh, Jonathan. Is Dana there?"

"No."

I paused before speaking again. "O . . . okay, well, I'll try her cell phone."

"She's at her parents' house."

"I see. So, did you get a chance to talk to her last night?"

"We're getting a divorce, Sylvia. But, I don't want to talk about it right now. I'll see you Monday."

"I thought you weren't coming in on Monday."

"I'll be there."

"Okay. And, again, thanks for the flowers. They're beautiful, but I'm starting to feel as if I'm at a funeral home or something."

Jonathan let out a soft snicker. "I'll cancel the ones I have set up for delivery on Monday and Tuesday."

"Please. There's no room in my house for any—"

"No explanation needed. I'll cancel them. Good-bye, Sylvia."

"Good-bye, Jonathan."

I could feel and hear the pain in his voice. Desperately wanting to know what went down, I hurried to call Dana's parents' house. When Mama Bell answered, she said Dana had gone horseback riding with her father. She asked me if I knew what happened between Jonathan and Dana, but I pretended not to know a thing. Mama Bell promised me she'd have Dana call me as soon as she got back.

Around five o'clock that evening, Dana called. She sounded like she was a basket case and said that she was on her way over to see me. Not knowing how I was going to react after screwing her husband, I prepared myself for an uncomfortable and awkward situation.

When the doorbell rang, I thought it was Dana, but when I opened the door it was Britney. She waved good-bye to someone in a Ford Escort and stepped into my house.

"What are you doing here?" I asked.

"I'm spending the weekend with you. You told me I could come over anytime I felt like it." She took her backpack off her shoulders and put it in the chair.

I closed the door. "Now, I don't remember saying all that, but you need to call first, Britney."

"Call for what? You don't ever answer your phone."

"You need to call just in case I have one of my li'l . . . little playmates over here or something."

She laughed. "You said that you weren't, but I bet you were wild back in high school, Sylvia."

"Okay, so I'm a hoochie mama now, but back then, trust me, sista girl was all good."

"If you say so," she said, following me into the kitchen. She sat on a stool in front of the counter, watching as I put the finishing touches on my spaghetti. Not wanting Dana to see her, I asked Britney if she wouldn't mind chilling in my room until we finished talking. Insisting that she didn't want to see Dana, she agreed.

Almost an hour later, I opened the door and Dana came in. She tightly embraced me and tears immediately rushed to the brim of her eyes. I rubbed her back, and then invited her inside so she could sit.

"Have a seat and calm down," I said. "I cooked some spaghetti. Would you like some?"

She shook her head, plopped down in the chair and took a hard swallow. "Maybe later. I . . . I just, girl, you . . . you don't know how I feel right now."

"No, I don't, but tell me what happened." I sat on the couch that was next to the chair. "I called you this morning and Jonathan said you were at your parents' house. He mentioned something about a divorce?"

"Yes." Dana covered her face. "He knows about Lewis and me. I tried to explain it to him, but he just doesn't understand."

"Did you expect him to, Dana?"

"No, but I at least thought he would understand what I've been going through. Then again, shit, I don't know. A huge part of me really thought he would forgive me."

"So, how do you know he won't forgive you?"

"Because you should have seen the look in his eyes. He was so disappointed and disgusted with me. I've never seen him cry before. He was hurt, Sylvia, and nothing I could say or do would change his mind."

"I hate to say this, but I—"

"I know, I know," she said, folding her arms and rocking back and forth. "Please don't say you told me so. I know I screwed up. I met Lewis at the Holiday Inn yesterday so I could tell him we needed to chill. I could tell Jonathan was getting suspicious and it was a matter of time that the truth came to the light."

"Chill, huh. That's all you intended to do with Lewis was chill? For how long, Dana? A month? Two months? Three? How long?"

"No, this time, I wanted it over. Lewis kept trying to talk me out of it, but I knew calling it off with him was for the best."

Frustrated with Dana, and at myself for even getting involved, I poured both of us a drink. I handed the glass of wine to her and sat back down on the couch. Dana rambled through her Coach purse for some Kleenex, and then took a sip from the glass. She leaned back in the chair, closed her eyes, and took a deep breath.

"I guess he's responsible for all of these flowers around here, huh?" she questioned.

"Dana, please don't start. Don't go digging up dirt on him because you messed up."

"I'm not, but he hasn't given me roses in years. Of course I'm going to be upset when I see you with all of these darn flowers."

"It was just a friendly gesture. Secretary's Day is over, and since it bothers you that much, I promise you I will never gripe again."

She laughed and wiped her runny nose. "Good. And since you're my best friend, and you seem to be the only person who can knock some sense into my husband's head, I need a favor."

"What?"

"I need for you to help me get my man back."

"Dana, look, I'm out of it. There's nothing I can say or do that will help you get Jonathan back, trust me." Not wanting to go there with her, I got off the couch and turned on the TV. I pretended that it had my attention, and I hoped she didn't notice me fidgeting.

"Sylvia, please. Just talk to him for me. Let him know how much I love him. Tell him I would never do anything to hurt him, please. He'll listen to you."

"No, he won't. If anything, he's going to be mad at me for knowing about you and Lewis and not saying a word. I'm sure he's put one and two together and figured out I lied to him about us being together on the weekends. I need my job, Dana, so keep me out of it."

I got up again, but this time I went into the kitchen. Dana followed me in her loud heels that sounded off on my hardwood floors. I pulled two plates from the kitchen cabinet, but when I asked again if she wanted any spaghetti, she declined and said that she didn't want any food to get on her white pantsuit.

"Thanks, though," she said, swinging her long hair over to the side. "I'm not staying. Daddy wants me to do something for him so I gotta get back soon. Think about what I said and help a sista girl out this time. I know I've always complained about you being in my business, but you might be the only person who can help me save my marriage."

After that comment, I couldn't even look Dana in her eyes. All I did was shrug. "I'll do what I can, Dana."

"Try hard and let me know if you make any progress. Thank you."

She kissed me on the cheek, gave me another hug and left. As soon as she closed the front door, Britney came out of my room with her hands on her hips.

"Oh, no she didn't cheat on my damn daddy!"

"Britney, watch your mouth and calm down."

"Sylvia, I know she's your friend, but she will not misuse him." Britney picked up the phone.

"Who are you calling?"

"My father, that's who. I'm telling him to come pick me up."

"Put the phone down, Britney."

Before I could say anything else, Britney left Jonathan a message about his conniving-ass wife, and told him to call her cell phone as soon as possible. After she told him she loved him, she hung up.

"I thought you cared about my father, Sylvia. How could you defend her when you know she's wrong for that?"

"I'm not defending her. It's up to Jonathan to do something about it. Not me, you, or anyone else."

"Then please don't try to talk him into getting back with Dana. I can't stand her and she can't stand me. He don't need to be with her anyway."

"Again, Britney, that's your father's choice. Now, do you want some of this spaghetti or not?"

"Of course," she said, sitting down to eat.

We ate dinner together. After dinner, we rented some movies and chilled out in the living room to watch them. No sooner had I slid in the first movie, than the phone rang. When I answered, it was Jonathan.

"Are you alone?" he asked.

"No."

"Male or female?"

"Young female."

"Britney?"

"Yes."

"Come see me."

"When?"

"Now."

"Where?"

"At my house."

"No way."

"Then at the office in one hour."

"Good-bye," I said, hanging up.

I looked at Britney. "Who was that?" she asked.

"A friend of mine I'm meeting for a drink."

"I thought we were going to watch some movies, Miss Hottie."

"We are, as soon as I get back. I won't be too long, but in the meantime," I said, taking *Training Day* out of the DVD player so I could see Denzel a little later, "save him for last."

I changed into my black silk short dress that crisscrossed in the front and tied around my waist. Pretending to be headed out for a quick night on the town, I put on my black strapped high-heeled shoes and sprayed on a tiny dash of perfume. Not having enough time to mess with my hair, I slicked it back with gel and flipped my ends.

I grabbed my purse and headed to the door. "I'll be back soon."

"Shooky-shooky, na. Look at you all glamorous looking. With that dress on, I will see you tomorrow morning."

I smiled. "Good-bye, Britney. I'll be home tonight."

On the drive to the office, I didn't know what to expect from Jonathan. Did he have something he wanted to tell me, or was he looking for comfort again. Either way, I went to offer my support.

When I got off the elevator, Jonathan stood in the doorway to the boardroom, watching me. He looked marvelous, casually dressed in black linen pants and a white crisp Ralph Lauren shirt. Slightly nervous, I opened the glass doors to the entryway and came face to face with him. He took my purse off my shoulder and put it in one of the twenty black leather chairs that circled the boardroom's table. When he closed the door and dimmed the lights, I knew exactly what he wanted from me. I stood with my back against the wall, and he stood tall in front of me with his arm resting above my head. He untied my belt and softly rubbed between my breasts with his fingers.

"You're the only peace of mind I have right now, Sylvia. Please don't walk away from me. I need you." He leaned in and kissed my neck.

"I won't," I said already dropping my dress to the floor.

I hurried to help Jonathan out of his clothes, and once they were off, we walked over to the boardroom's table. Jonathan took a seat in the chair and I maneuvered my way on the table in front of him. I opened my legs and he placed them on his shoulders. He massaged and pecked them with his melting soft lips. Feeling overly excited about what was about to go down, I laid back and lifted myself so he could remove my panties. After he did, he stood in front of me, and wasted no time putting his dick inside of me. While holding my legs apart, he worked magic on my pussy. I watched his dick disappear inside of me and return with heavy glaze on it. Immediately feeling myself about to come, I grabbed his muscular ass and dug my fingers into it. My actions caused him to stroke harder and much faster.

"Ri . . . right there, baby. You're hitting it! Daaaaamn, you hit it sooooo good!"

I came and was so ready to come again. I lay on my stomach and Jonathan got on the table with me. He pecked down my back, and then licked his tongue between the crack of my ass. He then parted my legs, and within seconds, the action continued.

After all was said and done, we worked well together. I knew exactly what he wanted and he gave me exactly what I needed. We fucked for hours in the boardroom, and we ended up with him sitting in a chair, while I was kneeled down in front of him with his steel damn near down my throat. I was determined to make him forget all about Dana, and by the way he couldn't contain himself in the chair, I figured she was the last person on his mind.

He raked his fingers through my messy hair and pumped my mouth to fill it. "Ahhhh, suuuck it, baby. Go all in for me."

All in I was. And after I finished swallowing, I licked my lips and sat sideways on Jonathan's lap. We both were exhausted, so I laid my head on his shoulder and wrapped my arms around his neck.

"I know this ain't right, but why does it feel so right when we're together?" I asked.

"I don't know, Sylvia. All I know is, if I didn't have you right now, I don't know what I would do. You've helped me with my business, my personal life, and let's not forget about my daughter. What is she doing at your place?"

"She's spending the night with me. And when you get a chance you need to call her. She's worried about you."

"I know. I got her message. I've been so out of it that I don't know what to say to her. Every time we talk, she's snapping and going off. I'm not in the mood for that right now."

"Well, get in the mood. I didn't tell Beverly; however, I did tell Britney I was going to tell you that she skipped school the other day. She called the office looking for you, and since you wasn't there, I picked her up from the park. Her so-called boyfriend, who she skipped school with, hit her and—"

Jonathan cocked his head back and frowned. "What? Hit her?"

"Yes, but I took care of it. Don't worry."

He leaned forward and I got up from his lap. "Put on your clothes. Let's go," he said.

I didn't argue with Jonathan and hurried to put on my clothes. When he suggested going back to my place together, I completely disagreed. I told him Britney seeing us together would only bring about many questions and assumptions. He disagreed so we left the office together and headed to my place.

When we walked through the door, Britney was lying on the couch, talking on the phone and watching *Scary Movie 3*. First, she looked at me, then at Jonathan as he followed in behind me. She told whoever was on the phone she'd call them back.

"Hi, Daddy," she said, standing up and giving Jonathan a hug.

He hugged her back. "Hey, baby."

"What is this I hear about your so-called wife?"

"Not now," I said. "Okay, Britney. You need to tell your father what happened the other day."

Jonathan turned on the light and looked at Britney's face that was still slightly swollen. "What's up with that? How you gone let some young punk put his hands on you without telling me?"

"I was going to tell you, but Sylvia took care of things for me."

"It's not Sylvia's job to take care of anything. You are my responsibility. I need his phone number so I can have a talk with his parents. That fool ain't got no business putting his hands on you."

Britney rolled her eyes. "I don't know how you plan on talking to his parents when they're never around."

"I'll find them. Make sure I get that info by tomorrow. If not, I'm going to your school."

"Daddy, that's embarrassing. You're fine and all, but I don't need you up at my school making trouble for me."

"Trouble? You haven't seen trouble, young lady, and you are in trouble for skipping school. I'm going to your school Monday to find out why they haven't told me about you skipping school. This stuff with you has to stop, Britney, and I mean it."

"He's right, Britney, it does," I said. "Besides, your father doesn't need any more stress to deal with. Do the right thing and get yourself together, okay?"

She looked at us and nodded. "I will cool out, I promise. The school already called Mama about me skipping, so there is no need for you to go there on Monday. Ju . . . just give me another chance and you will see a change in me."

Jonathan hesitated to say anything. He gave Britney another hug and kissed her forehead. She looked at me and pointed to his chest. "Was he your date?" she questioned.

I quickly spoke up. "No. I just happened to see him while I was out and told him you were here."

Britney looked at Jonathan. "Daddy, she lying, ain't she? That was you who called here, wasn't it?"

Jonathan looked at me. I closed my eyes and slowly moved my head from side to side. "Yes, Britney. I called Sylvia because I needed a friend to talk to. Just like you do when you need somebody."

Upset that he told her, I took a deep breath and headed toward the kitchen.

"You don't have to leave, Sylvia. I don't know who y'all think y'all fooling. I wasn't born yesterday."

"You were if you think anything is going on between your father and me. We are good friends, Britney. Nothing more, nothing less."

"Uh-huh," she said, tooting her lips. "Good friends with wrinkled clothes and messy hair."

Jonathan and I kept quiet. Later, he tried to convince Britney that we were nothing but friends, but she wasn't buying into it. He wanted her to go home with him, but she told him she wanted to stay the night with me. She agreed to stay with him Sunday night so that was cool with him. When he left, I walked him out to his car. Britney peeked out the window, watching us.

"What are we going to do with her?" I asked.

"I don't know, but I'm still trying to figure out what I'm going to do with you."

"That's a good question. Whenever you figure it out, be sure to let me know."

"I promise you I will." He winked at me and got into his car. I watched him drive away and thought about what a lucky bitch I was to be with him. If only our time together would last.

8

JONATHAN

While at home, I sat in my office and listened to Beverly over the phone as she called me all kinds of no-good motherfuckers. I didn't have the time or energy to argue with her so after she finished, I agreed with everything she'd said and hung up.

Sylvia called and said she and Britney would be over sometime that evening. I wanted to do something nice like cook dinner for them, but I couldn't seem to stop moping around the house about Dana and Lewis for nothing in the world. She'd been gone since our argument. I tremendously missed her. Why? I hadn't a clue, especially after how she played me. And Lewis, I had news for his sorry ass. After tomorrow, that son of a bitch was ass out. I couldn't wait to confront him about what I knew.

Around two o'clock, I went back to my office in the basement to do some work. When Dana came in and sat on the couch, I was paging through some documents from the Lawson case.

Dana looked so fine to me and my heart melted when I saw her. She was dressed in a blazing red Jones New York suit I bought her for Christmas last year. Her hair was full of curls, and by the look in her beautiful green eyes, I could tell she'd been crying. I checked her out from head to toe then I spun my chair around and pretended to be occupied. I opened the file cabinet behind me and searched for nothing.

"Jonathan," she said softly.

"What?" I said, refusing to turn around.

"Can we talk, please? I . . . I really need to talk to you."

"Not right now, Dana. I'm busy."

"Then when are you going to find time in your busy schedule to talk to me about our marriage?"

"I've already talked to you about our marriage. There is no marriage. There's nothing else to talk about, other than are you going to file for a divorce or shall I?" I turned to look at her.

With pain trapped in her eyes, she shook her head. "I've decided that I'm not going to give you a divorce. We've come too far together to let this go."

"You've decided? Since when did you start running shit around here? The only thing you decided to do was fuck Lewis. And, personally, I can't even see myself touching you ever again, knowing that you let a motherfucker like him have you."

"Baby, I was lonely," she said blinking the tears from her eyes. "He was there for me when you rejected me. The only—"

I hated for her to put the blame on me. "I don't want to hear it! Lonely my ass! Now, I'm not going to argue with you about this over and over again. I want out of this marriage! Now!"

"No, gotdamn it! It's not going to be that easy." She walked around my desk and came up to me. "I . . . I know how much I've hurt you but please know it was never my intention. It seemed as if you started loving your work more than you loved me. I know turning to Lewis was the wrong thing to do but I had to have something to hold on to."

I got up from the chair and walked away from Dana. Before I could reach my office door, I dropped my head and rubbed my eyes. I thought about how much love I still had for her and I refused to keep running away every time we spoke.

"Give me one week to think about this, okay? Do not call me or come here until I call you. Just know, Dana, that this is not going to go away overnight. You have been dishonest, you have hurt me more than anybody in my entire life has, and I don't know if this is something I will ever be able to put behind me."

She came up from behind me and put her arms around my bare chest. She rubbed it and laid her head against my back. "Never ever will I do this to you again," she whispered. "I'll call you next Sunday. Hopefully, you'll have good news for me. In the meantime, put your ring back on because this is not over yet. Don't go giving up on me because I will never give up on you."

I turned to face her. The direction of my eyes lowered to her lips and she inched forward to kiss me. The taste of her lips was so sweet that I couldn't pull myself away from them. Then I started to think about Lewis and backed away from her. We stared at each other without saying a word. Shortly after, Dana walked away and left.

I stood there feeling like a fool for even considering reconciliation with her. If anything, it proved to me how much love I still had for her. I was so damn caught up that it didn't even dawn on me that if we did work things out, I still had to face my feelings for Sylvia. She'd been there for me every step of the way. And even though my intention was to pump her for information, I found myself needing her more than ever. Besides, there was nothing in the world she wouldn't do for me. I truly knew that. In addition, her pussy was, without a doubt, the best damn pussy I'd ever had. She definitely knew how to please me, and being with her took an enormous amount of my stress away.

I stayed in the basement for a while, trying to get some work done. When I realized I'd spent most of my time thinking about Dana and Sylvia, I called it a day and went upstairs. I watched TV, wondering where Britney and Sylvia were, but they didn't show up until almost six o'clock. They carried grocery bags in their arms and took them into the kitchen. I offered to help, but they insisted they had everything taken care of. Once Britney came in with the last bag, we all stayed in the kitchen and unpacked the groceries.

"Y'all really didn't have to do this," I said with a growling stomach.

"Daddy, just move out of the way. Sylvia and me about to throw down in this kitchen."

"I don't know about all that, but we gon' try," Sylvia said.

"Is that my cue to leave the kitchen?"

"Yeah, Daddy. Why don't you go do something for the next hour or so?"

"Anything but work," Sylvia said.

"Fine. I'll go check out the football game, and when you ladies need me, holla." I kissed Britney on the cheek, winked at Sylvia, and went to check out the game.

As the Rams were on a roll, I was acting a complete fool. Sylvia came into my bedroom and put her hands on her hips.

"Now, I know the game ain't that good where you got to be jumping up and down, yelling like that."

"Actually, it is."

"Well, do you think you can pull yourself away from the game and come eat something?"

"In a minute," I said. "Give me about five minutes."

Sylvia shook her head and left the room.

I didn't make it to the kitchen until fifteen minutes later. And when I did, Britney and Sylvia had everything laid out for me. They cooked a meatloaf with mashed potatoes and gravy, macaroni and cheese, and a pan of homemade dinner rolls. For dessert, they baked my favorite, a German chocolate cake. Everything was set on the table, and they'd even dimmed the lights and had a few candles lit.

Not having a home-cooked meal in ages, I was over-joyed. I grabbed both of them around their waists and kissed their cheeks.

"Thank you," I said, looking mainly at Sylvia because I knew she was fully responsible for not only making me happy, but for making Britney happy as well.

"You're always welcome," she said, pulling away. She looked over at Britney. "I'll fix your daddy's plate and you can get mine and yours together."

"Nope. I'll get my plate and you and Daddy can stay in here alone. I'm going downstairs to watch TV."

"Britney," Sylvia said. "Your father and I do not need any time alone, so get your behind in that chair and sit."

She looked at me. "Daddy, if I don't want to stay upstairs with y'all, I don't have to, do I?"

"No. Actually, Sylvia and I could use a little privacy. I need to talk to her about something."

Britney licked her tongue out at Sylvia and she play-fully hit Britney on the leg with a towel. Their relationship meant so much to me. I was truly glad that Sylvia had become such an important part of Britney's life.

After Britney fixed Sylvia's and her plates, she headed downstairs to watch TV. Sylvia fixed my plate and sat at the table with me to eat. At first, she wouldn't even look at me. When I asked why, she said that she was nervous about being in Dana's house, sharing dinner with her husband.

"This isn't Dana's house anymore, Sylvia, so relax," I said.

"Jonathan, this whole situation makes me uncomfortable. The last time I spoke to Dana, she begged me to talk to you about getting back together with her. Honestly, I can't because I don't want you to work things out with her. I don't expect you to drop everything for me either, but for now, I'm enjoying every moment that I spend with you."

"Same here, but this situation is getting so complicated for me."

"Why?"

"Because I still love my wife, Sylvia. It's not fair to you if I pretend that I don't."

Sylvia stopped eating her food and she used her fork to pick at the meatloaf. "So, do you love her enough to forgive her for cheating on you?"

"Baby, I don't know. I've said in my mind that it's over but my heart is saying something different."

"Well, I'm going to back off until you decide what you want to do. I never intended to complicate your life more than it already is, but I couldn't hold back my feelings for you any longer."

"Thank you for not holding back because you're exactly what I need in my life right now. I know I've said this before, but I don't know what I'd do without you."

"You'll never be without me, but I don't want to be only a sex partner for you either. Also, I want to be a friend who you can talk to and come to for comfort."

"That you are. Sex with you is amazing and being with you sexually takes me to a place I've never been to with any woman. I just don't know if good sex is all we have in common."

"I feel you, but we'll see."

We finished up a quiet dinner together. Sylvia got extremely quiet when I told her I was going to give Dana my decision on Sunday. The only thing she suggested was for me to do what was best for me, and once I made my decision, to let her know what it was.

Sylvia cleaned up the kitchen, and not hearing a peep out of Britney, I went downstairs to check on her. While watching TV, she'd fallen asleep on the couch. I took her empty plate and went back upstairs. I gave it to Sylvia to wash, and after she finished, she said that she was getting ready to leave.

"You don't have to leave so soon, do you?" I asked.

"Yes, I do, Jonathan, because I don't want Britney to keep getting the wrong idea about us. She wants us together so badly."

"I know she does. But whatever happens, Britney is old enough to understand."

"You're right, and she is." Sylvia took her car keys off the table. "I'll see you in the morning."

"You most certainly will."

I opened the back door for Sylvia and let her out through the garage. In her tight Levi jeans, I watched her hips sway from side to side and decided not to let her leave so quickly. When I pushed the button to let the garage back down, she turned around.

"What are you doing?" she said with a smile.

I closed the door and stepped into the garage. "I forgot to thank you for dinner. It was delicious."

"But you did thank me."

"Not how I wanted to."

I took Sylvia's keys from her hand and put them on top of my Lexus. After I removed her jacket and unbuttoned her jeans, she knew damn well how I wanted to thank her.

"Jonathan," she moaned as she bent over the trunk of the car. "What if Britney wakes up?"

I spread her legs far apart, held her chocolate ass cheeks in my hands and slipped into her wet hole. "Then I'll just have some explaining to do. I'll explain that I just can't get enough of you."

"Me either," Sylvia said with a moan. "Damn you feel good in there. Sooooo good."

I felt relieved as I worked Sylvia over, and being inside of her felt like home. I was comfortable, and we didn't wrap it up until almost an hour later. By then, we were inside of the car, laughing.

"This is getting ridiculous," she said.

I placed my mouth on her breast and nodded. As her nipple hardened, she lifted my head and smiled.

"You don't like beds, do you?" she asked.

"As a matter of fact, I don't. I like spur-of-the-moment, 'right here and right now' sex."

"I can tell, but my ass is getting bruised up from not being on a comfortable bed. I'm still trying to recover from the copy machine, the hard tile floor, and the boardroom's table. Now, my stomach hurts from bending over on your car."

"Let me see some of the bruises you're talking about." I moved over and sat on the back seat next to Sylvia. She pointed out a few spots on her body, and I saw bruises on her thigh, her back, and on her ass.

"What a shame," I joked. "You really need to tell the man who keeps roughing you up like that to stop it."

"Yeah, you really should stop fucking me like this. I just might want to keep you forever."

I laughed, but my face fell flat when I heard Britney calling for me. Sylvia and I rushed out of the car to put on our clothes. All I had to do was put on my boxers and robe, but Sylvia had much more to do. By the time she slid into her panties, Britney opened the back door to the garage. She looked at Sylvia hiding herself by the passenger's side of the car and she watched me, as I stood with my hands in my pockets looking suspicious.

"Did I interrupt something?" she questioned.

"Naw, baby, we were just—"

"Just talking about something," Sylvia intervened.

Britney stepped into the garage and Sylvia picked up her jeans from the ground.

"Look," she said, sliding into them. "Your father will explain this to you. I'm going home." She buttoned her jeans, pushed the garage door opener, and told Britney and me good-bye. We stood and watched as she got in her car and sped off.

Britney looked at me with her arms folded. She cleared her throat. "Are you going to stop lying to me now? How long has this been going on between you and Sylvia?"

I put my arm around her shoulders and walked back into the house with her. When we got to the kitchen, Britney sat at the table and waited for an answer.

"Baby, Sylvia and I recently found comfort in one another. I have always been faithful to Dana, but I need somebody who can help me get through this."

"Help you get through this? It sounds to me as if you're using Sylvia. Do you at least love her?"

"No."

"Do you still love Dana?"

"Yes."

"Then, that's wrong, Daddy. What if you and Dana get back together? Have you even thought about how much that's going to hurt Sylvia?"

"Yes, I have."

"And?"

"And I'll have to deal with it when the time comes. Besides, who says Dana and I are going to work things out?"

"I know y'all will because you are so weak when it comes to her. You let her get away with murder, and I got a feeling that you're blaming yourself for her sleeping with another man."

"Yeah, well, a part of it is my fault. She doesn't know it, but there are some things I think I could have done better as a husband."

"Please. I know you don't want to hear this but Dana is a spoiled rotten bitch. When people don't do what she wants them to do, she will do everything in her power to hurt them. Personally, I hate her guts. I wish more than anything that you and Sylvia would stay together."

"Britney, don't be so hateful toward Dana. I don't know if Sylvia and I being together could be possible, but we'll just have to wait and see."

Britney invited one of her girlfriends over and I headed off to my room. I didn't get a wink of sleep, as I thought about Dana and Sylvia for the entire night. Knowing that the outcome wasn't going to be pretty, because someone was bound to get hurt, I felt even worse.

9

SYLVIA

Late last night, Dana called and we stayed on the phone for hours talking about her and Jonathan. Her urgency to talk was to tell me she was pregnant and didn't know what to do. She said the baby was, without a doubt, Jonathan's, and said she was positive of that because she and Lewis always used a condom.

I was devastated. Knowing how much Jonathan wanted a child with her, I found myself trying to convince her that the baby could be Lewis's. She assured me it wasn't and told me she intended to break the news to Jonathan this week, before he made his decision.

After we hung up, I was sick to my stomach and threw up all over the place. As we talked, I couldn't help myself from thinking about Jonathan fucking me. I couldn't stop thinking about how much love I had for him, and how much I knew he was also feeling something for me. And now a baby? There was no way in hell he would leave her if he knew she was pregnant with his child.

Surprisingly, though, Dana was one hurt sista. During our conversation, she cried and told me how much she regretted her relationship with Lewis. When I asked if she thought Jonathan would take her back, for the first time in her life, she seemed unsure. She asked me to pray for their marriage and told me how much she appreciated our friendship. She hadn't said those words to me in years. Thing was, I felt bad for her, even though I always said I wouldn't.

I dreaded going to work on Monday. I was happy about seeing Jonathan, but all the drama that was about to explode, I truly wasn't prepared for it.

I got to work about seven o'clock to get there before Jonathan, but he was already there. When I peeked in his office, his back was turned. He sat in his chair, gazing out of the window. I cleared my throat to get his attention. "Good morning," I said.

He swung his chair around. "Hey, good morning."

"Did you get a chance to talk to Britney?" I walked farther into his office, lusting by the look of him in his dark gray pinstriped suit.

"Yes, I did. I told you she would understand."

"Of course she understands. In her mind, she understands that she wants us together. Personally, I think her knowing about our involvement was a big mistake."

"I disagree, but I'm not one who has always been right about everything either."

"Neither have I, but she's your child. I'll let you handle her."

Jonathan went over to the coffee machine and started to pour his coffee. Knowing that I always poured his coffee for him, I walked over and took it away from him. "I can still do this, you know. Just because our personal lives have changed, I would like for our work relationship to remain the same."

"Suit yourself," he said, leaning against his desk. "I'm leaving around noon to go see what's up with Britney at school. I should be back no later than two or three. If you wouldn't mind doing a favor for me, I would really appreciate it."

I handed Jonathan his coffee. "What favor?"

"I need you to make arrangements for Lewis to be at my office around three-thirty today. Contact his supervisor and tell him it's imperative that Lewis sees me today."

"Jonathan, I don't know if that's a good idea. Why don't you make arrangements to talk to him after work?"

"Naw, I'm cool. My office will be just fine."

"Okay, if you insist. Just be careful because Lewis is a troublemaker. If Dana broke it off with him, I'm sure he's upset."

"He'll get over it," he said, taking a seat. "And there is no doubt that he has definitely caused some serious trouble for me."

"Yeah, well, so did Dana. We talked last night, and, uh, she seems pretty hurt by all of this. She told me you were going to make your decision about y'all marriage and I was kind of wondering . . ."

"Wondering where my head is?"

"I know where your *head* is, or should I say I know where it's been. I'm just wondering where your mind is?"

Jonathan laughed. "My *head* has had the pleasure of being where it's been, and my mind says to end my marriage. It's my heart that doesn't want to let go."

Wanting to know more about Jonathan's feelings, I got a chair and rolled it over next to him. He moved the coffee cup aside and locked his hands together.

"There's one thing I need to know," I whispered.

"What's that?" he whispered back.

"Is that heart of yours feeling anything for me?"

"Just a tiny bit," he joked, showing me with his fingers. "About this much."

"That's it, huh?"

"Yeah, that's it. Now, if you ask me how much my mind and my"—he looked down at his dick and cleared his throat—"and that's got for you, we're talking a whole different ballgame."

"So you enjoy having sex with me that much, huh?"

"So much that it's going to be hard to let go."

"Who says you have to let it go?"

"Nobody."

"Then don't even consider such a thing."

"Maybe I won't, but I need to know something."

"What?"

"What is it that you want from me? I need to know the truth, and I want you to be completely honest with me."

"Hmm, let's see." I closed my eyes, as I was in deep thought. When I felt Jonathan's lips touch mine, I opened my eyes.

"Sexy," he said. "You are one damn sexy woman."

"Yes, I am, but you got it going on too."

"Not like you, though. And tell me something else, while you're thinking about what it is that you want from me."

"What else?" I smiled.

Jonathan moved face to face with me and grinned. "What makes your pussy so damn good and juicy like that? I mean, damn!"

We burst into laughter. I blushed, and then responded. "It naturally comes that way."

"Well, I can't seem to get it off my mind. And if you don't exit my office in about five, four, three, two seconds, I'm going to hike up that short-ass flimsy skirt and go to work on you right here and right now."

I stood up and straightened my skirt. Then I rolled my chair back over to the table. Jonathan watched and waited on a response from me. I stood by the doorway and looked his way.

"In writing, I'm going to put down what I want from you. Trust me when I say that monstrous thing you got in your pants is something I can't hang with on a daily basis; I mean it. It is fulfilling, delightfully tasteful, and if

I were your wife, I'd have a gun to my head for fucking up something so good."

Jonathan looked at his watch and picked up a notepad from his desk. He rushed to the door, but I blocked him from leaving.

"Where are you off to so fast?" I asked.

"Check my calendar, Miss Secretary," he said, standing closely behind me. "I'm almost late for my seven for-ty-five meeting." He moved my arm from the doorway and placed my hand on his dick. "Do you see what those red panties you got on do to me?"

I squeezed his steel, then let go and moved aside for him to exit. "Later, I'm going to let you feel what it is that you do to me, instead of telling you," I whispered.

Jonathan smacked his notepad against his hand. "I can't wait."

He walked off and I watched as he opened the door to the boardroom.

I was on a serious high thinking about Jonathan and didn't know how in the hell I would ever come down. For today being Monday, this was normally a moody day for him. I was glad to see things starting to look up for him.

Not being able to concentrate on a darn thing, but writing down what I wanted from Jonathan, I took a break and went downstairs to get a bagel. When I saw Lewis standing in line at the bagel shop, I started to leave but I stood with my arms folded and pretended not to see him. After he got his order, he turned around and noticed me. He grinned, and then took a seat at one of the tables close by the door. On my way out, he reached for my hand. I quickly snatched away.

"Don't touch me," I hissed.

"Damn, baby. You know you be too hard on a brotha. I just wanted to tell you it was over between your girl and me. Therefore, me and you can hook up now—that's if you want to."

He winked and I seriously could have spit in his face. "What is with you, fool? Do you really think I'm interested in your stupid ass?"

He snickered, and then bit into his bagel sandwich. After he chewed, he reached for a napkin and wiped his mouth. "Yep," he said then nodded. "Someday you're going to apologize for disrespecting me. And when I fuck you, and I'm only going to only fuck you once, please don't go falling in love with me like your friend did."

"Love? Please. Negro, all you were was convenient to her. Just like you're only a convenient fuck for any woman in this place who's looking for something free. Sooner or later, your giveaways are going to run out. Mr. T would like to see you in his office around three-thirty today. Come prepared, and the next time you put your gotdamn hands on me, suggesting that I want you, please, think again."

I walked away and Lewis got up and followed me.

"Umph. Look at that ass jiggle underneath that skirt. Since I'm a man who knows women, I'd say you don't even have on any panties. And if you do, it's got to be a thong. Red, of course, since your skin is such a lovely chocolate. You seem like a red kind of gal."

I turned around and smacked the shit out of Lewis. He rubbed his cheek, and when the elevator opened, he stepped inside of it with me. I pushed the eleventh floor and when the elevator started to move, he stopped it.

"You're a feisty-ass something, aren't you?" he said, stepping up to me.

I smacked him again and pushed him back. "Lewis, I'm not playing with you!" I yelled. "G'on before you get hurt!"

"Hurt me, baby," he said, holding out his hands. Catching me off guard, he quickly reached up and grabbed my neck. "Don't slap me again, bitch! The only one who's going to get hurt is you."

He squeezed tighter and I grabbed at his hands, trying to stop him. I could barely breathe and my eyes were starting to water.

"See, now look at what you've gotten yourself into." He pushed my head back and watched as I gasped for air. When a tear rolled down my face, he reached up my skirt and fondled me with his fingers. He jabbed them inside of me then brought his mouth up to my ear. "Daaaamn, that pussy wet. That thong wet too and I'm sure it's because you're so excited about me." He placed his fingers on his lips and licked them. "Mmmm, delicious. And the next time you see me, don't be so hard on me, okay?" He released my neck and pushed the button on the elevator so it would move again.

I held my throat and tried to catch my breath. Before we got to the eleventh floor, he pushed the fifth floor and tried to get off. Gaining some strength back, I took my foot and kicked him, as hard as I could, right between his legs. He grabbed his dick and when the elevator opened, I jetted off and ran to the staircase.

Lewis came after me. I ran fast up the steps, and when I slipped and fell on one of them, he caught up with me. He grabbed my ankles, and as I started to scream, he pulled me down a few steps. I kicked my feet so he would let loose. Unbelievably strong, he held my feet together and unzipped his pants. I screamed louder and he fell on top of me. He pressed his elbow down on my throat and secured his hand over my mouth.

"Shut the fuck up," he said, moving my thong aside. He rubbed his dick against my slit and stared into my eyes, witnessing a very cold look. My look must've done something to him because he removed his hand from my mouth and got off me.

"You don't even deserve me," he said, zipping his pants. "But the next time I see you, you'd better keep your hands to yourself and have some respect for me or else I might not be so nice."

Wanting to kill his ass, I rose up, watching as Lewis ran down a flight of stairs and exited. Not knowing what to do, for a while, I sat on the bottom step and held my face in my hands. I couldn't even cry, but I knew this motherfucker was going to pay for what he'd done to me. Since I wasn't up for a bunch of people questioning me, I hurried to the bathroom, cleaned myself up, and headed back to my desk. Jonathan was still in his meeting so I left a note and told him I felt ill and needed to go home for the day. After I put the note on his desk, I got my purse and left.

No sooner had I hit the door, I got into the shower. My heart raced as I thought about Lewis putting his hands on me. I was so scared and seriously thought he was going to hurt me. More so, I didn't know what I was going to do. I felt every bit of violated, but the last thing I wanted was to be caught up in a scandal at work. Everybody would know about it, and as mad as Jonathan was at Lewis, if Jonathan found out, I wasn't sure what he would do.

Thinking more about what had happened, I finally got out of the shower and made up my mind to call the police. The nine and one touched my fingers, but for some reason, the other one I just couldn't push. I laid down the phone and sat back on my bed. Then I picked up my pillow and squeezed it closely to my chest. When the phone rang, I jumped. I looked at the caller ID and it was Jonathan calling from the office. I took a hard swallow and answered.

"Sylvia?" he said.

"Huh."

"Are you okay?"

"Yeah."

"I just got your note. You didn't seem ill when I saw you this morning, so what happened?"

"I, uh, started feeling ill right after you left."

"Oh, I see. It wasn't because of anything I said or did, was it?"

"No. My period came down on me and I wanted to come home."

"Damn, sorry to hear that."

I didn't respond.

"Sylvia," Jonathan said again.

"Listen, I'm cramping. Can I call you back?"

"Sure. I'm getting ready to go to Britney's school. I'll talk to you later."

I hung up, and thinking about the mess I'd gotten myself into, I started to cry. Lewis was going to pay. I wasn't sure when, how, or what I was going to do, but he had to go. And Jonathan, there I was fucking around with my best friend's man like it didn't even matter. Loving him as if he were my own and enjoying every moment that I spent with him. *How did this shit get so deep?* I thought. We were supposed to have sex one time and that was it. I hated that Dana was pregnant, and I was disappointed that Jonathan still loved her so much.

As I lay in bed thinking about how selfish I was, and feeling disappointed in myself for betraying my friend, I dozed off. What seemed like a few hours later, I was awakened by a soft knock at the door. I looked at the clock on my nightstand and it showed 4:14 p.m. Wondering who it was, I put on my robe and headed to the door. It was Jonathan. I rubbed my messy hair back then opened the door.

"Were you sleeping?" he asked, and then walked in.

"Yeah, I was." I closed the door behind him and went back into my bedroom. He followed, stood in the doorway, and I sat on the bed.

"You didn't sound too good over the phone, so I came by to make sure you were okay."

"I'm fine," I said softly. "How did everything go with Britney?"

Jonathan came farther into the room and sat on the bed next to me. "It went okay. She's been skipping school a lot, but she promised the principal and me that she would not do it again. If anything, I think that punk hitting her might have been a wake-up call for her."

"I hope so."

Jonathan placed his hand on my thigh and rubbed it. "Are you sure you're okay? You don't seem like yourself."

"I'm not." I stared into his eyes. "I hate myself for doing this to Dana, but I can't stop loving you. You don't understand the guilt and shame I—"

Jonathan placed his fingers on my lips, and then kissed me. Never listening to what I had to say, he leaned back then put me on top of him. I straddled his lap and untied my robe. When I slid it off, Jonathan rose up on his elbows, looking at my naked body. Then he rubbed his fingers between my coochie lips.

"I thought you were on your period," he said, looking at his finger.

I shook my head, and yet again, the clothes were coming off. Jonathan got on top of me and kneeled between my legs. He rubbed his hands up and down my legs, squeezed my hips, and then he placed my legs high on his shoulders. When he inserted himself, I tightly closed my eyes, as the feeling was always so right. He slow stroked me, causing my flow of juices to sound off in the room.

"Wh . . . why did you lie to me about your period, Sylvia? Did you not want to make love to me?"

I slid my legs off his shoulders and wrapped them around his waist. For now, I ignored his question and continued to bring him satisfaction.

For the next hour or so, Jonathan made passionate love to me. I had the pleasure of coming three times, and the last orgasm caused me to let out a loud cry that made him question me.

He rolled over and lay next to me, while holding me in his arms. "Okay, now," he said. "Tell me what's wrong with you. And don't lie to me, Sylvia, because I can tell by how your body trembled that something isn't right."

I laid my head on his chest and rubbed it. "Today, I realized how much I love you. When you asked me what I wanted from you, the truth is I want to be with you, Jonathan. I want a man who makes me laugh, who makes me feel secure, who gives me good advice, and who makes good love to me as you do. But no matter what you say, deep down I know that having you is impossible."

"No, it's not because I've made up my mind." He sat up and put a pillow behind him. I lifted my head off his chest and looked at him. "I thought about everything, Sylvia, and I'm not going to drive myself crazy thinking about it anymore. Tomorrow, I'm going to file for my divorce and move on with my life. As much as I still love Dana, there's no way for me to forgive her for cheating. I'll never be able to put it behind me, and I don't want you to keep torturing yourself wondering what I'm going to do."

Relieved, I was so glad to finally hear Jonathan say it was over. I wanted to tell him about Lewis, but I was so thrilled about his news that I didn't want to spoil the mood.

We stayed in bed for a while, and when I teased him about finally sexing me in bed, he insisted he hated beds and loved me all over again throughout my place. The bathtub was our resting place, and when I got out to answer the phone that wouldn't stop ringing, it was Dana. I wasn't going to answer, but since I wanted to make sure she wasn't on her way over, I picked up.

"Sylvia," she said.

"Yes."

"What are you doing?"

"I just got out of the shower. Where are you? Can I call you back?"

"I'm on my way over there to see you. I was calling to make sure you were there."

"I'm here but I'm getting ready to leave."

"Look, by the time you get dressed, I'll be there. I need your advice about Jonathan so stay put until I get there." She hung up.

Not knowing how far away she was, I panicked. I ran to the bathroom and told Jonathan that Dana was just moments away. When I suggested he leave, he remained in the tub and had the nerve to ask why.

"What do you mean by why?" I yelled.

"I mean, I'm not going anywhere. If she comes, she just comes."

"Oh, noooo. This shit ain't going down like this. Jonathan, please get out of the tub and put on your clothes. I do not want to be caught up in the middle like this."

Jonathan moseyed out of the tub and took his time putting on his clothes. I was so worried about him getting dressed that when Dana rang the doorbell, I was still in my bathrobe. When I opened the door, he sat on the arm of the couch with his back turned while on his cell phone. Dana came in and her eyes widened when she saw him. I closed the door behind her.

"He interrupted my shower and now you. What is it that the two of you want with me?" I tried to play it off, but I wasn't so sure if Dana was buying it.

She looked me up and down, and then looked over at Jonathan, as he talked on the phone. "How long has he been here?" she asked.

"He got here right before I was getting ready to take my shower."

"When I called, why didn't you tell me he was here?"

"Because you hung up on me, that's why."

"You still could have told me." Dana's eyes shifted to Jonathan as he ended his call. "Hi, baby," she said.

He sucked his teeth and glared at her. "Don't go babying me, Dana. It isn't even like that between us and you know it."

I took a deep breath, feeling some heavy shit about to go down. "Dana, can I get you something to drink?" I asked.

"No, thank you. However, you can allow my husband and me some time alone—that's if you don't mind."

"I was on my way out anyway, so take all the time you need." I headed to my room and Jonathan yelled for me not to go.

"Sylvia, sit down. This is your place and you don't have to go anywhere." He stood up and removed his car keys from his pocket. "I'll see you at work tomorrow," he said, looking at me. "And, Dana, that was my partner on the phone. Those papers I want you to sign will be ready tomorrow."

"But I . . . I thought you were going to think about this," she said, starting to tear up.

"I did. I thought for as long as I could, and the only solution I can come up with is a divorce."

Saying nothing else, he walked to the door.

"Noooo." Dana rushed up behind him. "Not now, baby, please. I need you," she cried. "Not only that, but we need you. I can't raise this child without you." Jonathan swung around with a frown on his face and glared at her. "Yes, my dear," she said as tears streamed down her face. "We're having a child. All this time you've wanted one, and, finally, I'm pregnant."

Jonathan's eyes shifted to me, then back at Dana. He shook his head. "There's no way it's my child. Don't fucking do this to me, Dana!" he yelled.

"I swear to God it's yours," she said. "I never had unprotected sex with Lewis, I swear."

He quickly swung the door open and slammed it behind him. Dana opened it and yelled for him to wait. When he sped off in his car, then she closed the door.

"Sylvia, what am I going to do?" she sobbed, and then walked up to hug me. "He hates me!"

I hesitated to put my arms around her, but I did. "No, he doesn't, Dana. He just needs time. Give him time, okay?"

"But I need him now more than ever." She backed away from our embrace. "What am I going to do if he divorces me? Girl, tell me, what am I going to do?"

Dana plopped down on the couch, looking a mess. Feeling as if I couldn't give her any advice, I went into the kitchen to get her some water. When I handed it to her, she refused to drink it.

"That's okay. I need to go to the bathroom."

I moved aside, but as soon as she came out of the bathroom, I saw her stop in front of my bedroom door to look in. Knowing what a mess Jonathan and I had made, I rushed up to her with the water again. There was no doubt that the smell of his cologne escaped from my bedroom.

"Here," I said. "Drink this. It's cold and it will help to calm you."

She took the glass of water, but continued to stare into my bedroom. When she walked inside to look around, my heart dropped to my stomach. "A strong drink is the only thing that will calm me, and, no offense, but you really need to clean up this room. Why are your pillows all over the floor?"

"Before Jonathan came, I was doing my sit-ups on the floor. I don't have any floor mats so I use my pillows."

Dana hesitated, and then took a sip of the water. "Why was he here anyway?" She looked at her watch. "It's kind of late, isn't it?"

"Dana, you know Jonathan is always stopping by here. I left work ill today and he stopped by to check on me."

"Are you okay?" Finally, she walked out of my room.

"Yeah, I'm fine. This period of mine just drives me crazy. You know how bad my cramps can be."

"Yeah, I remember. I remember you crying so hard in Mr. Douglas's class in high school and he wouldn't even let you leave."

We laughed and sat in the living room for the next hour, reminiscing about the good old times we used to have. Before she left, she apologized for being such a snobby-ass friend over the past few years and said being with Lewis made her a different person. I truly missed our wonderful friendship, but I also knew that there was no way in hell we would ever get it back.

After she left, I called Jonathan to speak to him. When he didn't answer his home phone, I called his cell phone and he didn't answer that either. Knowing exactly where he was, I put on my clothes and headed to the office.

10

JONATHAN

A baby? I thought, while sitting in my office with my hands pressed against my forehead. *Why now?* Dana and I had been trying to have a child for years. The doctors said our chances were slim. The big question, of course, was whose baby was she carrying? If anything, I knew there was a fifty-fifty chance that it was mines, but what if it was Lewis's? *Damn,* I thought. *What a fucking mess my wife had gotten us into.*

Then again, what if she was lying? She'd been playing the lying game for years so why should I believe her when she said she's pregnant? It probably was a last resort for her, and if she thought that a baby, who I wasn't even sure was mine, was going to stop this divorce from happening, then she was out of her mind. There was no doubt that I had to go through with this divorce. My feelings for Sylvia were getting stronger and a big part of me wanted to continue our relationship. It wasn't that I was in love with her, but I loved so much about her. Most of all, I loved how she'd been able to keep me out of this funk I've been in. It seemed like every time I dropped my head, she was there to pick it up. Anything I needed, she had been in my corner. Yes, I hated she was Dana's best friend, but I couldn't do anything about that. Sylvia's and my friendship had grown into something special. I'd be a fool to let it go for Dana.

I looked at my watch. It was already one o'clock in the morning. Something told me Dana was probably at our house waiting for me, so trying to avoid her, I stayed at the office. Around 1:30 a.m., I went to the gym room to work out. Once I finished, I showered and went into the sauna to relax. As steam filled the room, I laid my naked body back on the bench and covered myself with a towel. I closed my eyes, and, again, I started talking myself into forgiving Dana. I mean, what if the baby was mine and I wasn't a part of his/her life? That would kill me. If anything, I had to know the truth about the baby before I made up my mind about what to do.

Still in deep thought, when the door opened, I turned to see who it was. The room was filled with steam, but I could clearly see that it was Sylvia. She had a white towel wrapped around her and headed my way. I sat up and laid my towel on the bench next to me. She dropped her towel, and then sat sideways on my lap. Knowing what I was going through, she wrapped her arms around my neck and comforted me.

"How much more of this are you going to take?" she whispered. "You're a strong man, Jonathan, and it kills me to see you so torn like this."

I rubbed the side of my face against her breasts and closed my eyes. "You are my guardian angel, Sylvia. Lord knows I wouldn't know what to do without you. Every time I think it's the end of the world, you always show up."

"Well, I almost didn't find you. I saw your car in the parking garage and looked all over for you. Noticing the lights on in the gym is what made me come in here."

"I'm glad that you found me." I massaged Sylvia's left breast and began to suck it.

"Jonathan, no," she moaned, and squirmed around on my lap. "We . . . we can't keep doing this."

"Says who?"

"Says me." She lifted my head and looked at me. "What about the baby? What if the baby is yours?"

"What if I don't want to talk about it? What if I just want to make love to you right now and not think about anything else?"

Sylvia stood up and reached for her towel. She dragged it on the floor and moved toward the door. I stood up and gazed at her plump ass, and when she turned around, she looked me up and down. She tossed the towel in the air and smiled. "Oh, what the hell? I can't leave you like this."

"No, you can't." I walked up to her. We wrapped our arms around each other and I rubbed my nose with hers. I pecked her lips a few times then squeezed her tightly in my arms. "Woman, you feel so good."

"And so do you."

We stood for a while holding each other and Sylvia glanced down at our arms. "You know, I didn't think I was that much darker than you."

"You're not," I said, laughing. "Actually, I'm darker than you."

"No, you're not. Look," she said, putting her arm next to mine.

I looked at our arms. "And I still say I'm darker than you. What difference does it make anyway?"

"Because you know, the blacker the berry, the sweeter the juice." Sylvia kneeled down in front of me. She went to work on my goods, and as I tried to keep my balance, she stopped and looked up at me. "Yep, your juice is much more sweeter than mine."

"Let me be the judge of that." I helped Sylvia off the floor, spread her legs apart on the bench, and crawled in between them. To me, she was so much sweeter than I was, and over a period of time, we went back and forth debating who had the sweetest juice.

"Okay," she said, taking deep breaths after her orgasm. "You win; mine is sweeter. Now, would you please cut the foreplay and fuck me like you said you would?"

I remained kneeled in front of Sylvia while she sat on the bench. She wiped the sweat from my forehead, and I wiped it from her face. "I didn't say I wanted to fuck you, Sylvia. I asked if I could make love to you. Don't go putting false words in my mouth. Besides, you were the one who said you couldn't handle my loving on a daily basis."

"I did, didn't I? But"—she reached for my dick and put it inside of her—"I could never imagine myself being without it. Now, shush and handle your business. I've waited long enough."

I laughed, leaned in, and let the stroking begin.

We went at it like we were the last two people on earth, and our chocolate bodies dripped with sweat. But when we heard the loud sound of a door closing, it alarmed us. We stopped in action, and not knowing who it was, I quickly slid myself out of Sylvia. We got off the floor, Sylvia covered herself with a towel, and I wrapped mine around my waist. I asked Sylvia to chill, while I left the sauna to see who was there. When I looked around, there was no one in sight. I even went into the workout room and saw no one. Curious, I headed back to the sauna. Sylvia stood by the door and waited for me.

"Who was it?"

I shrugged my shoulders. "I don't know. I didn't see anyone."

"But somebody was in here."

"I know, but don't worry. It could have been anyone." I lifted Sylvia's wrist to look at her watch. "Sometimes the janitors come in and clean up around this time."

Sylvia looked at her watch too, and saw that it was ten minutes after four in the morning. "Where did the time

Slick 121

go? If you want me to come in for work, you'd better let me get out of here."

"Yeah, I'd better get out of here too. I have to be in court by nine, Crissy and I are supposed to have a late lunch, and I promised Britney she could stay the week with me. I still haven't had a chance to meet with Lewis yet, but I'm eager to speak to him."

We put our clothes back on, and after I walked Sylvia to her car, she left. As I strutted toward my car, I noticed a piece of paper underneath the windshield wiper. I grabbed it and got inside of my car. I unfolded the paper, and inside was a note from Lewis. He asked me to meet him at CJ's at seven o'clock this evening, saying that it was imperative that we spoke. Having every intention of meeting him, I balled up the paper and threw it in the trashcan on my way out of the parking garage.

I hurried home to shower, took a quick two-hour nap, and was in court by nine. My court case ran over until almost three o'clock, so I cancelled lunch with Crissy. I then called the office to see if Sylvia would pick up Britney for me and chill at her place until I got finished with my meeting with Lewis.

"Jonathan, just be careful, okay?" she said.

"I will, and tell Britney I'll be home no later than nine."

"Will do. Are you tired?"

"Very. If I don't do anything else tonight, I'm going to get some rest."

"I agree. It's been crazy today, but I'm leaving at four o'clock so I can be on time picking up Britney."

"What's been going on? Anything I should know about?"

"Not really. You have about fifteen messages waiting for you from your clients. Beverly called twice, but I don't want to repeat what she said. Dana called looking for you, and the rest is all office gossip. You don't want to hear about that, do you?"

"No, I don't. And I have a feeling that this office gossip been going on all day long, especially since I'm not there."

Sylvia laughed. "Now, you know I'm not going to lie to you, but, baby, I haven't done shit all day long. I haven't the strength to pick up a piece of paper, let alone file one. I am drained from what you did to me, and you have no one to blame but yourself."

"So, you're slacking?"

"Terribly bad."

"Then go home. You ain't doing me no good by being there."

"All you had to do was say the word, Boss Man. I'll stop to get Britney and we'll see you later."

I hung up, and once again, thanked the Lord for Sylvia. Dana had been calling me, so I pulled my car over in front of the courthouse and called her back.

"What is it, Dana?" I asked with an attitude.

"I need some time alone with you. Tonight, I'm coming to the house and you need to prepare yourself to talk to me."

"I'm busy tonight."

"Damn it!" she yelled. "Is this attitude of yours because you're seeing someone else?"

"Dana, you need to understand that I'm not on your fucking time! You're not going to snap your fingers and I'm gonna come running. That's just not going to happen."

"But what about our child?" she cried. "How can you abandon us like this? Fine, I made a mistake, but don't make your child pay for it too. I'm so stressed out that I may lose this baby. You don't want that to happen, do you?"

"You're forgetting the most important thing here. What if it's not my damn child, Dana! What if you are having another man's baby!"

"But it's not. It's one hundred percent yours. I swear!"

"Well, your word isn't worth a damn anymore. You will have to prove to me that the child is mine, and more than anything, I need to know if you're really pregnant. You're so fucking full of games, I don't know what the hell to believe."

"I wouldn't lie to you about anything like this."

"Like hell! If you lied to me about being with another man, you'd for damn sure lie to me about a baby, especially since you know how much having a child means to me."

Dana was silent, and furious once again, I hung up on her. Since I was on a roll, I called Beverly to see what the fuck her beef was about. When she didn't answer, I left a message for her to call me back.

Before meeting with Lewis, I went to Cardwell's and had dinner. Around 6:45 p.m., I headed to CJ's. I looked around for Lewis, but he was nowhere in sight.

Soon after the waiter seated me in a booth, I saw Lewis come through the door. He looked around for me and when he caught my eye, he headed toward me. Trying to figure out Dana's attraction to this cocky, arrogant fool, I checked him out in his baggy blue jeans, black fitted tank shirt, and fake-ass diamond earring in his ear.

He came over to the booth, and held his hand out for me to shake it.

I brushed him off. "Naw, man, none of that. You know more than I do that only friends shake hands."

"Awww, Mr. T," he said, sliding into the booth. "I thought you were better than that. I would have never thought you, of all people, would trip off a brotha like me banging your wife."

I snickered and tried my best not to let him get underneath my skin. "Is that what you're doing? More than anything, I assumed you were using her."

"That too, but I really did start liking her ass, though. So, when she had the nerve to try to cut this shit short, I couldn't let that happen. And even though I had some backup booty at the hotel, Dana trying to take her lovely self away from me was quite damaging."

"Shit, I truly understand how you feel. After all, she's a dynamite-ass woman. She cooks, cleans, and will fuck your brains out when she wants to."

"Yeah, buddy! That pussy be on overtime. But, not like that secretary you got. You know, Sylvia?" He slammed his hand on the table and laughed. "Now, that dark chocolate, 'smack it up and lay it to the side' sista is bad!"

I held my hands tightly together in front of me. Bringing Sylvia into the mix, he definitely had my attention. "So, what else about Sylvia, Lewis?"

"Nuttin'." He shook his head. "She's just a bad motherfucker when it comes to sex, that's all I'm saying. When I had the pleasure of poking that pussy on the elevator yesterday, and then again on the stairs, I was a li'l bit disappointed in myself when I found out she ran to give you some pussy later. She was so drenched when I pulled those red panties aside and when—"

My face twisted and displayed a whole lot of anger. I couldn't hold back, so I cut him off. "What in the hell do you want from me? Cut the bullshit, Lewis, because I know you're after something."

"Come on now, Mr. T. I'm just trying to free you from a life of trifling conniving, and dick hungry–ass women. You didn't expect for me to let you have all of the fun, did you? Share some of the pussy, damn."

"Fun? Do you think this game you're playing is funny?"

"Hilarious. It's so funny that you're going to help me keep a little chump change in my pockets."

"So, money is what you're after?"

"Yeah, just a li'l bit, though."

"Man, what in that fucked-up mind of yours would make you think I would give you any of my money?"

"Well, you've already been giving me some through Dana, and I truly appreciate all that you do for me. But now you're going to give me some on your own free will."

I couldn't help but to laugh. This Negro was a clown. "Lewis, you know what, you are sick. It puzzles the hell out of me how Dana could stoop so low with a boy like you, but I guess it lets me know how desperate she was. Tomorrow, get your shit out of my mailroom. If you ever come near my wife or my secretary again, I'm gonna kill you." I started out of the booth.

"Mr. T, Mr. T, Mr. T, if I were you, I wouldn't leave so soon. Now, since I took a lot of time planning this shit out, you have got to stay and listen."

Foolishly, I stayed at the booth, wanting to know what else Lewis had to say. "Make it quick. I have some business I need to tend to."

"Please. All the hell you got to do is go somewhere and fuck your secretary. Earlier, I watched y'all for a good li'l while, and I feel cheated because she did not suck my dick the way she sucked yours. You must be on cloud nine having your cake and eating it, too, especially since Sylvia and Dana are friends. It's just a matter of time you'll be kicking down a threesome, won't you?"

"Maybe, or maybe not. But you sound a little jealous. A brotha like you shouldn't be wasting so much time and energy on my love life. Especially when the women say you got it going on like you do. Hopefully, watching me last night will help you better yourself in the bedroom. If not, then don't expect to get your dick sucked well like I do." I slid out of the booth.

"In one week, Mr. T, I need five hundred thousand dollars. If not, everybody in the workplace will see these pictures I have of you and Sylvia fucking like wild animals, your wife will know that her best friend is a backstabbing bitch, and not only that, but she'll be able to use these pictures against you in court and take you for every dime you have. Then there's your beautiful, young teenager daughter you got—"

Before I knew it, I reached over and grabbed Lewis by his shirt. I tightened my fist and punched him so hard in his face that my knuckles cracked. He picked up the glass of water on the table and slammed the glass on the side of my face. My vision blurred from the water being in my eyes, and I wasn't sure if the glass had cut me. All I know was we went at it. The people around us cleared out and the manager and a few waiters ran over and tried to break us apart.

"Stop this," the manager yelled. "Stop or I will call the police!"

While standing in the way, the manager got knocked in the face with a punch. He rushed away, and still seething with anger, I pounded Lewis's face and tore up his ribs with my fists. When I put him in a headlock, he lifted me over his shoulder and slammed me on the table behind us. I crashed on the table then hit the floor. Lewis lifted his foot to kick me, but I grabbed that motherfucker and tried to break it away from his body. I twisted and turned his ankle, causing him to lose his balance. When he fell to the ground, I took my size-thirteen leather shoe and punted it between his legs.

Lewis rolled over on his stomach and grabbed his dick. Shortly after, four police officers came rushing through the door. They aimed their guns at me.

"Lift your hands where we can see them! Now!"

I slowly placed my hands behind my head and two of the officers cuffed me. The other two cuffed Lewis, who was still lying face down on the floor.

After they sat me in a chair, they picked up Lewis and sat him in another chair. Blood dripped from his nose, his shirt was torn off, and his eye looked as if he just had a fight with Mike Tyson. I, on the other hand, wasn't in good condition either. The sleeve to my jacket was torn, blood streamed down my face and onto my white shirt, the taste of thick blood was stirring in my mouth, and my entire body was stiff as a board.

When the cops inquired about what had happened, I told them the partial truth. Since the manager and waiters knew me well from coming there all the time, they added a little somethin' somethin', and the cops immediately took the cuffs off me. I told them I wanted to press charges against Lewis, and when all was said and done, they stood Lewis up to haul him off to jail.

After I found my wallet that had skidded on the floor, I paid the manager $1,000 for the damages we'd caused. I knew the damages were much more than that, considering all the wasted food, the drinks that were on the floor, and the many people who walked out because of what went down. And since he'd kept me out of jail, I planned to come back tomorrow with a check that covered the entire inconvenience.

"Thank you," he said, shaking my hand. "That young punk should've known better."

"Yeah, but so should I."

Disgusted that I allowed things to go this far, I went to the bathroom to see how much damage had really been done to my face. The cut wasn't as bad as I'd thought, so I gathered a bunch of paper towels and pressed against my face to stop the bleeding. The police had asked if I needed an ambulance, but I declined. The only other things were a cut inside my mouth that wouldn't stop bleeding. And as for the soreness in my body, I couldn't do anything about it.

When I came out of the restroom, one of the officers waited for me. The other two still hadn't left with Lewis yet.

"Are you going to be okay, Mr. Taylor?" the officer asked.

"Yes, I'm fine. I thought I needed some stitches, but I think I'll be okay."

I looked at Lewis and he grinned. "This is not a laughing matter, young man," the officer said to Lewis. "You're in serious trouble."

I walked up to Lewis and stood face to face with him. "I told you this shit wasn't funny. And if you still think it is, laugh it off in that fucking jail cell tonight. Going against me, Lewis, you'll lose. Just like you lost out today, you're going to lose out again."

He gathered spit in his mouth and let it out in my face. With the police standing there or not, I punched him so hard that it sent him and the officer standing to his right to the ground.

"Okay, Mr. Taylor," the other officer said, grabbing my arm. "Now, you're going to jail."

I quickly wiped the spit off my face and showed no resistance. The officer cuffed me and escorted me out to his police car. He placed me in the back and closed the door.

After the other officers placed Lewis in another car, they stood outside and talked for a while. When the officer hopped in the front seat, he straightened his rearview mirror and looked at me.

"Mr. Taylor, why did you say anything to that stupid punk? You know he was just trying to work you over, man, don't you? Thugs like him are a waste of time."

"I'm well aware of that. He just had my damn blood boiling."

The officer laughed. "Yeah, well, a fancy lawyer such as yourself should know better, right?"

"I guess, but a fancy lawyer such as myself will kick ass when I need to."

We both laughed this time and the officer pulled off.

"Is your car parked around here?" he asked.

"It's in the parking garage to your left."

The officer pulled over to the left, opened the door, and uncuffed me. "Have a good night, sir. Next time, let the courts handle it, okay?"

"They always do, don't they?" I smiled, thanked the officer, and headed to my car.

What a night, I thought as I got into my car. It was almost nine o'clock, so I hurried home to wash up and change clothes so I could go get Britney from Sylvia's place. To save some time, I called Sylvia's place to see if they could meet me at my place, but I got no answer.

Thinking hard about what Lewis said, I knew that motherfucker was out to destroy me and everyone around me. I had to watch my back, and at the same time, have everybody else's, too. I was so mad at Dana for allowing this fool to have so much control, and Sylvia? There was no way in hell she let him fuck her after hating him so much. When I thought about her mood yesterday, and about her suddenly leaving the office, my mind started playing tricks on me. Was there a chance she was fucking that nigga too?

Rushing home, when I pulled in the driveway, Dana's car was there. I was in no mood for the drama tonight. All I wanted was to see my daughter and to lie in a nice, comfortable bed.

No sooner than I went inside, I saw Dana on the couch. She was ready for me to listen to another one of her sob stories. I walked right past her and headed to the bedroom. Seeing how roughed up I was she followed behind me.

"What happened to you? Were you in a car accident or something?"

"Yeah, I wish that's all it were." I pulled off my bloody shirt, slid out of my shoes and went into the bathroom. Dana came in and wet a towel while I started to run water in the tub. When I stepped out of my pants and eased into the tub, she came over and wiped the side of my face with the towel.

"How did this happen?" she asked again.

I moved my head so the towel wouldn't touch it. She tried to wipe my face again, but I snatched the towel from her hand. "This is what happens when you fuck around with stupid, ignorant, lowlife sons of bitches."

Her mouth hung open. "Did you and Lewis have a fight?"

"You're damn right we did. And I feel like such a fool for stooping so low tonight and fighting with his ass."

"But wha . . . what made you fight with him? I mean, baby, it is over between us. I love you and there is no reason for you to fight with Lewis over something that belongs to you."

"Whatever. Look, let me enjoy my bath alone, all right? I'll talk to you when I get finished."

Dana left quietly and closed the door behind her.

I let the jet bubbles massage my body for a while, shaved, and then gargled with Listerine to kill the soreness in my mouth. When I came out of the bathroom, Dana was lying across the bed while flipping through an *Ebony* magazine. She closed it, laid it down on the nightstand, and then she reached for her purse and pulled out some papers. After she handed them to me, I sat on the bed next to her. I was somewhat nervous, thinking they were our divorce papers, but when I saw they were papers from her doctor's office confirming the pregnancy, I was a slight bit relieved.

"I told you I didn't lie. And I'm also not lying when I tell you this child is yours. We've waited so long to have a baby, and I'm so afraid that I'm going to lose it."

I placed the papers on Dana's lap, and then I lay back on the bed. I looked up at the ceiling and placed my hands behind my head. "Just move back in for now. I don't want to cause the baby any harm. Besides, when Lewis gets out of jail, I don't want him trying to hurt you."

Dana moved back and laid her head on my arm. She turned sideways to look at me. "Thank you. I don't want to be away from you another day, and going forward, I'm going to show you what a wonderful wife you have."

"Dana, I'm only asking you to come back because I want to protect what's mine. As for our marriage, I can only take it one day at a time. I'm not making you any promises. If this living arrangement doesn't work out for me, I will let you know."

She nodded, and then kissed my cheek. When I closed my eyes, she rolled on top of me and rubbed the cut on my face. "I'm so sorry."

I grabbed her hand and started to rise up. "Yeah, I'm sorry too, but move. I need to go call Britney."

Dana raked her hair to one side then she reached for my hand and placed it on her breast. "It's been awhile for us. The only way to break the ice and get you out of your misery is for me to show you just how sorry I really am." She leaned forward to kiss me, but I turned away. She grabbed my face and pressed her soft lips against mine.

Enjoying the sweet taste of her lips, I kissed her back. The kissing became intense, so intense that I rolled on top of her and hurried out of my robe. I lifted her skirt and tore off her panties. She kicked off her high-heeled shoes, and as soon as her legs opened, I pushed my dick inside of her. Almost immediately, I let out a deep sigh, feeling relieved. My pace was slow at first, but then I was so excited to be in her pussy that I picked up speed. Dana's head was hanging off the bed, and it was squeaking loudly as we got our fuck on. She gripped my ass while I took deep strokes inside of her and was very apologetic.

"I'm so sorry, baby, please, pleeeease forgive me. I love you, Jonathan, only yoooou."

I was so caught up in the moment with Dana that I didn't even hear Britney and Sylvia. Sylvia called my name, and when I snapped my head to the side, I saw them standing in the doorway with blank expressions covering their faces.

Dana rose up on her elbows and I got up off her. My dick was dripping wet with her juices, and by the time I covered myself with the robe, Sylvia had run out of the house. Britney ran after her. I tightened my robe and hurried out of the room. Dana stayed on the bed, calling for me to come back.

I ran outside, but Sylvia had sped off. Britney pushed my chest and stormed back into the house. She picked up the kitchen phone and dialed out. Thick wrinkles lined my forehead and I snatched the phone from her hand. "Watch yourself, all right?" I yelled. "I'm sorry it had to be this way but—"

"But, my ass," she yelled back. Tears poured down her face. "You are such a liar. I hate you, Daddy! That bitch has made nothing but a fool out of you and—"

I slapped Britney across her face and grabbed her arm. "Stop it! Don't you dare talk to me that way, Britney! I am your damn father and you will respect me!"

She snatched away. "How in the hell do you want me to respect a man who doesn't even respect himself?"

"Britney," Dana yelled as she came into the kitchen with a frown on her face. "Why are you over here yelling at my husband like that? I know you're not thrilled about me being here but—"

"Dana," I shouted. "Let me handle this!"

"No, no, no, no," Britney smirked with a devilish look in her eyes. "Since you want to put your fucking hands on me, I got something for you." She looked at Dana. "I'm not mad that my father is a sucker for you, bitch! I'm just furious that he's not man enough to tell you he's fucking your best friend. That's right. Sylvia's been getting a piece of the action too, so don't think for one minute that you got yo' shit under control."

Dana's eyes shifted to me and began to fill with water. She opened her mouth, but no words came out. I grabbed Britney by her arm again, and held her with gritted teeth. "Either go downstairs and cool the fuck off or get the hell out of my house. One or the other, Britney!" She pulled her cell phone from her pocket and slammed the back door behind her.

I walked past Dana who was still standing in shock. She walked slowly and calmly into the living room where I had taken a seat on the couch.

"Take your best shot, Dana," I said, holding out my hands. "Everybody else has today so go for it."

She eased down on the coffee table in front of me, and moved her head from side to side. "Ple . . . please tell me she just lied to me. It can't be, Jonathan, there's no way."

I sat silent for a while and then opened my mouth. "I was hurt—"

"Noooooo," she yelled and fell to her knees. "Not Sylvia! You did not have sex with my friend, did you?"

I stared at Dana, and when I didn't say anything, she screamed and punched my chest. She smacked my face about five times, and when I'd had enough, I tightly grabbed her wrist. "Stop it, please. If you're that angry then leave," I said casually.

"You're damn right I'm getting the fuck out of here!" She stood up and smacked my face again. "I knew you were fucking around with her all this time. I knew it!" She stormed into the bedroom and continued to talk her shit. When I heard the sound of broken glass, I quickly got up and went into the bedroom. Dana had thrown something into the glass shower and glass was shattered everywhere. She was kneeled down on the bathroom floor, screaming "why" at the top of her lungs. Did she really have to ask why? She was shaking so badly that I kneeled down and put my arms around her.

"Don't you touch me!" she yelled.

"Look, I know this hurts but you have got to calm down."

"Fuck you, Jonathan!" She got off the floor, and then grabbed her purse from the nightstand. After she pulled out her keys, she gave me an evil stare and jetted.

After she was gone, I picked up the broken glass in the bathroom then lay across my bed. I was exhausted from all that had happened today, but couldn't even close my eyes to rest. By one o'clock in the morning, I looked at the phone, wanting to call Sylvia and apologize, but I couldn't. I knew she was upset with me, and thinking about how much she was hurting, I tried to make some sense out of what I had done. I felt terrible for slapping Britney, but when I called her cell phone she didn't answer. I left her a message and told her we needed to talk.

11

SYLVIA

After seeing Jonathan making love to Dana, I cried the entire way home. Yes, she was his wife, but since I finally realized that he used me, lied to me, and persuaded me to do everything in the world for him, I was devastated. All I needed was a gun so I could shoot myself for being so stupid. I praised his ass; I gave him so much credit, and didn't even realize that he was just like any other man who wanted to get laid.

The visualization I had of him fucking Dana and her squeezing his black ass stayed in my mind. I couldn't wait to get home. When I got inside, I slammed the door and fell hard on my couch. The phone rang off the hook. Knowing that it was probably Jonathan, I picked it up and threw it against the wall. It broke off into tiny pieces before hitting the floor. That didn't solve my problem because the other phone started to ring. When I got up to throw that one as well, I looked at the caller ID and Dana's number appeared. Not wanting to talk to her either, still, like a fool, I answered.

"What?" I said.

"Don't what me, you whore! Who do you think you are sleeping with my damn husband? What kind of friend are you, bitch?" she yelled.

"One you should have never trusted! Now, don't call here disrespecting me! When you want to talk to me like you got some sense, call back!" I hung up, but Dana called right back. Foolishly, I answered again.

"You have got some nerve hanging up on me. I am on my way to come kick your trifling ass!"

"Listen, bony bitch, if you want to keep that child, you'd better stay as far away from me as possible. I mean it."

Dana hung up, and ten minutes later, she had the nerve to be banging on my door. Now, this heifer knew for a fact that I had always had a li'l hood in me, so I didn't know why she was tripping. I wanted so badly to snatch her up in here, but I couldn't. I let her bang on the door, scream and holler for me to open it, and allowed her to make a damn fool of herself. Moments later, somebody called the police, and she finally got in her car and left.

I was drained from all the bullshit, and when Britney called and told me what she had said to Dana, I could have killed her.

"Why in the hell would you tell her that, Britney?"

"Because I hate her, Sylvia. I'm sorry. I didn't want to be the one to tell her, but she worked my nerves. Please don't be mad at me. I . . . I just don't want her and my daddy to get back together."

"Britney, you know better. Do you have any idea what you've done?"

"Yeah. If anything, I opened the door for you and Daddy to be together."

"No, baby, it's not that simple. Jonathan doesn't love me. He loves his wife. I should have never interfered but I was too busy trying to satisfy my own needs."

"Well, I'm sorry. After he smacked me, I was so mad that I couldn't hold back on telling her."

"Smacked you?"

"Yes. And even though I'm furious with him, I'm kind of worried about him. He had an open cut on his face and I noticed scratches on his hands. I think he had a fight with somebody."

"He didn't tell you how he got the cut?"

"Nope. But he not too long ago called and apologized for hitting me. When I called him back, I asked him and he confirmed that he had a fight."

"Really? Did he say with who?"

"No. He wouldn't tell me but I think it was with the guy Dana was tripping with."

I took a deep breath and sighed from my mounting frustrations. "Thanks for calling, Britney, I have to go. Get some rest so you can get up for school tomorrow."

"Don't worry, I am. Would you do me a favor, though?"

"What?"

"I know you're upset with my daddy, but please call him. He—"

"Britney, no. I am not going to call your father right now, but he and I need to figure out a way to put closure to this. You're his daughter. You be the one to spend time with him and comfort him when need be. Me, I'm done. I've hurt myself too much by getting involved."

There was silence before Britney spoke again. "Bye, Sylvia."

"Good-bye."

Since I had no intentions of going to work, I stayed up until four o'clock watching TV. Lorenzo called and wanted to come over, but I wasn't in the mood. Jonathan was still heavy on my mind but I knew there wasn't a chance in hell I could face him this morning. Before I went to sleep, I called the office and left a message on his voicemail, saying I was sick and wasn't coming in.

Around seven in the morning, I got up and called a temp agency to have someone replace me for the rest of the week. Realizing that I needed more time away than I anticipated, I called my sister, Debra, in Chicago and asked if I could drive down and spend some time with her. We never really got along, but she insisted it would be good to see me.

After my shower, I looked in my closet for a few pieces to take with me. When the phone rang I knew, without a doubt, it was Jonathan. Anxious to give him a piece of my mind, I snatched up the phone.

"Hello," I said sharply.

"Sylvia, why aren't you here?"

"Because I'm taking a vacation."

"No. Vacations are supposed to be planned out and approved by me. Never are they to be spare of the moment like this."

"Look, I'm not feeling well today, so I'm not coming in. I'll come in when I get better. Besides, I called a temp for you this morning. She'll work out fine until I get back."

"No, she won't. You should see this chick they sent over here. I need you now. I have three meetings today, a slew of phone calls to return, and I have to be in court by three."

"That's not my problem. Handle your business because I'm for surely going to handle mines."

"I thought we agreed to keep our personal lives aside from our business relationship."

"We did and I am. Can't you understand I'm not feeling well?"

"And can't you understand that I need you?"

"For what, Jonathan? To fuck every time your wife gets you down? I'm not going to play the fool for you any longer. After what I witnessed yesterday, we're done."

"I have never considered you or wanted you to be a fuck thang for me. Yesterday was a big mistake. I had a fight with Lewis and Dana just caught me—"

"Stop there because I don't even want to hear it. You seemed to be the aggressor in that bed yesterday, not her."

Jonathan's tone was calm. "So, maybe I was. That still doesn't change what I've been feeling for you."

Feeling myself giving in to him, I sat on the couch and started biting my nails. "When are you going to stop this? You have no feelings for me, remember? All you have feelings for is for what's between my legs. I can't do this with you anymore. It hurts too much." My voice started to crack and I swallowed to clear the lump in my throat.

"Okay, then fine. If you say it's over, it's over. At least come to work so you can help me with all this stuff I have to do."

"No!"

"Please!"

"I said no!"

"Then you're fired!"

"You can't fire me, because I quit!" I slammed down the phone.

In a rage, I sat my behind down at my desk and quickly typed up a resignation letter. After I finished, I put on some clothes and hurried to the office. I stormed off the elevator, and when I entered Jonathan's office, he wasn't there. I glanced at his calendar and it showed he was in a meeting in Boardroom A. I laughed to myself when I saw the jacked-up, ghettofied secretary the temp agency sent and headed to the boardroom.

Not even giving a care about Jonathan being in a meeting, I quickly opened the door, excused myself, and slammed my typed resignation down in front of him as he spoke.

"There you go, Mr. Boss Man! And don't even think about asking me to come back because I won't!"

Shocked, more so embarrassed, Jonathan stood up and unbuttoned his suit jacket. He excused himself from his meeting with Mr. Bradford, Crissy, three other executives, and a secretary who took notes. I rolled my eyes at all of them and headed for the door.

By the time I reached the elevators, Jonathan pushed the entryway doors open and stepped up to me with a frown on his face. He grabbed my arm and swung me around. "Why in the hell would you do that to me?"

I snatched away. "Because you can use me all you want to, but firing me was the worst damn thing you could have done to me, especially after all I've done for you." The elevator opened and I got inside of it. Jonathan followed.

"I have never used you! Making love to you was always in the back of my mind. This doesn't have anything to do with me trying to chase after some pussy, woman, don't you get it!" The elevator opened and a lady stepped inside, looking at us. "We're getting ready to go somewhere private and talk about this," he whispered.

The elevator opened to the lobby, where we exited. "Please go make things right with your wife. With the baby, I'm sure she's demanding a lot of attention. You're so good at comforting her and I'm sure she needs you more than I do."

"Sylvia," Jonathan said, calmly. "I will handle my situation with Dana but you need to understand my position."

"I thought I did," I said, continuing to walk ahead of him. "But what could have possessed you to have sex with her after what she did to you?"

Jonathan took my hand and pulled me into the stairwell. He sat on the steps, and as usual, had my attention, as he looked out of sight in his brown silk suit. He covered his face with his hands and rubbed it. When he removed his hands, he looked at me with my back against the wall in front of him.

"I never ever wanted to hurt you, Sylvia. Yesterday, after meeting with Lewis, he made me feel so unworthy of my wife. I just felt like if I had sex with her I could somehow compete and show her what she'd been missing out on. Then, when he told me that he had sex with you, I couldn't get the thought out of my mind."

"What? He told you he had sex with me and you believed him?"

"Come on, Sylvia, he knew what color panties you had on the same day you pretended to be so sick. Then you lied about being on your period and you wasn't."

I folded my arms and pursed my lips. "So, you believed him?"

"Shit, I don't know what to believe anymore. It's not like you would tell me if you did have sex with him, especially since you know how I feel about his ass."

My whole face was scrunched. He acted like I was some kind of whore or something. I didn't appreciate what he'd said. "Damn you, Jonathan. What kind of woman do you think I am? Just because I'm having sex with my friend's man, it doesn't make me a crazed-ass woman who wants sex from everybody. The only thing I'm guilty of is loving you so damn much that I can hardly think straight." I started to get choked up.

Jonathan stood up and embraced me. He planted a soft kiss on my forehead and apologized. "Forgive me. I'm just so fucked up right now, and believe me when I say you are the last person that I want to hurt."

I wiped a tear and nodded. "I know. But the other day, Lewis tried to rape me. He and I tussled on the staircase and he lifted my skirt and touched me. I didn't want to tell you because I was afraid of what you might do. I didn't want you getting into any trouble, and you already had a lot on your plate."

Jonathan backed away from me with a puzzled look on his face. "Why . . . why didn't you call the police? Damn, Sylvia, you should have called the police! I swear I'm sick of this motherfucker! He has been nothing but a pain in my gotdamn side!"

"Baby, just calm down." I saw the fury in Jonathan's eyes. "I promise you Lewis will be dealt with."

"You damn right he will." Jonathan opened the door. "Are you coming back to work?"

I shook my head. "No."

"Suit yourself," he said, and then walked out.

Allowing Jonathan time to cool off, I walked down the street to get something to eat at Taco Bell. My mind was on overload. I wasn't sure if I was still going to Chicago. If anything, I needed to somehow make as much peace as I could with Dana, and I needed to put closure to my relationship with Jonathan. Loving him so much was more than I could seriously handle.

12

JONATHAN

After what Sylvia told me, I decided to deal with Lewis my own way. I immediately dropped the charges and wanted him released as soon as possible. In my eyes, Lewis dragging everyone into court with his bullshit and spending measly time in jail was not the solution. I had other plans for him, and being a lawyer or not, this damn fool was going to pay.

Dana was on a rampage. She called and made all kinds of threats, and when I got home, her car was in the driveway so I kept on driving. I drove to the Renaissance and got a room, then called Britney to let her know where I was. More than anything, I felt so bad for slapping her, but I made it clear to her that I wasn't going to stand for her verbal abuse. She explained how mad she was and told me she would never speak to me in that manner again. When she questioned me about Sylvia, I told her I'd call her later.

Badly needing some rest, before I went to sleep, I called an important and close friend of mine, Jaylin, who always had the solution for dealing with fools like Lewis. When one of his ladies answered the phone, it didn't surprise me. She gave the phone to him.

"John-John," he said with enthusiasm in his voice. "What's up, man?"

"Plenty. I just hope you and your cousin, Stephon, wouldn't mind taking care of a li'l something for me."

"Would that be in reference to shaking down some sistas, or with something else?"

"This is on a more serious level."

"You mean something like that problem I had with that white bitch's husband, Mr. McDaniels?"

"Yeah, something like that but more intense. Can you come by the office tomorrow so we can talk?"

"For you, yes. I'll see you around nine o'clock in the morning."

"Thanks, man. See you soon."

The next day, I felt well rested. I woke up early, went home to change clothes, and headed to the office. I was shocked to see Sylvia at her desk. When I walked up to her, she put up her hand.

"Don't say nothing to me. Just g'on," she said.

"But how are we supposed to get some work done if we're not communicating?"

"By the way you look at me, I can always tell what you want. So, if you want something, don't talk, just look."

I sat my briefcase on Sylvia's desk and folded my arms. I looked at her and she walked over to the file cabinet, pulled out a file, and gave it to me. It was the file on the Johnson case. She must have somehow known that I needed it.

"Anything else?" She grinned.

I picked up my briefcase, stood in my doorway, and looked at her again. She rolled her eyes. "Hell, no. I am not going there with you again."

"Yes, you will," I said with a smile

"No, I won't."

"You wanna bet?"

"You're darn right I do," she said, getting out of her chair. She followed me into my office. "How much money you got?"

"Plenty. But I'm not going to take your money like that."

"Naw, you won't be taking my money," she said, walking over to the coffee machine. She poured my coffee, and as soon as she handed the mug to me, Audrey and Jackie came in with boxes of Krispy Kreme doughnuts.

"Would you guys like some doughnuts?" Audrey asked, then walked past Sylvia and headed toward me. She opened the box, and after I removed one doughnut, she placed the box on my desk. Jackie and Sylvia grabbed a doughnut, and as we all stood around in my office loudly talking and laughing, there was a knock on my door. The ladies turned around, and when they saw Jaylin, they stood with their mouths hanging wide open and eyes bugged.

"Now, why didn't nobody invite me to the party? That's what I wanna know," Jaylin said, stepping into my office with an off-white linen suit on. The suit was off the chain, and he had a few buttons undone so the women could see his buff chest. Doing it Jaylin's style, the diamonds on his Rolex watch were sparkling and his healthy, curly hair was trimmed to perfection, as was his goatee. I stood up and introduced him to Sylvia, Audrey, and Jackie.

"Lord, have mercy on me," Jackie said with lust locked in her eyes. She reached out to shake his hand. "Honey, you are gorgeous. What color are your eyes?" she asked, and then squinted to look at them.

Jaylin smiled and checked her out from head to toe. "They're gray. And thank you for the compliment." He winked. "You don't look too bad yourself." He looked at Audrey and Sylvia. "Nice to meet you, ladies," he said, as they headed out.

Audrey held her head down and Sylvia stopped to reach for the knob on my door to close it.

"Before I go, do you need anything else?" she asked me.

"It depends on how far you're going."

"I'll be right at my desk."

"Then no."

She looked at Jaylin who had already taken a seat. "Can I get you some coffee or something else?"

He turned around. "As fine as you are, you should never ask a man like me that question. But, if you want to, you can pass those digits to me before I get out of here."

Sylvia smiled then looked over Jaylin's shoulder at me. "I just might have to do that," she said then closed the door.

"Umph. What a chocolate delight right there. John-John, why in the hell didn't you tell me you had all these lovely-ass women walking around up in here? All I work with are a bunch of old white folks, and with a secretary who occasionally sucks my dick. Was that your secretary?"

"Yeah, man," I said, taking a seat. "She's the best darn secretary any man can have."

"Really, now," Jaylin said suspiciously then took a seat. He crossed his leg over the other. "You, my brotha, have added that pussy to your collection, haven't you?"

"Man, hell naw. I have a wife who I'm mad as hell with, and my secretary has been there to offer her support."

"Support, huh?" He leaned forward and whispered, "That's what we're calling it these days? By the looks of things, she's supporting your ass very well. You can't fool me, John-John, I've been in the game for too long. I sense shit like that."

I held out my hands, feeling defeated. "All right, damn. We got a li'l somethin' somethin' going on, but that's not what I want to talk to you about."

Jaylin sat back and stroked his goatee. "Shit, and there I was thinking you were a better man than me. When you pull off that Rolex, that fancy-ass expensive gray suit, and those eight hundred dollar lizard skin shoes, you still the same damn man as I am."

"Sounds like you hating a li'l bit," I said with a smirk. "Why you checking a brotha out like that?"

"Don't front. I know you already peeped my shit when I came through the door. And don't try to hang because you can't. Altogether, I'm busting about six grand on me right now. And that doesn't even include the jewelry."

"Bullshit," I said, standing up. "Negro, these shoes cost me twelve hundred dollars, the suit was two grand, shirt was five hundred, and check out these diamond platinum cufflinks," I said laughing, and pulling them off so he could see them. "These cost me seventeen hundred dollars, pimp."

Jaylin observed my cuff links. "Daaaamn, where did you get these from?"

I snatched them and sat back down in my chair. "None of your business."

We laughed, and then got down to business. I spent the next few hours giving Jaylin the scoop on Lewis. He was surprised to find out Dana cheated on me and was more surprised when he realized how much love I still had for her. He told me he and Stephon knew all kinds of fellas who could take care of things for me, and he assured me that I had nothing to worry about, especially since I had saved his ass many times before. When he asked me if I wanted Lewis dead or alive, I wasn't really sure how to answer. All I knew was that I wanted him out of our lives for good. If that meant doing away with his ass, I really didn't care.

Since Jaylin was a man of his word, I trusted whatever he decided to do. He told me he wouldn't tell me who, what, when, or where things would go down, but promised that Lewis would be history. Being in my position, the less I knew the better.

Before he got ready to leave, we shook hands and Jaylin stayed in my office to use my phone. I opened the door and Sylvia was on the floor by her desk while organizing my files.

She smiled at me and I smiled back. "Dana called. I threatened to call the police on her, but you'd better talk to her soon and watch your back."

"I will."

I shook Jaylin's hand, again, and agreed to walk him out. Before he left, he stood by Sylvia's desk and flirted with her.

"Pssss, Sylvia," he whispered. "What's up with that number?"

"You know, if things weren't so complicated right now, maybe I would. And who knows what the future holds. Maybe I'll see you again."

Jaylin laughed then looked over at me. "Is he treating you okay?"

Sylvia looked at me and smiled. "Remarkably well."

"That's good, but if you ever think you may want a pay increase, I'm always in the market for a secretary."

"I'll keep that in mind."

I lightly pushed Jaylin in the back and nudged him toward the exit door. "Hands off, man. Don't you already have plenty of women?"

He laughed and walked toward the elevator with me. "Plenty, but there is always room for plenty more. Just tell me something, though," he said.

"Yes, Sylvia is off the chain. Both in and out of the bedroom."

"Damn, I knew it." Jaylin covered his eyes with his shades. "And here my underwear cost more than your whole damn outfit and I can't even get a number."

"You silly, man. And I can't believe you out searching for more women and you got, uh, what's her name?"

"Scorpio Motherfucking Bad-ass Valentino. Nokea was tripping so I had to let that go. For now anyway."

"Naw, she probably had to let you go for being a naughty man. Either way, I'm sure the two of you will work things out, as y'all always do."

Jaylin shrugged and we continued to talk as we waited for the elevator to open. No sooner had it done then Dana rushed off and swung wildly at me like she had lost her mind. I ducked and tried to get control of her, but she was seriously out of control. She yelled for Sylvia, and when the receptionist questioned what was going on, I asked her to call for security.

Jaylin and I, both, had to restrain Dana. When she elbowed him in the jaw and brushed up against his suit, he got mad.

"Hold up, baby. Watch my damn suit now," he said with a twisted face. He looked at me and shook his head. "Man, you need to get some control over this shit. Your wife is crazy!"

"Who are you calling me crazy?" Dana hissed as I held her arms behind her. She struggled to get away from my grip. "You don't know me."

"I'm glad I don't," Jaylin fired back. "Regardless, you need to calm this shit down."

Security rushed up the steps, and I turned Dana over to them. I told them to make sure she didn't get back in. They escorted her out, and told her if she came back that she would be arrested.

Making sure everything was cool, Jaylin and I walked to the parking garage together.

"John-John, that was some wild shit. I don't know how you can stand there and let a woman swing on you like that. If it had been me, her ass may have hit the floor."

"Man, those punches don't hurt. Besides, I was taught to never put my hands on a lady, no matter what."

"Good for you, but that courtesy went out the window years ago. These women out here today are crazy. I'll mess somebody up getting at me like that, and she's the one who brought that shit on herself, too. I know she's your wife but that was ridiculous. And as fine and classy as she is, she should know better."

"Yeah, well, obviously she doesn't. I'm starting to see a side of her I didn't even know existed. And fine or not, I don't like it one bit."

"John-John, please," Jaylin said, opening the door to his Mercedes-Benz and giving me dap. "Stay up, and we'll holla soon."

"No doubt."

Jaylin shut the door and sped out of the parking garage. I headed back upstairs to my office. Truly behind on my work, I asked Sylvia to stay late and help me get caught up. Since we had so much to do, there was no time to discuss our personal situation. And by the time we had almost everything in order, we left the office together around 8:30 p.m.

I walked Sylvia to her car. When I opened the door, and leaned down to kiss her, she held her hand in my face.

"Do you understand what no means?" she asked.

"No," I said, leaning in to kiss her. She turned her head, but I turned it back toward me. I pecked her lips and forced my tongue in her mouth. When she reached up and rubbed the back of my head, I knew I was in business. Soon after, she backed away and wiped her lips.

"Now, go home, please," she said.

"Only if you'll go with me."

"Listen, if you don't talk to Dana, she is going to lose her mind and mess both of us up. Please go see what she wants."

"I already know what she wants, and I'm not worried about Dana right now."

"I am because I don't want anyone to get hurt. Please, please do your best to put some closure to this mess, okay?"

"I intend to. Right after you let me make love to you tonight."

"You are a persistent little something, aren't you?"

"Only when it comes to something I want. Follow me to the Renaissance. I assure you it will be worth your time."

"There's no doubt in my mind that it will be," Sylvia said, reaching for her door to close it.

On my way to the Renaissance, I was all smiles. I checked my rearview mirror, several times, to make sure Sylvia followed me. After the valet parked our cars, we headed to my room and tore it up. Sylvia wasn't holding back and neither was I. More than anything, I realized that night that I not only needed her, but I also loved her. There was no way for me to move forward without her.

13

SYLVIA

I was so caught up in this mess with Jonathan that I didn't know what to do. We spent the entire week avoiding Dana and screwing the hell out of each other. Thing was, I truly enjoyed our times together. I didn't even care about my friendship with Dana because Jonathan was everything I needed. Just maybe, all of this would somehow work out for us. I knew how much he cared for me, so anyone standing in the way certainly had to move on. Including Dana. Jonathan promised me he would make time over the weekend to talk to her, but I didn't know how successful that conversation would be.

What made me more irate about the whole thing was she continued to call my house, and yell and scream at me like it was all my fault. When she implied I wasn't good enough for Jonathan, and implied that I didn't have enough class to be with a man like him, that really made my blood boil. How dare she say that when she was the one running her supposed to be classy ass around here acting like a fool? On Friday, she cut Jonathan's tires so he couldn't go to work, and he just called me this morning and told me she was outside with a bat, threatening to smash the windows to his car if he didn't talk to her. He said that after he called the police, he was on his way to get a restraining order against her. He advised me to be careful and encouraged me to get one as well.

I really wasn't worried about her crazy butt. Whatever was going to go down, so be it. Jonathan was being too nice for me. If he would just put Dana in her place, or maybe kick her tail one good time, she'd be all right. I understood his position, though. He always tried to do the right thing, but that was him and this was me.

Since it was a beautiful day outside, I put on my workout clothes and headed for Forest Park to jog. I called Britney's house to see if she wanted to go with me, but Beverly said she was still in bed after coming in at four o'clock in the morning. I told Beverly she should have torn her behind up, but all she did was laugh. The shit wasn't funny to me because they knew better letting Britney get away with too much stuff. If somebody didn't start putting their foot down, Britney was going to one day find herself in serious trouble.

I parked my car by Steinberg Skating Rink, and by the time I jogged to Lindell Boulevard, my heart raced fast. I put my hair in a ponytail and sat on a bench to catch my breath. When a man in a pickup truck blew his horn and flicked his tongue in and out at me, I presented my middle finger and started to run again.

I was almost on DeBaliviere when I saw Dana charging my way. She didn't have a bat or any other objects in her hands, so I bent down, placed my hands on my knees and tried to catch my breath before she approached me. Since she was in high heels, I started to take off, but maybe it was time that I listened to what she had to say.

"You are a dirty bitch, Sylvia," she said, moving close to my face.

I backed up. "Dana, I'm not going to stand out here and argue with you. Now, if you got something to say, say it and be done with it. Just know, though, I'm not going to be too many of your bitches."

"All I want to know is what possessed you to sleep with my husband? Not only that, but how in the hell could you do this to me? You knew—"

"Dana, let me stop you right there. All I knew was that you were playing Jonathan for a fool. I told you over and over again I didn't like it one bit, and when he came to me for comfort, it was hard for me not to be there for him."

She put her hand on her hip and got teary-eyed. "But . . . but you were supposed to be my friend, Sylvia. I trusted you with my husband and with my secrets. How could you do this to me?"

"I honestly can't say that I'm sorry because you opened up the door for another woman to love him. Unfortunately, that woman just happens to be me. I told you that you were going to lose him, Dana. You put all of us in this uncomfortable situation and I'm sorry it has to be like this."

"So, you're blaming me for you being trifling, huh? Out of all of the men in St. Louis, you want my damn husband? I'm telling you now, there's no way in hell I'm going to lose him to you or to any other woman. What you walked in on the other day, prepare yourself to walk in on it again. Jonathan still loves me, and when he realizes how much joy and happiness this child is going to bring us, you are going to find yourself left without."

I shrugged and pursed my lips. "If you say so, Dana. Now, do you mind if I get back to my workout?"

Dana narrowed her eyes and glared at me. "You have no damn regrets, do you? And by the way you're talking, you are still fucking him, aren't you?"

"Don't worry about what I'm doing. That ain't your business. But, if I am still screwing him, it's because he can't let go."

Dana slapped the shit out of me, causing my head to jerk to the side. Instead of punching her ass, I gave her a hard push that sent her to tumbling to the ground.

"Backstabbing bitch," she yelled, as I jogged away. "I hate you, Sylvia! I hate you!"

I kept on jogging, but Dana wouldn't let it go. While driving in her car next to me, she cursed and yelled at me. When I tried to veer off and take a shortcut, she was finally out of my sight.

Shortly after, I heard a car skid and a loud crash. My head snapped to the side and all I saw was smoke. I quickly ran to see what had happened. The front of Dana's Jaguar was mangled. The Lincoln Navigator she'd run into was smashed as well, but not like her car.

Panicking, when I saw her unconscious and blood dripping down the side of her face and matted to her sandy-brown hair, tears welled in my eyes. I couldn't tell if she was dead or alive. Afraid to touch her, I watched as a jogger pulled her limp body from the wrecked car. He reached for his cell phone, handed it to me, and yelled for me to dial 911. I called and the dispatcher said help was on the way.

Pacing back and forth, I watched as the paramedics put Dana and the lady in the Lincoln Navigator on stretchers and into ambulances. Thank God they were both still alive. The police asked if anyone saw what had happened, so I stepped forward and explained how she must have taken her eyes off the road. After seeing how nervous I was, the officer offered to take me to Barnes Jewish Hospital to make sure Dana was okay.

It was a few hours before the doctors came out and told me anything. I lied and told them I was her sister. When the doctor asked for her husband, I told him Jonathan was on his way. Dana was lucky, so the doctor explained. Not only was she unconscious, but also she had a broken nose, a fractured rib, had lost a lot of blood, and as for the baby, they could not save it.

Feeling as if this was my fault, I sat in the waiting room and released many tears. My entire body ached. I had a throbbing headache that wouldn't go away. Fearing to call Jonathan and break the news to him, first, I wanted to see Dana. The doctor led me to intensive care, and when I got a glimpse of how messed up she was, I couldn't get myself together. A few nurses helped me stand and they escorted me back into the waiting room. One of them gave me some pain medicine for my headache, and after I calmed down, I called Jonathan. He answered, but I remained speechless.

"Is anyone there?" he repeated.

"Jonathan," I said softly.

"Sylvia? Talk up, I can't hear you."

"Dana's in the hospital."

"What?"

"Dana was in a car accident. She's in the hospital."

"What hospital? Is she okay?"

"I don't know," I said choked up.

"Where are you?" he yelled.

"Barnes Jew—"

The call ended.

When Jonathan came busting through the doors, I was still in the waiting area with rattled nerves. He went straight to the nurse's station and the nurse took him back to intensive care. I didn't even have the guts to look at him and tell him what had happened. I figured he'd want some answers, so I hung around and waited for him.

Finally, after about an hour of being with Dana, Jonathan came out, appearing devastated. His tie was loose, his shirt hung out of his slacks, and his jacket was thrown over his shoulder. His eyes searched around, and when they connected with mine, he slowly walked toward me. I stood up and held my arms out for a hug. We embraced, as I cried on his shoulder. When I let go, we sat down. Before he said anything, he used his cell phone to call Dana's parents. Agitated by their many questions, he told them where Dana was and hung up.

"Are you okay?" he asked, rubbing my messy ponytail back.

I took a hard swallow and shook my head. "No."

"What happened? When you called, I had just gotten back from getting a restraining order."

I placed my hands over my face and closed my eyes. "We got into an argument and everything just . . . just happened so fast."

Jonathan moved my hands away from my face and I opened my eyes. "So, you were with her when this happened?"

"No, but she . . . she was yelling crazy stuff at me as I jogged, and . . . and she must have taken her eyes off the road."

Jonathan shook his head, displaying disgust. "I can't understand why she insisted on acting like this. Did you say anything to her?"

"Yeah, we went back and forth for a while. When she slapped me, I pushed her down."

"So, how did y'all have a physical confrontation if she was in the car?"

"At first when we argued, she was out of the car. Then, when I jogged off, she got in the car and came after me."

"So, when y'all argued, why did you push her on the ground?"

"Because she slapped me, that's why," I said with attitude.

"So you pushed her on the ground, knowing that she was pregnant?"

I cocked my head back and wasn't feeling Jonathan's questions. "After she slapped me, she's lucky that's all I did to her."

Jonathan stood up and took a few steps. He slowly turned. "Do you know she lost the baby?"

I nodded. "Yes. But are you implying that my push had anything to do with it?"

"Shit, Sylvia, I don't know. Why couldn't you just walk away from her?"

"I tried! I tried to be calm about the situation, but she wouldn't let it go."

"And I'm sure you didn't either," he said, raising his voice.

I jumped up from my chair. "Hold on one damn minute! I know—"

Jonathan looked over my shoulder and so did I. We saw Dana's parents come in. Mama Bell hugged him then she gave me a hug too. Mr. Bell did the same, and they all headed back to see Dana. I waited for about fifteen minutes before I left.

Since Forest Park was close by, I jogged back to my car. I sat and listened to some soft music for a while. My mind, however, was going a mile a minute. I couldn't believe Jonathan's response. I already felt guilty, and I didn't need any additional pressure from him. If anything, he should have been man enough to talk this shit out with Dana before it got out of hand. He knew how crazy she'd been acting and he didn't do nothing about it but get a restraining order. What in the hell was that supposed to do? A restraining order didn't mean shit to Dana, especially when her father had connections and money to get her out of any trouble she'd get herself into.

Overwhelmed, I went home and took a hot, bubbly bath. I wanted so badly to hear from Jonathan but he didn't call. I'd even thought about calling him, but I quickly changed my mind. I knew he was busy trying to make sure Dana was okay, so I allowed him all the space he needed.

By Monday morning, I was hurt like hell. I expected to hear from Jonathan, but when Crissy came through the door and went into his office, I had a feeling something wasn't right. She didn't say anything to me, until after I listened to her conversation with Jonathan on the phone.

"Line one," she said.

I picked up. "Hello."

"I'm not going to be in for a while. Crissy is going to take care of things for me. If you wouldn't mind showing her where she can find the files for the cases I have coming up, I'd appreciate it."

"I'll do what I can." My throat ached, so I swallowed. "How long are you going to be out?"

"For at least a month. Dana's conscious now, but she has a long road to recovery. Losing the baby was quite damaging for her."

"I'm sure it was. Not only for her, but for you as well."

"Yeah, it was."

"Well, I'll do what I can to help out Crissy. If you need anything, just call."

"I will," he said and then hung up.

I was crushed and rushed to the bathroom to release my emotions. I knew working for that bitch Crissy was going to drive me crazy, but stupid me was still trying to be there for Jonathan, as I'd always been.

When I got back to my desk, I gathered Jonathan's files and took them into his office to give to Crissy. She was on the phone. I reached out to give them to her, but she mouthed for me to put them down on Jonathan's desk. As I was on my way out, she put the caller on hold and asked me to sit. Not feeling up to her bullshit, I let out a deep sigh and took a seat. When she got off the phone, she opened her purse and slid on some lipstick.

"Does this look okay?" she asked wiping around her lips while looking at her compact mirror.

I shrugged my shoulders. "Yeah, I guess."

She closed the mirror and glared at me. "Sylvia, what is it about me that you don't like? I have done nothing to you, and you always come at me with such an attitude."

"I feel the same way about you, Crissy. You're always walking up in here like somebody owe you something and I don't owe you nothing."

"I do not come off like that. I get along with everybody in this place, with the exception of you. You have an attitude, honey, and you know it."

"Maybe I do, or maybe I don't, but don't worry about my attitude. For the next month, we have to work together, so the faster we put all this chaos behind us the better."

"I agree. So, if you wouldn't mind filling me in on what Jonathan's been doing, we can start from there."

"I'll do what I can."

I spent the entire day running around the office for Crissy. Around three o'clock, she said that she was tired and headed for home. Not wanting to stay either, I asked her if I could also leave and she suggested that we leave together.

We walked to the elevator and didn't say much of anything to each other. By the time we reached the parking garage, Crissy told me to have a good evening and went to her car. Unbelievably, we made it through the day without scratching each other's eyes out. I guessed, just maybe, she wasn't so bad after all.

Jonathan hadn't called to speak to me all week long. Crissy said he called the office to check on things, but he never asked to speak to me. I was dying inside, but I put up a front like everything was all good.

On Friday, as I gathered my things to leave, Crissy came out of Jonathan's office and thanked me for helping her out this week. When I nodded and didn't say anything, she displayed a puzzled look.

"Girlfriend, I don't know what's been ailing you this week, but I am sick and tired of seeing your long face. Besides, I know something is going on in that big head of yours, especially since you haven't gone off on me all week long."

I laughed. "Trust me, I've wanted to go off on you, but I kept my peace."

"Go off on me for what?" She put her hands on her hips and grinned. "I've been nothing but nice to you this week, girlie. If you had gone off on me, I would have gone right back off on you."

"I'm sure you would have."

We laughed and Crissy suggested we go across the street to CJ's to have a drink. Having nothing else to do, I decided to go.

Crissy and me had a ball at CJ's. Both of us had gotten tipsy and we talked about all kinds of mess. When she called me a black bitch, not just a bitch, but a black bitch, I put down my drink and looked at her.

"Watch it now, heifer. We ain't that cool where I'm going to allow you to disrespect me."

She threw her hand back at me. "Oh, Sylvia, get over it. What's with you Black women when it comes to being called a bitch? Black bitch, white bitch, purple bitch, whatever. Who gives a damn?"

"I do, white bitch, only because we ain't that cool. It's okay for my girls to call me a bitch, but when any man or a white bitch such as yourself crosses the line, I don't play that."

"So, let me get this straight: a man or any white bitch can't call you a bitch, but it's okay for your friends to call you a bitch?"

"Yes."

"Well, that doesn't make sense. It's just like the issue you guys have with being called the N word. What difference does it make whether it's said by me or by someone from your own race?"

"Big difference. And to avoid yourself getting your ass kicked, don't ever call me either one."

Crissy laughed and shook her head. "I like you, Sylvia. You wanna know why?"

"Because I'm a black bitch who will tell it like it is, that's why."

"You're right. And even though I pretend that you irk the hell out of me, you make my day with your jacked-up attitude. I love it!"

I gulped down another shot of Martell and so did Crissy. When this brotha came over and tried to holla at both of us, Crissy suggested having a threesome. Excited about her offer, he bought both of us another drink. Several minutes later, he insisted he was ready to go, but Crissy went off on him.

"What in the hell do we look like, man?" she slurred. "A bunch of fucking whores?"

"Now, I didn't say all of that," he said, trying to compromise. "I thought you ladies might have wanted to have a little fun tonight."

"We are having fun, brother. And we're going to have a lot of fun as soon as you get your ass away from here."

The brotha frowned and looked at Crissy like he was getting ready to go off. I quickly intervened. "Hey, listen, my girl here is kind of messed up, all right? But, either way, we're really not interested, okay?"

"That's all y'all had to say," he snapped then walked away.

I looked at Crissy. "You better watch that shit. That brotha was about to hurt both of us."

"Please," she said. "What is it with these men anyway? Why must everything revolve around having sex?"

"Well, when you come off suggesting a threesome, what did you expect?"

"I was only kidding. Besides, I'm not interested in screwing around with a black man anyway. That's, of course, with the exception of your boss, Jonathan. He is definitely one man who I would fuck the mess out of. Tell me, is he a good lover?"

"Why in the hell do you think I would know anything about that?"

"Sylvia, please, girl. You know darn well that you've screwed him. There's no way you would have interrupted that meeting like you did if you weren't screwing him."

"Well, believe it or not, I can't answer that question for you."

"Then I'll just have to see for myself."

"Go ahead. If you think he'll screw you then go for it."

"I've already tried," she said, ordering herself another drink. "You better not tell anyone this or else I'm gonna kick your butt."

"Please. You always talking about kicking somebody's butt and can't fight a lick. Anyway, I better not tell nobody what?"

Crissy leaned in and whispered, "That Jonathan and I worked late one night and I stripped naked in my office for him. I threw myself at him and he—"

"He what, girl?"

"He looked at me like I was out of my mind. I consider myself to be a great catch, but he told me he wasn't interested. When I asked why, he said because he was a married man and he loved his wife. I respected that, until I had my suspicions about him screwing you."

"Well, you're wrong about that."

"Bullshit, Sylvia. Now, I was honest with you. You can at least be honest with me and tell me how good it is."

I laughed at Crissy and took another sip of my drink. Trusting her not to tell anyone, I admitted to having sex with Jonathan.

"I knew it!" She slammed her hand on the table. "But, like, give me some juicy details. Is it everything that you could imagine?"

"Yes, and then some. He's a great lover, and I'm truly missing the hell out of him this week."

"So, that's why you've been all quiet and shit."

"Pretty much. Other than that, I dreaded working for you."

Crissy rolled her eyes. "Get over it, bitch. I'm the best darn thing that could have happened to you."

"All right, trick. Watch the bitches because I will still mess you up."

"I can call you a bitch all I want to. You only said I couldn't call you a black bitch. Besides, I'd like to consider us as being homegirls now, right?"

"Hell no! You are too damn stuck up to be considered one of my homegirls."

"For your information, I am more hip than any of your homegirls are. 50 Cent is the man, so is Nelly, and Jay-Z. I love me some Jay-Z."

Crissy stood up and tried to rap. Several people looked over at us and shook their heads.

"No way," I said, standing up. "You are not about to embarrass me up in here. Put that drink down and let's go."

Crissy laughed, and after she finished her drink, we left. We stumbled back to our cars, and after we stood yakking for at least another hour, we went our separate ways.

***

When Crissy came into work on Monday morning, she said hello and walked into Jonathan's office. Giving her a taste of my attitude, I followed in behind her.

"Say, bitch, can I get you a doughnut or something this morning?"

She laughed. "A doughnut would ruin this awesome figure I got, girlie. I do not want to look like your fat ass, so I'd better watch it."

"You call that a figure?" I joked.

"You're darn right I do," she said, then smacked her flat butt. "Girlfriend, you wish you had it like this."

I patted my butt. "Honey, I got it like that and then some. You should be wishing that you could pull it off like this."

"Hell, no. That's too much behind. You should be ashamed of yourself for squeezing that big butt into those tight skirts."

"Jealousy will get you nowhere, Crusty. And I'm going to get you that doughnut in hopes that it goes to your butt and fattens it up."

She laughed out loud. "You do that, *Shanana,* and while you're at it, get me some freaking orange juice, too."

We laughed and I went downstairs and got Crissy and me breakfast. When I gave it to her, she thanked me and told me to keep up the attitude.

As hard as I tried not to think about Jonathan, he stayed on my mind for the remainder of the day. I hadn't been away from him for more than two days, and not seeing him at work tormented me. I, at least, hoped that he missed me as much as I missed him.

14

JONATHAN

I hoped and prayed that Dana would get well soon. The doctor said she could leave the hospital next week and I was thrilled to hear that. She really didn't say much to me, except for she was sorry for acting like a fool and she hoped I wasn't upset with her for losing the baby. I apologized to her as well, and told her I held myself accountable for mostly everything that had happened. If anything, I should have listened to her when she begged for attention, and I never should've consulted in Sylvia for advice or comfort. It wasn't that I regretted being with Sylvia, but knowing how much hurt our being together would cause everyone, I should have never overstepped my boundaries.

Thing was, though, I didn't have the courage or guts to tell Sylvia I planned to work on my marriage with Dana. I knew my news would devastate her. The last thing I wanted to do was hurt her again. At this point, though, I really didn't have a choice. If I walked away from Dana at a time when she needed me the most, I would never be able to forgive myself.

On the day Dana left the hospital, her parents and I brought her home. Mama Bell stayed and cooked all of us a wonderful dinner. When Britney called, I invited her to come by, but she declined and insisted she didn't want to be around Dana. I told Britney she would have to deal with Dana and me being together, and after that, she ended the call.

When Dana's parents decided to leave, it was almost ten o'clock that night. I was exhausted, and after I walked them to the door, I went into the bedroom where Dana was. She didn't have her strength back yet, so I basically had to wait on her hand and foot. Her waist and head were wrapped in bandages because of her ribs and the gash on her forehead. Feeling badly for her, I sat on the bed and placed her feet on my lap. I rubbed them and she smiled.

"You haven't rubbed my feet like that in ages." She closed her eyes. "That feels so wonderful."

"The last time we made love I rubbed your feet. You just don't remember."

"That's right, you did. I can't wait to get better so we can work on having another child."

I looked down at the floor, thinking about the loss of our child.

"Jonathan?"

"Yeah."

"You do want to try again, don't you?"

"Of course, I do, Dana. One day at a time though, baby. First, I want to make sure you get better."

"I hope you're not worried about what the doctor said. They've always said my chances were slim, but, hey, we proved them wrong, didn't we?"

"We sure did, and we'll do it again."

I continued to rub Dana's feet until she fell asleep. After she did, I went to the kitchen and got a slice of cake, then ate it in the living room while reading the newspaper.

Finding myself thinking hard about Sylvia, I reached for the phone next to me to call her. I must have picked up the phone and hung it up ten times before letting it ring. When a deep voice answered, I was almost speechless.

"Hello," a manly voice said again.

I cleared my throat. "Is, uh, Sylvia there?"

"Who's calling?"

"This is her boss, Jonathan. I need to ask her something."

"Aw, hold on. She's getting out of the shower so wait a minute."

I took a hard swallow, as I waited for Sylvia to get on the phone. Shortly after, she did. "Hello," she said.

"Hey, it's me."

"Who?"

"Jonathan, Sylvia."

"Aw, hey, what's up?"

"Have you heard from Crissy?" I said, trying to think of anything to ask her, other than who was there with her.

"Yeah, I saw her at work today. She said that she had a date tonight, so maybe she's just not answering her phone."

"Hmm. So, have the two of you been getting along okay?"

"As a matter of fact, we have. But, listen, I'm gonna have to call you back, okay?"

"Sure."

"And Jonathan, please give Dana my best."

"I most certainly will," I said.

She hung up.

For hours, I sat around thinking about Sylvia fucking another man. I thought I recognized Lorenzo's voice and knowing that he was inside of her ate at me all night long. I even thought about calling her back, but I couldn't. Really, I didn't know what in the hell to say. It messed me up that she wasn't even tripping off me and had decided to move on.

By morning, my jealousy had seriously taken over. After I cooked breakfast for Dana and me, I told her I was going to the office to get something. I promised her I would be right back, and told her I would bring back some of her favorite ice cream from Velvet Freeze. She smiled and told me to hurry.

When I got to the office, from a distance I saw Sylvia down the hallway, while leaned against the wall with her hands on her hips. She talked to Audrey and looked out of sight. Her straight, long hair was combed back and was flipped on the ends. She had on a brown leather short skirt that showed her sexy chocolate legs that I missed touching. After she saw me, she swished her hips from side to side and headed my way. I couldn't help myself from wanting her so badly.

"Back so soon?" she said, smiling.

"I just stopped by to pick up something. I didn't see Crissy in my office. Is she here?"

"No, she's in court." Sylvia walked past me and went to her desk. All I got was a whiff of her sweet-smelling perfume. She looked down at her calendar. "Crissy is going to be out for the rest of the day. After court, she's going to the St. Louis Cardinals game."

"Okay, well, I'll just get what I came for then." I went into my office. It was neat as a pin and nothing seemed to be out of place. Trying to make conversation with Sylvia, I called her into my office.

"What's up?" she asked, peeking her head in the door.

"Have you seen my, uh, blue folder? It had a lot of important papers in it and it was on my desk."

"No, I haven't seen it. Last Monday, when Crissy came in, there was nothing on your desk."

"Damn!" I said, looking around. "Do you think you can help me look for it?"

She looked at her watch. "Yeah, I guess. I don't know what I'm looking for, but if I see a blue folder, let you know, right?"

"Please."

I sat at my desk and turned around in my chair. I pretended to search for the folder in the file cabinets behind me. Sylvia looked on my bookshelves, and then squatted down and searched in the file cabinet next to the one I looked in. I glanced at her sexy ass, and it took everything I had not to dive on top of her and fuck her brains out.

After looking through two drawers, she looked at me while holding the drawer open. "How's Dana doing?"

"She's fine."

"Is she home yet?"

"Yes."

"That's good."

"Very."

She stood up and walked toward the door. "I'm going to take a look in my file cabinets. Maybe you or I put it there by accident."

I turned my chair around and released a deep sigh. "Close the door for me." She stared at me then slightly rolled her eyes. "Please, just close the door."

She closed the door, but stood in front of it. "What do you want?" she asked.

"Who was at your house last night when I called?"

Her eyebrows rose. "Why?"

"Because I want to know. Was it Lorenzo?"

"I can't believe you have the nerve to sit there and ask me who in the hell I've been entertaining."

"That's not what I asked you. I asked you if the brotha who answered the phone last night was Lorenzo."

"That's none of your business. From now on, stay the hell out of my life and do not question me about my personal relationships."

"Okay, so you're mad at me for not calling. I just needed time, Sylvia. You have no idea what I've been going through."

"No!" she yelled and pointed her finger at me. "You have no idea what I've been going through!" A tear fell from her eye, but she smacked it away. "Right about now, I don't give a shit what you've been through. If anything, you at least owed me an explanation! That's all I wanted, but as usual, you failed me once again." She opened the door and walked out.

"Syl—"

I leaned back in my chair and shook my head. Feeling as if I never should have come here, I grabbed my keys to go. When I walked out of my office, Sylvia was at her desk with her back turned.

"I'll see you in a couple of weeks."

She ignored me and didn't say a word. Not wanting her to get loud again, I headed home.

In deep thought about Sylvia, I forgot about Dana's ice cream. When she asked for it, I told her they were out of Heavenly Hash and promised her I would go back later to get it.

Later that day, I rented us some movies to watch. I stopped to get her ice cream, and when I got home and entered the bedroom, she was on the phone with her mother. Her parents had been calling her like crazy, checking to make sure everything was okay. They were really starting to be a pain, but I tried not to trip. I understood their concern, but when her father kept making comments like, "You better treat my baby girl right," and insisting that we'd better work things out, it kind of pissed me off. I was too damn grown for anyone to tell me what to do, but out of respect, I chilled and kept my mouth shut.

Dana struggled to make it to the bed, and when I saw her standing in the doorway, holding herself up, I walked over and picked her up. She wrapped her arms around my neck and kissed me on the cheek.

"I love you," she said, as I carried her over to the bed and laid her down.

"I love you too." I sat next to her.

She placed her hand on my cheek. "Do you really? I know we've been through a lot these past several months, and I just hope you still love me as much as I still love you."

"I wouldn't tell you that I love you if I didn't. I know we've been through a lot as well, but, sometimes, a marriage has to be challenged to make it stronger." I leaned forward and gave Dana a kiss. After we finished, I pulled the DVDs out of the bag.

"Okay, which one do you want to see first?"

Dana opened the container of ice cream. She put the spoon in her mouth and licked it. "Uh, that one."

She pointed to a horror flick, so I put it in the DVD player, and quickly went to the kitchen to pop us some popcorn. When I got back to the bedroom, I turned down the lights and jumped into bed with Dana. She laughed as I tickled her feet.

"Stop," she said. "Believe it or not, that hurts."

"No, it doesn't."

"Yes, it does. When I laugh, it makes my stomach hurt."

"Oh, I forgot about that. Sorry."

We were tuned in to the movie, but when Dana reached for the popcorn, I snatched it away so she wouldn't get any.

"Come on now, baby, stop this and give me some."

"No. You're going to have to work for this popcorn." I tossed some up in the air so she could catch it with her mouth. She opened wide and the popcorn fell in. She snatched the bag, and then held her head, applying pressure with the tips of her fingers.

"Are you okay?" I asked.

"Yeah, I'm fine. I just got a little dizzy. But now, it's your turn."

She tossed up the popcorn and I tried to catch it with my mouth. By the time I did, popcorn was all over the bed. We laughed as we picked up the pieces and aimed them in each other's mouths.

The movie started to get good, so we chilled out and watched it. By the time it was over, Dana had fallen asleep in my arms. I kissed her forehead and rubbed my hands up and down on her soft cheeks. Thinking back to the last time we had so much fun together, I realized it had been years. Hopefully, things were getting back to normal, and all the hurt I still felt would soon be a thing of the past.

After several more weeks, Dana was back on her feet. I was excited about going back to work, but she wasn't happy about it at all. I promised her it was over between Sylvia and me, but Dana wouldn't let the memory of Sylvia and me being together die. She wanted me to fire Sylvia, but I told her that was something I just couldn't do. When I suggested her trying to mend their friendship, she told me I was out of my mind. In the meantime, I asked her to forget about what had happened in the past and to try hard at moving on.

I tried to move forward my damn self, but no sooner had I stepped back into the office than I found it was difficult for me to be around Sylvia again. On purpose, I went in late just so she wouldn't think I was in a rush to see her. Trying not to be an asshole, I did the norm for a Monday morning and walked right past her, Audrey, and Jackie, as they stood outside of my door running their mouths. I slammed the door hard, and shortly after, when I heard a knock, I yelled for whoever it was to come in.

Sylvia peeked her head through the door. "Would you like for me to tell you where Crissy left off? She and I went

over everything on Friday, and if you want me to, I'd like
to fill you in."

"Yeah, come on in. Sit down so we can get started."

Instead of sitting, Sylvia went over to the coffee machine, poured my coffee, and then placed the mug on my
desk. Afterward, she took a seat in front of me.

"Thanks," I said, answering the phone when it rang.
"Jonathan Taylor."

"Hi, baby," Dana, said. "Can you believe I'm missing
you already?"

"Already?"

"Yes. Are you busy?"

"A little bit, why?"

"No reason. I didn't want to be alone all day, that's all."

"Well, I'll wrap up things around three o'clock. I'll see
you then, okay?"

"Thank you. I love you."

I looked up at Sylvia who was biting her nails and
pretending not to be listening. "I love you too," I said
and then hung up.

Sylvia glared at me and narrowed her eyes. "Are you
ready now?"

"Been ready."

For the next several hours, Sylvia went over everything
that Crissy had worked on. She told me how close Crissy
and she had gotten and said it was a lot more exciting
working for Crissy than it was working for me. When I
told her she could always move on, she said that moving
on was definitely in her plans. I didn't ask when or where
she intended to go because I knew it would only start an
argument between us. Basically, I let her comments roll
right off my back.

As three o'clock neared, I packed my things and got
ready to go. I stopped at Sylvia's desk and told her to hit
me on my cell phone if she needed anything. Completely

forgetting about Britney's band concert tonight, Sylvia asked me if I had planned on going.

"Damn, that's right. It is tonight, isn't it?"

"Yes, Jonathan. And things like that you shouldn't forget."

"I know, I . . . I was so eager to get back to work today that I forgot."

"If you don't come, she's going to be really disappointed."

"Oh, I'll be there. It just slipped my mind."

"Okay, then I'll see you later."

"So, you're going too?"

"I wouldn't miss it for the world. Besides, if I didn't go, she would kill me."

"She probably would."

I told Sylvia she could leave early, and then headed for home to spend time with Dana. When I told her about Britney's concert tonight, she insisted that she wanted to go. She explained how it was time she supported Britney more and said that she was willing to give their relationship one more try.

Later that evening, Dana and I put on our clothes and left to go to the concert. She looked dynamite in her red Dana Buchman pantsuit that was accented with white pearls. She didn't have the time or patience to curl her hair, so she put it in a neat, slick ponytail, which looked perfect to me.

When we arrived at Britney's school, the entryway to the auditorium was jammed with people. Having height over just about everyone, I looked around to see if I could see Britney. When I saw her in the far corner talking to Beverly and James, Beverly's boyfriend, I took Dana's hand and walked over by them. From a distance, Beverly spotted us and immediately walked away. Britney smiled and ran up to give me a hug and kiss.

"Hi, Daddy," she said, wiping her lipstick off my cheek.

"Hey, baby girl. What time is this thing supposed to get started?"

"Soon, I hope," Britney said, looking at Dana. "Dana, I heard about your accident. I . . . I'm glad you're okay."

"So am I. It really could have been a lot worse, but I'm thankful that it wasn't."

Britney nodded and looked back at me. "So, Daddy, where are we having dinner at tonight?"

"Dinner? Who said anything about dinner?"

"Nobody, but I'm hungry. Can we go to Morton's? Please?"

"We? Who are we?"

"You know, all of us. Me, you, Mama, James, Sylvia, her boyfriend, and oh, yeah, Dana."

I had no idea Sylvia was bringing a date. "And, let me guess. I'm supposed to pay for all of this, right?"

"Well, you the only one who got some for real money."

"We'll see," I said. I wasn't up to having dinner with Beverly and Sylvia, or with their men.

Britney hugged me again and went back into the band room. Knowing that the concert was about to start, Dana and I found a seat, after she stood around running her mouth with several ladies she knew from the neighborhood.

No sooner had we taken a seat, than Sylvia came in with Lorenzo. They sat two rows in front of us not even knowing that she had my attention; I couldn't keep my eyes off her. Interrupting my gaze, Dana reached over and touched my hand. I held her hand tightly in mine and squeezed it. She smiled then kissed me.

"What was that for?" I asked.

"Just for being you," she said.

I nodded then looked for Britney as the band came in.

I was so damn proud of Britney, and I watched her throw down on her flute. Over the last few months, she had changed so much. I knew Sylvia was somewhat responsible. During the concert, though, my eyes wandered. I couldn't keep them off of Sylvia and Lorenzo. I watched as he rubbed her legs, he leaned in to kiss her a few times, and she even rubbed the back of his head like she always did mine.

When the lights came on for intermission, I told Dana I needed to go to the restroom. She insisted she needed to go as well and stood up with me. She walked in front of me, and as we passed by Sylvia's row, I saw her look over at us. Our eyes connected, but when Dana took my hand, Sylvia turned her head.

After I used the restroom and washed my hands, I looked in the mirror to straighten my tie. Lorenzo came in and caught me completely off guard.

"Jonathan, right," he said, reaching his hand out for me to shake it.

"That's right. Lorenzo, correct?"

"Yeah," he said. "Sylvia told me so much about you. She's always bragging about what a great boss she has."

"Yeah, that sounds like Sylvia."

"Anyway, Jonathan, good seeing you again. I'm glad I came tonight. That band out there is phenomenal."

"Aren't they," I said and then turned to leave.

As soon as I left the restroom, I saw Sylvia leaned against the wall, waiting for Lorenzo to come out. I waved at her and she gave me a simple wave back. I heard Dana calling my name, so I walked up to her. She wanted to introduce me to a few people that she knew.

"This is my husband, Jonathan," she said loud enough for everyone to hear. I shook hands with everyone, and after conversing for a while longer, we all went back into the auditorium. Again, Sylvia and I caught each other's eyes, as Dana and I were on our way back to our seats. Dana held my hand and did not let it go until the concert was over.

We all waited for Britney in one big circle, but no one had anything to say to each other but James and me. He asked if I could do anything about a ticket he'd gotten and I referred him to someone who could help.

Knowing how uncomfortable Dana was about seeing Sylvia, I wrapped my arms around Dana to put her at ease. She held me tightly around the waist, and when Britney came out, it was such a relief. She gave everybody a hug and thanked us for coming. When she suggested dinner again, nobody wanted to go. Everybody made excuses, but when she pleaded with us, we all changed our minds.

Britney rode in the car with Dana and me. She and Dana made good conversation, and when we got to Morton's, we all went inside.

Since it was rather crowded, they seated us in a private room. The waiters showed us samples of the steaks we could order, and after everyone ordered, you could hear a pin drop in the room. Britney was the only one making conversation with everyone, and when she didn't talk, I turned to Dana for small talk. Just by looking at her, I noticed how uncomfortable she was. Beverly and Sylvia quietly talked to James and Lorenzo.

The food came and I could barely eat in peace. I couldn't keep myself from looking at Sylvia, and when she got up to go to the restroom, the direction of my eyes followed her out the door. Shortly after, she came back and glanced at me before taking a seat.

That was it for me and I was ready to go. I finished my wine and asked Dana if she was ready. She nodded, and when I let it be known to Britney that we were leaving, she thanked us again for coming and gave both of us a hug.

I pulled out my credit card and looked for the waiter so I could pay him. When James and Lorenzo saw the American Express card in my hand, they offered to chip in. I told them no, and after I paid the waiter for dinner, Dana and I said good-bye to everyone and left.

The drive home was quiet. My mind wandered while Dana's head was leaned back on the headrest. Her eyes were closed and I figured she was in deep thought. But when I looked again, she had fallen asleep.

I carried Dana to the bedroom, knowing that she needed some rest. As for me, I took a shower, changed into my pajama pants then I climbed into bed with her. As I pulled the cover over me, she turned in bed to face me. I could see that she had already gotten up and changed into her nightgown.

"I hate to keep bringing this up, but can I ask you something without you getting defensive?" she asked.

"Of course. And I never get defensive when you ask me anything."

"Sometimes, yes, you do, but, uh, are you in love with Sylvia?"

"No. Why did you ask me that?"

"Because you did not take your eyes off her for one moment tonight. It made me very uncomfortable, and I know she saw how you watched her."

"Dana, just because I might have been looking at her doesn't mean I'm in love. Besides, I wasn't looking at her that much. She is attractive, so what man in his right mind wouldn't look?"

"Not how you were looking at her, though. And attractive, she is not. Forgive me if I'm wrong, but I read a little bit more into it than just that."

"You're reading what you want to read into it because of our past history. I told you before that it was over between us, so therefore, you have nothing to worry about."

She placed her hand on the side of my face and rubbed it. "If you say so, baby. Only if you say so."

I straightened my pillow and turned to face the wall. Dana moved closer and whispered in my ear. "Would you be so kind and make love to me tonight?"

I turned around to face her. "Are you sure you're ready? I didn't think you were ready for that yet."

"I am, but you have to take it extremely slow."

I lay on my back. "Why don't you get on top and go as slow as you would like to."

Dana straddled my chest then brought her pussy up to my mouth for me to taste her. As I licked her insides, I moved my hands up her silky nightgown and massaged her breasts. We were both excited, and after I made her come, she backed away from my mouth and worked her wet pussy up and down on my growing dick. Not having sex for a while, I came fast. We took a short break, and after that, my wife and I made love throughout the entire night. I tried to be as gentle as I could, but certain positions I put her in, she insisted she wasn't ready for yet. Not wanting to hurt her, I let her direct me and she had no problem doing so.

By morning, we lay on the floor where we ended up last night. It was already seven o'clock, so I hurried up and showered, then changed into my work clothes. I woke up Dana and told her to get in bed. She did and I gave her a long, juicy kiss before leaving.

On my way to work, my cell phone rang. I didn't recognize the number, but I answered it anyway.

"John-John," he said, and I knew it was Jaylin.

"What's up, man?"

"You, my brotha. But, uh, you got company. Right now, if you look in your rearview mirror, you're being followed by a black Cutlass Supreme, right?"

I looked in my rearview mirror and saw the Cutlass. "Yeah, who is it?"

"It's the man of the hour, Lewis. Along with a friend of his, and they've been following you for a couple of days. Today, however, is not going to be their lucky day. I'm about to tell you what to do. Don't ask any questions, John-John, just do it."

"The plan is in motion. Now tell me what to do."

"As soon as you merge onto Highway 40, slam hard on your brakes and let him run into the back of your car. Get out and make the biggest damn scene you have ever made about the damages to your car. When the police get there, because they've already been called, make sure they run a police check on both of the brothas and make sure they search the car."

"So, let me get this straight: you want me to tear up my fucking car? I don't know about that shit, man."

"Trust me, it'll all be worth it. It's a gun in his car that was used in a carjacking that injured a white woman. And in the trunk, there's enough cocaine in a suitcase that's going to send those motherfuckers to jail. For quite some time, I might add, especially after the police get a look at the long-ass criminal record those two fools got. Thing is, the brothas don't even know the shit is in there. So, quickly, do like I told you and don't forget to thank me later."

Jaylin hung up.

The highway was half of a mile down the road, and as soon as I turned onto it, I slammed on the brakes. Traveling so closely behind me, the Cutlass hit me in the rear and sent me flying forward with my seatbelt on. It took me a few seconds to gather myself, and when I got out, the back of my Lexus was fucked up. The Cutlass's front end was smashed, had antifreeze dripping from it, and was smoking.

Lewis and his friend rushed out of the car, slamming their doors.

"Are you following me, motherfucker?" I yelled.

His friend pulled out a gun, but when he heard the police sirens coming, he ran up the hill and tried to cross over a tall fence. The police saw him and ran to catch him. The other police car pulled behind the Cutlass and two officers got out.

"What's going on here?" a heavyset officer asked while looking over at the other officer who already had Lewis's friend in handcuffs. He was frowning and couldn't stop talking shit to the officer. I shook my head and explained what had happened.

"I was on my way to work, Officer, and this gentleman slammed into the back of my car. He used to work for me, and I recently had him arrested over a confrontation between us. His friend suddenly pulled a gun on me, I guess, trying to settle our dispute."

The officer slammed Lewis's friend on the ground then searched his pockets.

"Motherfucker, you gotta be so rough?" Lewis's friend yelled at the officer.

"Shut up. I don't want to hear another word from you."

Lewis stood there and didn't have a damn thing to say. When the officer asked for our driver's licenses, we handed them over. One officer walked back to the police car, and the other one asked Lewis if he could search the car.

"Feel free," he said being stupid and not even knowing his rights. He hadn't a clue what the hell was about to go down.

With my arms folded, I stood next to my car and waited. When four more police cars showed up I laughed to myself. They all pulled their guns and yelled for Lewis to get down on the ground. He placed his hands behind his head and slowly kneeled down.

"Wha . . . what the fuck is this all about?" he shouted and appeared confused.

"Close your mouth and stay there!"

Two officers laid him and his friend out in the grass while more officers tore the car apart. They found another gun, and when they opened the suitcase, it was stacked high with cocaine packages.

Lewis's eyes bugged and he shook his head. "This . . . this is a gotdamn set up! I've been set up!"

One of the officers pointed to him. "Sit there and shut the fuck up!"

I walked up to one of the officers, pretending not to know what the hell was going on. They told me Lewis and his friend were wanted for questioning pertaining to three carjacking cases, a drive-by shooting on the north side, and a robbery. All, of course, fabricated charges, but what the hell? I hated to see black men go down like this, and it was kind of hard to watch the officers toss out so much disrespect. But, Lewis had fucked up, and he was about to pay for doing so.

Before I left, the officer thanked me for helping them crack such a large drug case and he called a tow truck to come get my Lexus. They put Lewis and his friend into separate police cars, and I placed my business card against the window so he could see it.

"If you need a lawyer," I said with a smirk on my face. "Call me."

"Fuck you, motherfucker," he shouted and spit on the glass. I laughed at him, and when my taxi came, I jetted.

15

SYLVIA

Nobody knew how much I missed Jonathan but me. Hell, he didn't even recognize how much I still wanted him. I hid my feelings very well and used Lorenzo like it wasn't funny to get over Jonathan.

Working for Jonathan and seeing him every day was tough. There were times I didn't even want to go in because I knew how much seeing him in his sharp, tailored suits would weaken me.

After Britney's concert the other night, I was so sick to my stomach after seeing him with Dana that I asked Lorenzo to drop me off because I wanted to be alone. I cried the entire night and prayed to the Lord, asking Him to help me get over Jonathan. It was obvious he had moved on with Dana, and she didn't have a problem trying to let it be known. Every time I looked their way, she would grab his hand or rub herself up against him. When I saw how affectionate he was with her, it tore me apart.

During work, I fought hard not to bring up anything about what had happened between us; after all, it had been awhile since we were last together. And if it seemed as if he tried to avoid me, I was, without a doubt, trying to avoid him.

I stood by the restroom door talking to Jackie. She asked me if I'd seen the news on Channel 4 about Lewis being arrested. I told her I hadn't, and when she gave me the scoop, I was shocked. I knew Lewis was up to no good and was thrilled that he was finally behind bars. My prayers on that end had been answered.

I rushed to Jonathan's office to tell him, but as I walked into his office, he was on the phone laughing with his back turned.

"Thank you, thank you, thank you," he said then paused to listen. "Yeah, man, I'm picking up my car today." He laughed out loudly. "I owe you big time, Jaylin, but to answer your question, no, you can't have her because I'm not quite done yet."

I cleared my throat, and when he swung around in his chair and saw me, he told Jaylin he would call him back.

I ignored what Jonathan had said because it was obviously said to make Jaylin believe we still had something going on. Jonathan had been hyped all week, so I figured his sex life with Dana was probably back on track.

"I didn't mean to interrupt, but did you hear about Lewis on the news?" I asked.

"Yes. As a matter of fact, I did. By the look of things, he's going to jail for a very long time."

"I would say so too, but don't y'all run background checks on people before y'all hire them? I didn't know he had all that mess going on."

Jonathan shrugged his shoulders. "I guess his bad record must have slipped through the cracks. I'm not in charge of that stuff, so there's no telling what happened."

"Well, I'm glad he's behind bars. In the meantime, do you mind if I leave early?"

"Why?"

"Because, I have some business to take care of."

"What kind of business?"

"Jonathan, look, when I leave this place, I don't have to tell you where I'm going or who I'm with. So, again, do you mind if I leave early?"

"I don't mind, but the only reason I asked is because I care about you."

"I'll be okay, trust me. I don't think I'm going to get in any trouble being with your daughter at the movies."

"How do you get to spend so much time with her and I don't?"

"Because, we talk almost every day, and she feels comfortable having girl talk with me."

"Girl talk, huh? I hope y'all not having the same girl talk you be having with Audrey and Jackie."

"Please. Britney and my conversations are on a completely different level. She's a good girl, Jonathan. She's a little on the wild side, but that's okay."

"Well, I can't express enough how much I appreciate you being there for her. If it wasn't for you, she'd be lost. Beverly's so wrapped up with the men in her life that she doesn't have time to even deal with Britney's issues. I get kind of caught up myself, but—"

"Let's just hope and pray she stays on the right track. She's been begging me to go see this crazy comedy movie with her, so I told her I would pick her up from school."

Jonathan looked at his watch. "You'd better get going. Tell her I'll see her this weekend and thanks, again, for being there."

"No problem."

I left to go pick up Britney from school. She stood outside my car and talked to this nice-looking young man for a while. I blew the horn and she gave him a hug and said good-bye. She got in the car with a huge smile plastered on her face.

"No way, *chica*. I've seen that look too many times before. Don't even think about getting yourself involved. He is definitely a heartbreaker and you don't need that kind of drama in your life."

"Whateverrrr," she said, looking out of the window. "Look at him, Sylvia, he is soooo fine."

"Yes, he is," I said, driving off. "He so fine that you don't even need him."

She laughed. "Would you rather I be alone then?"

"I'm not saying that, but I would rather you get your grades together first then worry about all that other stuff later."

"My grades are together." She reached in her purse and pulled out a piece of paper. When she gave it to me, I saw it was her report card. She had two As, three Bs and one C.

"Okay," I said, shaking my head. "That's definitely an improvement, and I'm proud of you. But knowing that you can do better, you still got some work to do."

"I know, but I'm proud of myself too. Last semester, I don't know if Daddy told you or not, but I had four Ds and two Fs. If I keep this up, I won't even have to go to summer school."

"That's good. And be sure to call your father and let him know about your report card. I'm sure he'll be pleased when he finds out."

She pulled out her cell phone and called Jonathan to tell him about her grades. When she asked him to meet us at the movie theater, I looked over at her and rolled my eyes.

"Now, why did you ask him to join us, Britney? If this is one of your attempts to get us back together, it's not going to work. Jonathan and Dana are happy, and I have moved on with Lorenzo. Stop interfering, okay?"

"Interfering? I'm not interfering. I just want to see my father, that's all."

"Fine, Britney, whatever you say."

The movie didn't start until five o'clock. Britney and I stayed in the lobby until Jonathan came in. When I saw that he'd changed into his polo shirt and Levi's, my heart melted. He looked spectacular in just about anything he put on.

Britney ran up and gave him her report card. After he looked at it, he hugged her and smiled. I was sitting on a bench, so they came over by me. Jonathan asked if I'd seen what a great job she'd done.

"Yes, I did. And I told her how proud of her I was."

"Yep. Sylvia's so proud of me, Daddy, and she said when school lets out I can stay with her."

"Wait a minute. Don't be lying on me. I did not say that. Besides, over the summer, I'm taking a loooong vacation. The last thing I need is your butt chilling at my place and I'm not there."

"Please," she begged. "Would you at least think about it?"

"No, Britney, there's nothing to think about."

She sadly looked at Jonathan. "Daddy, would you ask her for me? She'll listen to you."

"Baby, I don't know if that's a good idea. Sylvia might have some other things to take care of."

Britney rolled her eyes at both of us, and we went into the theater.

Like father like daughter, Britney and Jonathan were all into the movie. I was quite occupied thinking about Jonathan, so the movie really didn't hold my attention. I was glad when it was over, and since Jonathan's car was outside, he offered to take Britney home. They both thanked me and waved good-bye.

Before going home, I stopped at Dierbergs to shop for groceries. After I filled my tank at Quik Trip, I headed for home. When I pulled up, I saw Jonathan sitting in his car. He got out and came up to me, as I removed the bags from the trunk of my car. I handed him a few bags so he could help, but he dropped them to the ground. He looked at me, as I slammed down the trunk.

"Do you even miss me?" he asked.

I took a deep breath and walked past him. He grabbed my arm, but I turned away, trying not to face him. "Sylvia, I must know, please. Because I . . . I'm missing you like hell."

I turned to face him. "Please don't do this to me. I have finally—"

He stepped up to me and placed his lips on mine. Dying to feel the taste of his lips, I dropped my bags, heard my eggs crack and watched my oranges roll on the ground. I pulled Jonathan closer to me, and eager to feel each other, by the time we reached the front door, his shirt was unbuttoned and my skirt was up. I fumbled around for the key and was already moist as he rubbed his hands on my pussy.

When the door flew open, I quickly helped him out of his jeans and we fell on the floor right by the front door. I tightened my legs around his waist, and when he entered me, a loud gasp escaped from my mouth. Tears rushed to my eyes, but I blinked them away. This was such an emotional moment for me, especially when Jonathan came closer to my ear and whispered, "I love you." By then, we had already fucked our way to the hallway, and I stopped the motion to look at him.

"Wha . . . what did you just say to me?" I asked.

He ignored me, rolled me over on my stomach, and eased his steel back inside. He watched my ass grind against him, and as I was now on my hands and knees, he held my hips and guided us in the perfect direction. My pussy couldn't stay quiet, and the sounds of him stirring my juices could be heard through the silence. Jonathan broke some of that silence, and said exactly what I needed to hear.

"Damn, you just don't know, Sylvia. I'm happy to say it again. Yes, I'm in love with you. Not only just in love with this amazing-ass pussy you got, but I'm in love with everything there is about you."

After hearing that, I got down to business and worked his dick as best I could. I was on a serious high and nothing in the world could bring me down. Not even Lorenzo, who had decided to stop by without calling, or Dana who had been ringing Jonathan's phone like crazy. We were so into each other that nothing outside of us being here together even mattered.

Jonathan had my legs spread far apart while I lay back on the kitchen table. He looked down at the goodness of him sliding in and out of me.

"Yo, you should really see this," he said, smiling.

"If it's anything like it feels, I'm sure it looks good," I moaned.

Jonathan released one of my legs and lightly rubbed my clitoris with the tips of his cold fingers. I was about to explode, and when I did, I squeezed my fists and pounded his chest.

"Damn you!" I squealed. "I'm never going to get over you. I love you so much, but what are we going to do, baby? We cannot keep doing this."

"I agree," he said, helping me down from the table. "I've been thinking about what to do for a while, but, baby, I don't have an answer for you right now."

"The sad thing is I don't have an answer either. I guess we're going to have to take this one day at a time and see where things go."

"It's all we can do."

We took a shower together, and not even wanting to leave, Jonathan cuddled in bed with me until two-thirty in the morning. When I asked what he planned to tell Dana, he told me he'd think of something. We walked outside and picked up my busted groceries bags that were still there. I watched Jonathan slowly drive off in his car.

As usual, I didn't get a lick of sleep. It felt so good having Jonathan back in my life again, but then there was a side of me that knew this would never work itself out. There was too much at stake. Dana would never give him up, and if Mama and Papa Bell found out I was interfering in their daughter's marriage, they would kill me. That didn't even include the people at work who would think I was a backstabbing bitch for sleeping with my best friend's man, let alone wanting to marry him.

Focusing too much time thinking about this on a Saturday morning, I went for a quick jog. When I got home, I cooked breakfast, but as soon as I sat at the table, the doorbell rang. Not knowing who it could be at nine o'clock in the morning, I looked out the window and saw Dana. I wasn't up for arguing with her and when I told her I wasn't, by yelling through the window, she insisted that she just wanted to talk.

I opened the door, and all she did when she came in was look me up and down in my stretch workout suit that fit every curve in my body. She was dressed casually in jeans and a pink and yellow shirt that matched her high, spiked heels. I went back into the kitchen and she followed me. As I sat at the table, she leaned against the counter and stared at me.

"Why can't you just leave us alone, Sylvia?" she asked calmly. "I am here today to beg you to stop seeing my husband. I can't believe that after all that's happened, you still refuse to let him go."

I bit down on my toast and chewed. Once I finished, I responded to her. "You might not believe this, Dana, but I never intended for things to go this far. I'm sorry but . . . but I love him too. I have tried to get over him, and I have tried to move on, but I . . . I can't. So as far as letting him go, right now, I can't make you any promises. I don't know what's going to happen between us, but whatever does, you might have to be woman enough to move on."

Dana's mouth hung wide open and she pointed to her chest. "So, you're asking me, his wife, to move on? I can't believe you, Sylvia. Every time I talk to you about this you sound as if you don't have any sense at all. The only thing you care about is you. You say that you care about Jonathan, but are you even aware of what this is doing to him? If you don't care about me, which it's apparent that you don't, at least think about what this is going to do to him, to his career, and to his family."

"I have thought about it. Pertaining to him, I'm the best thing that ever happened to him. In reference to his career, I have supported him almost every step of the way. And as for his family, they don't even like you, Dana. They have always wanted us together. When I think about this, all I can say is that's what you get for fucking a good man over. If you had never cheated on him, lied to him, and deceived him, none of this would have happened. Yes, my feelings would have always been there, but Jonathan loved you with everything he had; you fucked that up and you have no one to blame but yourself. The sooner you start to realize that, the better off you will be."

"No marriage is perfect, Sylvia. Yes, I've had my faults and I have paid for them dearly. But there is no way, and I've said this before, there is no way I'm going to hand Jonathan over to you, or to any woman, on a silver platter. Our vows said for better or worse and I'm sticking to them."

"You're right and you should. But don't skip over the part about being faithful. You throwing all this other mess up in there, but the bottom line is you should have appreciated what you had. Most women would love to have a man like Jonathan, so when you say that you are not going to hand him over on a silver platter, trust me, you already have."

Anger covered Dana's face and she narrowed her eyes while glaring at me. "So, I guess this means you're not going to let him go, huh?"

My look was stern. "No, I'm not. Jonathan will have to end this. And from what I know, he's not ready to let go any time soon. My suggestion to you: deal with it or move on."

"Oh, trust me when I say you'll have to deal with it too. You'll have to deal with him being my husband, and making love to me every single opportunity we have. He's not going to end anything, because we'll be allowing him to have his cake and eat it, too. What man would want to end it? I'm aware that he was over here last night. And, yes, he lied to me when he got home, but look at what kind of man he's turning out to be. He never used to lie and play games like this before. You're creating a man who, eventually, you're going to wind up hating."

"No, Dana, the Jonathan I know will make a decision soon. He's not going to go back and forth for long; it's not his style. All I can say is, you'd better prepare yourself. I've prepared myself for the good, the bad, and the ugly. I only hope that you've done the same."

Dana took her keys out of her purse and headed to the door. She opened it and turned around. "You're going to lose out, Sylvia. And when you do, I'm going to enjoy every moment of it."

"I feel the same way, Dana. Good-bye."

16

JONATHAN

There was no doubt about it that I was torn between two women. I wasn't trying to have my cake and eat it, too, but I couldn't find it in my heart to let either one of them go. Dana's and my marriage was somehow getting stronger, and we spent more time together during the week and on the weekends. As far as our sex life, it was off the chain, as it had always been. Now, she cooked dinner for me, kept the house spotless, and forever checked in to let me know where she was. Basically, our marriage was back to what it was years ago. There was nothing I could complain about, other than her parents still bugging us every once in a while.

Then, of course, there was my ongoing relationship with Sylvia. Seeing and being with her was like a breath of fresh air. At work, she was my support system when things weren't going as well as I wanted them to, she had become a second mother for Britney, and making love to Sylvia was the best. We had sex more than Dana and I did because there was something about the way Sylvia made me feel that I couldn't let go of for nothing in the world.

It had gotten to the point where I knew both Dana and Sylvia knew about each other. Dana, being my wife, I couldn't find it in my heart to flat out tell her the truth. Whenever I'd come in late nights, I'd make up any excuse that I could. Some of the shit didn't even sound right, but all she would do was glare at me and not say a word. And if she did try to elaborate on where I'd been, I would get defensive and insist I didn't want to talk about it anymore.

Sylvia, on the other hand, coped with my situation. She was well aware that I was intimate with Dana, and Sylvia had seen us out and about together. The only thing she'd asked me was to make up my mind soon because she had no intentions of sharing me with Dana for the rest of her life. I understood how she felt and was doing the best I could to make this situation as comfortable as possible for everybody. I knew both of them wanted answers soon, but every time I thought my mind was made up, something would put me right back where I started.

Our company's annual dinner dance and salute to excellence awards ceremony was what finally opened my eyes. I was voted Best Businessman of the Year, and when Crissy called my name to accept the award, I felt as if it wasn't truly deserved.

With Dana and Sylvia sitting at the same table as I was, I glanced at both of them and took a hard swallow. I lowered my head and tightly closed my eyes. Not being able to say anything but thank you, I quickly stepped away from the podium and walked off to the restroom. For the first time in my life, I looked in the mirror and didn't like who I saw.

Just yesterday, Sylvia and I stayed at the office late to finish up some things. Always wanting each other so badly, we ended up in the ladies' room fucking each other's brains out. Today, however, there I was sitting at a table with my beautiful wife next to me, holding my hands and knowing that I didn't come home until midnight. The hurt from watching Dana and me put on this charade like everything was so perfect in our marriage was written all over Sylvia's face. There was no doubt I had to end this and end this soon.

When I got back to my seat, Sylvia was voted Hardest Working Woman, and she was at the podium accepting her award. Crissy and I both nominated her because it was truly deserved. When the crowd stopped clapping, she stepped to the microphone. She lowered it to her mouth then she immediately looked up at me as tears trickled down her face.

"Over five years ago," she said tearfully, "I suffered a tremendous loss. My husband was killed in a car accident, and shortly after that, I lost my job of fourteen years due to the company I had worked for downsizing." She paused to take a deep breath. "After that, I truly wanted to crawl under a rock and die but someone wouldn't let me. He opened many doors for me, and he became the best friend I always wanted to have. Whenever I needed anything, he was always there for me. He never judged me, he never criticized me, nor did he ever make me do anything I didn't want to do. All I ever needed was a friend to listen to me, to guide me in the right direction, and to put me in my place when I got out of line." Sylvia paused again and looked down at the floor.

When she looked back up, she wiped her tears and stared at me again. "It's been so easy being there for you, Mr. Jonathan Tyrese Taylor, because you have always been there for me. Truly from my heart, thank you for your nomination and I'll do my best at continuing to make you happy."

Everybody stood up and clapped, surprisingly even Dana. When Sylvia came back to the table, I gave her a tight hug and didn't want to let go. She pulled away and reached down for her glittery purse that was on the chair. She said good night to everyone and quietly walked out of the room.

After the ceremony was over, Dana and I rode in silence back to our house. She knew where my mind was and really didn't say much to me.

At home, we took off our clothes in the bedroom, and as I got ready for bed, she came into the closet and took my hand. She escorted me out of the closet and asked me to have a seat on the bed. After I did, she reached for my hands and held them in hers. She touched my wedding ring with her finger and rolled it around.

"I know you don't love me anymore and—"

"Baby, yes, I do. I just—"

She pressed her fingers against my lips. "Listen, please. I have no one to blame for this mess but myself. If I could do this all over again, I would definitely do things differently. But we both know it's too late for that. You have love for another woman, and as much as it hurts me, I can't make your heart feel any differently. Tonight, I realized that Sylvia's and my friendship was over years ago. The word friend is something that we called ourselves when, in reality, we had never been there for one another. You were the friend she'd grown to love and you were the one whose shoulder she could cry on, not me. How could I blame her for falling in love with a man as wonderful as you are?"

I swallowed the lump that was locked in my throat. "So, what are you saying?"

Dana's lips quivered as she continued to talk. "I'm saying that I'm throwing in the towel. We need to end this so we can both get on with our lives. You deserve so much better, and if being with Sylvia is going to make you happy, then go be happy."

I grabbed Dana around the waist and placed my head against her chest. She rubbed my head as I started to show my emotions. "I'm sorry, baby," I said. "Only the Lord knows how much I wanted this marriage to work. I never stopped loving you, even until this day, but there is still so much anger and hurt inside of me that I don't know what to do with it."

"That's why you have to let it go. I'm not mad at you. Again, all I want is for you to finally be happy."

Knowing that our marriage was finally over, Dana and I made love to each other for one last time. And even though I was excited about having sex with her, the feeling was quite different this time. I was relieved all the lies were over, and everything was out in the open. More than anything, I was eager to tell Sylvia I would soon be a free man. I wasn't trying to rush off and marry her or anything, and my intentions were to still take our relationship one day at a time. But, when I got to the office on Monday and shared the news with her, she had some plans of her own.

"So, it's over," she said with a shrug. "And you're a free man. A free man who wants to screw and date anybody he chooses to?"

"Sylvia, all I'm saying is, give me time. I do not want to jump out of one marriage and right into another one."

"How much time? Just how long do you want me to wait for you, Jonathan?"

"I don't know. All I know is that I love you, and I want to be with you. However, us getting married so soon is out of the question. Hell, Dana hasn't even moved out yet."

"When is she supposed to move out?"

"She's moving out this weekend. We're going to have a quiet and speedy divorce, but I . . . I don't know, baby. I don't know what else you want me to do."

"Well, I don't want you to sit around and think that all you're going to do is have sex with me when you want to. I want the full package and I deserve it. Sex is something I can get from any man. If you love me like you say you do, then you'd better think hard about this."

Sylvia had pissed me off. My voice went up a notch and I pointed my finger at her. "I have thought about it, more than you know. I'm not going to spend too much more time on this and I got all of this work to do around here. As of right now, marriage is out! I'm not going to be pressured by you or anyone else, Sylvia, and I mean that shit!"

Furious, she got up, walked out, and slammed the door.

What in the hell did she want from me? I was getting a divorce and Sylvia still wasn't satisfied. I thought she would be ecstatic, but I was so wrong. How she could even think I wanted to jump right back into another marriage just puzzled the hell out of me.

The rest of the workweek was quiet. Sylvia hadn't said much to me, and since I was so busy running back and forth to court, I really didn't have much time to say anything to her either.

On Friday, the news hit fast. Mr. Duncan had finally lost his battle with prostate cancer and the entire place was in mourning. Already pretty much planned out, Crissy, Mr. Bradford, and I stayed in a meeting all day and worked out the final details pertaining to the business. Not wanting to take over her father's 60 percent of the company, Crissy agreed months ago to transfer 40 percent to me, 40 percent to Mr. Bradford, and keep 20 percent for herself. She said her time in the office would be minimal, since she was part owner of five elegant restaurants in St. Louis; she had three beauty shops, and a slew of commercial property to manage, now that Mr. Duncan was no longer around. She was his only child and he pretty much had her set for the rest of her life.

After our meeting, I looked around for Sylvia but she was gone. It was already six o'clock in the evening, and by the way she'd been acting, I didn't expect her to hang around and wait for me. Then again, maybe I did. I'd wanted to take her to dinner tonight but I didn't have time to tell her.

On the drive home, I thought about Sylvia and called her at home to see if she wanted some company. She didn't answer, so I drove by her place to see if she was there. Her car was parked in the driveway, so I went to the door and knocked. It took awhile for her to answer, and when she did, she cracked the door and looked out at me.

"You should have called," she said.

"I did, but you didn't answer. Open the door."

"I have company right now."

"What?" I said in disbelief. "What do you mean by you have company?"

"It's like I said. I have company so you need to come back later."

I got pissed and my scrunched face displayed it. "Come back? I don't think so. You need to open the damn door."

She closed the door and slid off the chain. When she moved aside to let me in, I was furious with her. Every time she didn't get her way with me, she always ran off to another brotha for comfort. I placed my hands in my pockets and looked at her with much anger.

"Is this how you want it to be?" I said, raising my voice. "Must you go fuck somebody every time things don't go your way?"

She pursed her lips, then folded her arms and glared at me. Getting no response from her, I went into her bedroom, but no one was there. I looked into her other rooms and they were empty as well. After I went into the kitchen to make sure the coast was clear, I walked back into the living room where she continued to stand with her arms folded.

"Why must you play so many games?" I asked.

"Why must you think I'm so trifling like that?"

"I never said you were trifling. I believed when you said you had company."

"Then believe me when I tell you I'm in need of a husband, not a fuck buddy. Anything less than a husband will not suffice."

I opened Sylvia's door and slammed it behind me. At this point, I'd gotten sick and tired of hearing it. She wasn't going to get a marriage out of me until I was ready. And right now, it was the last damn thing on my mind.

When I got home, Dana had packed up the rest of her things. Tomorrow was the big day. She seemed so hurt by moving out, and not having her around the house was going to be difficult for me.

After I helped carry most of her things close by the front door, for the movers to put on a truck tomorrow morning, we spent a nice quiet evening together. We talked about our plans for the future, and when she asked about my plans with Sylvia, I didn't quite know what to say.

"So, if you love her so much then why aren't you going to marry her?"

"It's funny because she's been asking me the same question. Not only that, but it's so strange how men and women think so differently. In my eyes, just because you love someone doesn't mean you have to marry them. There are so many other things we take in consideration that women don't."

"Well, it's not like I want you to marry her because I would be devastated if you did. My thought, however, is that you are going through too much right now. I'm not really sure if you love her as much as you think you do. And if it is love, it's a love that will never last."

"Why do you say that?"

"Because, baby, you fell in love with me. The first time we made love, we were eight months into our relationship. By then, you'd gotten to know me well. You loved my style, my personality, my ambition, and my mind. With Sylvia, I can't say that you ever really focused on getting to know her that way. You expressed your feelings for her by having sex with her. Quite often, I'm sure, but when you think of her, do you only think about having sex, or do you think about other, simple things, like taking walks in the park, or going on vacations together, maybe even having a child together? I know those are only a few things you thought about with me. If you're ending this to be happy, just make sure you are."

I listened to Dana, and we stayed up the entire night talking and drinking wine together. A lot of what she'd said made sense because I really hadn't thought much about doing anything other than having sex with Sylvia. Very few times did I think about dinners, vacations, or simply just going to the movies, but it was definitely nothing to brag about. It wasn't that I didn't want to do those things with her, but since our sex life was so spectacular, it was hard for me to focus on anything else.

The movers took the last of Dana's things to the truck. She was moving into a condominium not too far from me, and she promised to stop by and check on me some times. I kissed her forehead, as she held me around the waist and shed some tears.

"Look at it this way," I said with my arms around her. "How many couples are able to end their marriage and still have respect for each other?"

She nodded. "Not too many, but it still hurts so much."

"I know it does, baby." I wiped her tears. "But you're an amazingly strong woman. You'll be able to put this behind you in no time."

"I hope so," she said still holding me tight. She finally let go and blew me a kiss as she walked out the door.

After the movers left, Dana got in her car and followed. I went back into the house, and feeling a bit down, I called Britney so she could come spend the weekend with me. Lately, she'd been playing me off a lot, but she was at an age where nothing seemed to matter but boys, mo' boys, and mo' boys.

Beverly brought Britney over around six o'clock that evening, and since she knew Dana had moved out, Beverly finally came into the house to speak. She stood in the foyer and gazed into the immaculate great room.

"When did you all fix up the place like this? I didn't think Dana had good taste."

Britney carried her bags into her bedroom. "The last time you came into this house was over seven years ago. It has been updated since then. Would you like to see the rest?" I asked.

"No, that's okay. By the looks of things, somebody's got some money. I was wondering when I'm going to get a raise on my child support. Britney is expensive and I can't afford her."

"Shut up, Mama," Britney said, walking by. "You don't do nothing for me anyway. Stop standing there and pretending that I'm breaking your bank account, when in reality, Daddy is the one who pays for everything."

"Britney," I shouted at her. "Don't talk to your mama like that."

"But she gets on my nerves."

"I'm sure you get on hers too. Watch your mouth, all right?"

She nodded and rolled her eyes.

"See, that's your child," Beverly said to me. "That mouth is going to get her hurt. You've created a monster and I can't do nothing with her."

"You're the only monster around here," Britney snapped.

"Look. Why don't both of y'all chill out? I can't believe y'all disrespecting each other like this. First of all, Beverly, don't be calling her a monster. She's been through a lot and you and I should have—"

Beverly cut me off and started yelling. "I don't even want to hear it! You're always taking up for her, no matter what she does. You and I should have put our foot in her ass a long time ago, and if we had, none of this smart-talking bullshit would be going on."

"Well, we didn't. So now, we just got to deal with it."

"You mean you got to deal with it. She's been begging to stay with you or Sylvia for the summer and I don't care what she does."

"Just give up like you always do. I asked you a long time ago to let her stay with me, but you weren't trying to hear it."

"Well, I'm hearing it now. Do whatever." Beverly looked at Britney. "Since you're calling the shots, say the word and I'll have your things to you by tomorrow."

"Please do," Britney said, storming off. "I don't want to live with you no damn way."

Beverly opened the door and stepped on the porch. I followed her and closed the door. "Maybe it's for the best," I said, trying to calm things down.

"Maybe so," Beverly said, pulling some tissue from her purse and dabbing her watery eyes. "I am so sick and tired of Britney. Nothing I do is good enough for her, Jonathan. I'm tired of her disrespect, and if you think she's going to treat you any differently, you are wrong. She doesn't give a damn about anybody but herself."

"I know I got some work to do, but I can't give up on my baby girl. I'll come by next week and get the rest of her things, okay? "

Beverly nodded and walked off to her car. I went back into the house and looked for Britney. She was in her bedroom and was on the phone with one of her friends.

"Get off the phone. We need to talk," I said.

She talked for another minute or two then told her friend she would call her back. "Daddy, I was in the middle of something."

"Listen," I said, sitting next to her on the bed. "You have got to stop talking the way you do. Cursing, especially in front of me, is not only disrespectful but a young lady such as you should have more respect. I haven't raised you to be a thug. And I for damn sure didn't raise you to curse at your mother like you do. She's been through a lot, and you can't blame her for everything that has happened in your life."

Britney laid her head on my shoulder. "I'm sorry, Daddy. And I don't blame her, but I do not like her. I never said anything to you about this, but she's always hated me because you and her didn't stay together. She said because I was born, that's what drove you away. Every time I used to get in trouble, she'd tell me how much she hated me and wished I were dead. I was a little girl when she said those things, but I still remember them like it was yesterday."

I hugged Britney and wiped the tears from her eyes. My baby girl was hurt and I could have killed myself for not letting her move in with me sooner. I promised her things would get better and she promised me she would keep up the good work in school and continue to make me proud.

The office was closed Monday so everyone could attend Mr. Duncan's funeral. It was short and served its purpose. There wasn't a bunch of people falling all over his casket and the condolences were kept to a minimum. In less than thirty minutes, it was all over. Crissy invited everyone to her house in Frontenac for dinner and drinks. When I asked Sylvia if she wanted to ride together, she said that she wasn't feeling well and wanted to go home. Giving her all the space she needed, I drove to Crissy's house alone.

A house wasn't the word to describe the humungous place that sat on acres and acres of land. A mansion would have been more suitable and it definitely had it going on in the inside. Crissy gave me the grand tour and I was floored. The mansion had six bedrooms, eight bathrooms, and a finished lower level that had everything from a kitchen to a theater room. Old-fashioned crown molding surrounded the upper level of the house and every faucet inside was made of gold. Why she even needed so much space, when she lived alone, puzzled the hell out of me. She said the house was used for entertainment, and she insisted that she had a party almost every weekend of the year.

The house had gotten jam-packed. I took a seat in the billiards room and talked to Audrey. Together, we had about eight drinks and were both quite tipsy. Trying to stay focused on our conversation about Mr. Duncan, we found ourselves slipping into a conversation about having sex.

"I'm sorry to hear about your marriage, but, then again, I'm not," she said. "I was wondering when you were going to give a sista like me a chance to show you bigger and better things."

"A chance to do what?" I asked.

She leaned over and licked my ear, then whispered, "A chance to show you what you've been missing."

"Exactly what is it that I've been missing?"

"I can show you better than I can tell you."

"Show me where?"

"If you look over to your left, there are some stairs that lead to a nice quiet room on the lower level. There are so many people here that no one would ever know we're missing." Audrey stood up. "I'll see you in a bit, right?"

I nodded and finished up the rest of my drink. Reminding me a little bit of Dana, Audrey was definitely my kind of woman. She was classy, full of ambition, and had already proved to me that she was a freak.

When I noticed no one watching, I walked down the steps to find her. I knew exactly where the room was because when I toured the house with Crissy, she showed the room to me.

I went into the room and Audrey was on the bed with her legs crossed. She smiled, and when I closed the door behind me, she walked up to me. She started to unbutton my shirt, but I grabbed her hand.

"I don't feel comfortable doing this here," I said. "Let's go to your place."

"No, I don't want to wait."

She continued to unbutton my shirt and she also removed my belt. Getting no response from me, she reached for my hand and placed it on her ass. I massaged it, and finally on the rise, I lifted her black dress and slid her panties down to the floor. She backed up and lay on the bed. I moved forward and snatched off my shirt. As soon as I lay on top of her, and felt the warmth from between her legs, I had a change of heart. I pecked her cheek and got up.

"You know, I can't do this," I said, zipping my pants.

She rose up on her elbows. "No, I didn't know, and why not?"

"Because, I don't want to be the morning news tomorrow. In addition to that," I said, putting my shirt back on, "I don't have relationships with people I work with."

"Since when, Jonathan? It's obvious that you're fucking Sylvia, and you are sadly mistaken if you think nobody knows."

"It's called speculation, Audrey. Everybody suspects we're sleeping together. Nobody really knows what happens between us when we're alone."

"I know because she tells me. You're so worried about me running my mouth but what about her? It's okay that she tells everybody, huh?"

"Well, if she's told you that we've been together sexually, then she lied. That happens on occasion when people start fantasizing about being with you. You know what I mean?" I opened the door. "Good night, Audrey. I hope this doesn't ruin our friendship. I'll see you at work tomorrow."

I went upstairs, looked for Crissy through the overly crowded house, and after I found her, I gave my good-byes.

17

SYLVIA

I wasn't trying to be hard on Jonathan, but I wanted him to know that I hadn't planned on being his bed buddy for life. He made me many promises about us being together and I held him to it. Now that Dana was out of the picture, Jonathan and I were, basically, in the same situation. Nothing had changed, and if I had left it up to him, it never would. Again, I tried to stick to my words, but the day after Mr. Duncan's funeral, I was right back in his arms. He'd come over to my place singing the same old song about how much he missed me and how things were going to get better between us. Hoping that they truly would, I gave in to him that night. There was something about the way he made love to me that I just couldn't do without. I knew he loved me, so my heart told me to be patient with him. My mind, though, said I was a fool.

During lunch on Tuesday, I damn near lost it when Audrey told me she had sex with Jonathan the day of Mr. Duncan's funeral. Having too much info about the size of his dick, the thickness of it, and knowing how he loved to massage an ass, I knew there was some truth to her story. While everyone was still at work, I didn't get my clown on, but as soon as the place cleared out, I stopped him on his way out.

"Do you have a date, since you're rushing out of here before me?" I asked.

"Come on now, Sylvia. You know I don't go out on dates."

"Well, maybe you should. By all means, if you're having sex with other women, then maybe you should be entertaining them as well."

He placed his briefcase on the floor then folded his arms. "Okay, let's hear it. Who am I having sex with now?"

"You know who. And don't tell me she lied on you because she knew the exact size of that," I said, pointing to his dick.

Jonathan stared at me then leaned down in my face. "I'm getting tired of the bullshit, Sylvia. Your friend is a fucking liar and whatever you and I have going on is none of her damn business." He picked up his briefcase. "Keep this up and I won't have a problem ending this. I'm still here because I love you, but I will not be ridiculed by another woman again." He walked off.

Mad because he had quickly flipped the script on me, I called his cell phone but he didn't answer. I even left work and went to his house but he wasn't there either. Knowing what condominiums Dana moved to, I drove by her place and his car was parked outside. That was enough to send me over the edge. Not only was he lying about fucking Audrey, but also, that bastard was still screwing around with Dana.

I calmly drove home, typed up my resignation that provided two weeks' notice, and took my butt to bed. By morning, I was hyped and ready to give my resignation to him. He didn't have to worry about ending this shit with me, because as far as I was concerned, today, it was over.

No sooner had he strutted through the door, than he walked past me and didn't say a word. He went into his office and read my resignation letter on his desk. He yelled for me to come into his office and told me to close the door behind me.

"What is this?" he asked, shaking the letter in his hand.

"What does it look like? Didn't you read it?"

"So, you're bailing out on me again, huh?"

"I'm not bailing out. I'm leaving because I can't take this crap anymore."

"What crap are you talking about, Sylvia?"

"You are not going to keep using me, Jonathan. It's bad enough you fucked Audrey, but going back to Dana was low. If you were going to do that, then you should have never filed for a divorce."

Jonathan sucked his teeth and bounced a pen on his desk. "So, you still believe what Audrey told you? And not only that, but you've been checking up on me?"

I shrugged my shoulders. "Hey, a sista gotta do what she gotta do."

"Okay, then, sista." Jonathan dialed Audrey's extension and told her to come to his office immediately. When she said that she was on her way, he shot me a dirty look.

"Every morning when I saw you, you used to brighten my day. You coming through that door would put me at ease. What in the hell has happened to you, woman? When I clear this shit up, I want you to keep your word and leave this office in two weeks."

Audrey knocked on the door. "Come in," Jonathan yelled. She came in and closed the door behind her. She looked shocked to see me, and when she saw the frown on Jonathan's face, I suspected she could tell what was up.

"Have a seat," Jonathan said.

Audrey took a seat and looked over at me. "What's this all about?" she asked in a soft, innocent tone.

"This is about rumors, games, and lies," he said. "I will not be part of the bullshit that goes around in here. The other day at Crissy's house, after Mr. Duncan's funeral, did you and I have sex?"

"Wha . . . what difference— "

Jonathan slammed his hand on his desk. "Answer the damn question!"

Audrey jumped in her seat. "We . . . we came close."

"Close, maybe, but did I stick my dick inside of you? That's what Sylvia wants to know."

Audrey looked at me, again, and then answered Jonathan's question. "You would have, if we had gone to my place like you suggested."

"Would've, could've, should've! Can you attest to what this motherfucker here feels like inside of you?" Jonathan said, grabbing his dick. "I need some type of evidence here because I'm getting convicted of some bullshit I didn't even do!"

"No, we did not have sex, but it's not like you didn't want to."

"If I had wanted to, Audrey, I would have. Believe it or not, for some men, it is not all about the pussy. And since we're on a roll, you told me that Sylvia shared with you some intimate details about our relationship, right?"

I looked at Audrey. "I told you what? I have never told you Jonathan and I were intimate, Audrey."

"Ya see," Jonathan said, standing up. "Case closed." He pointed his finger at me. "I didn't even confront you about what she said because I knew she was a liar and I trusted you. If I could get the same damn thing from you, then we might have a little something to work with." He snatched his briefcase off his desk, and slammed the door on his way out.

Feeling like such a fool, I let Audrey have it. "Bitch, why did you have to lie like that?"

She threw her hand back. "Girl, Jonathan is so full of it. I don't care what he said, he wanted to have sex with me."

"Well, he didn't, even though you said y'all did. But why did you lie on me? You know damn well I never told you Jonathan and I had sex."

"I was just joking around when I said that."

"Audrey, please get out of my face. You have no idea what you might have caused me."

Audrey rolled her eyes and left Jonathan's office. I hung around until six o'clock, in hopes that he would return but he didn't. I felt so badly for not trusting him and for giving him my resignation. Never seeing him so angry with me, I knew I had to keep my word and be out of his office in two weeks.

The following week was extremely difficult for me. When Britney told me Jonathan only went over to Dana's house to drill some holes in her walls so she could hang her curtains, I felt even worse. He barely said anything to me and spent minimal time at the office. Our conversations pertained to business and business only, and when I asked if I could cook him dinner on Thursday night, he declined. He said he and Britney had plans to go to the movies. Not wanting to get my face cracked again, I didn't even bother to ask if I could go.

What was supposed to be my last week in the office, Jonathan didn't even come in on Monday or Tuesday. He finally came in on Wednesday, and the only reason he'd shown up was to start the interviewing process for my position. He didn't waste any time putting an ad in the paper, and all kinds of resumes and applications came in.

By the end of the day, he had interviewed at least eight women for my job. While he was looking though the applications that were spread out over his desk, I knocked on his door and asked if I could come in.

"Any luck?" I asked.

He nodded and continued to look down at one application in particular. "Umm, maybe so."

"Can I take a look at it?" I said, pretending not to be hurt. He quickly passed the application over to me then picked up another one.

I glanced at the woman's work experience. "Well, it looks like she has the experience. Which one was she?"

"The light-skinned one with the short hair and dark blue pantsuit on."

"You mean the one with the workable ass, model-shaped legs, and friendly smile, right?"

"Yep, that's the one," Jonathan said, and still not smiling.

"No go. Let me see another application." He passed another application to me. I looked at it and this chick had the credentials as well. "Okay, now, which one was she?"

He looked up like he was in deep thought. "She . . . she was the one with the black skirt on, the royal blue blouse, and had long braids."

"Right, but she also had thick lips, big-ass breasts, and if I'm not mistaken, that skirt was damn near up to her ass."

"That would be the one," he said, looking down at another application.

"Jonathan," I whined, then placed the application on his desk.

"What, Sylvia?" he said with seriousness in his eyes.

"I don't really want to leave."

"But you have to."

"Says who?"

"Says me."

"But I changed my mind."

"You can't do that. You gave me two weeks' notice and I'm preparing myself to find a replacement."

"Again, you don't have to, especially since I don't want all these beautiful women hanging all over you and falling in love with you like I did."

"Well, too bad. I'm not going to keep going back and forth with you about this. Every time you get mad, I have to worry about you quitting your job. Have you found another one yet?"

I pouted and lowered my head. "No, but I will. In the meantime, you still have a couple of days to decide if you want me to keep my job."

"Don't do me any more favors," he said, as I walked toward the door. "Besides, there's no way in hell I'm going to allow my wife to work for me. That doesn't work out too well."

I halted my steps and turned my head. "What did you say?"

"I said that I need to find a replacement for you because I want to marry you. My divorce will soon be final. I'm getting kind of lonely not having a wife around."

Stunned by his words, I couldn't even move. I felt the tears trying to escape from my eyes, and my entire body was numb. Jonathan asked me to sit on his lap, and after I did, I damn near broke his neck as I wrapped my arms around him and squeezed.

"I'm sorry for being such a bitch, baby, please forgive me for not trusting you. I just needed to know where things stood between us."

"You gotta trust me, Sylvia. A marriage is based on trust, and without it, we'll have nothing."

"I know. It's not that I ever really doubted you, but I was so angry with the way things were going and I got frustrated."

"Well, like I said, my divorce will be final soon and we can finally move on, okay?"

"I love you," I said, kissing all over him.

"Wait a minute," he said, as I started to unbutton his pants. "I need a bed tonight. My back is killing me from making love to you in these awkward places. But first, I got two days to find a replacement for you. By Friday, one of these ladies is going to be my new secretary. We need to figure out which one."

"I already know which one. I liked the old lady with the long gray ponytail and beige polyester suit on. She was really nice." Jonathan handed me her application. The woman hadn't worked since 1982 and had the nerve to be honest on her application.

"I will train her, baby, I promise you I will," I said.

"No, that's okay. I kind of like this one." Jonathan pulled out the application from the light-skinned chick with the workable ass and friendly smile.

"I'm sure you do like that one," I said, snatching the application and looking at it again.

"Look, baby, this gal knows her stuff. She's worked for a law firm before and she can type eighty words a minute."

"Quick hands, huh? If she even looks at you the wrong way I'm gonna kick her butt."

Jonathan laughed. "So, we're in agreement with this right?"

"I guess so."

"Done deal. Now, let's get the hell out of here so I can tap into some of that good pussy tonight."

"You know, you really shouldn't talk like that. You have so much class about yourself and hearing you speak that way is sometimes so hilarious."

"You think? I came from the hood, baby. No matter how high up I get, the hood is still in me."

"I might be wrong for saying this, but there was nothing hoodie about growing up in Hazelwood in the 1970s. But I love yo' wannabe hoodie, proper-talking ass."

"Not like I love yo' greasy, fried chicken–eating, baby back ribs cooking ass."

I cocked my head back. "What's wrong with my chicken and ribs? I thought you liked my cooking."

"Baby, I do but that shit will kill me. I can't be eating like that all the time."

"That's because I done spoiled you. You too busy eating everything else, you done forgot what good food taste like."

"Now see, you just started something. Ain't no way I'm waiting until we get to your house tonight. You need to assume the position right now, baby. Please remove the clothes."

All he had to do was ask. We got down in his office, and we were known to always start in one place and end up in another. We put the finishing touches on the boardroom's table again, and after I complained about my back pains, we went to my place and he gave me a backrub that made me feel better.

I was happier than I had been in my entire life. Jonathan agreeing to marry me was all I needed to hear. There was no one or nothing that could stand in the way of our happiness, or, at least, that was what I'd thought.

18

JONATHAN

Everything was going according to plan. My divorce from Dana was final, Britney was on the honor roll and was now in the eleventh grade. Sylvia had moved out of her place and moved in with us. As for my new secretary, Courtney, she was working out just fine.

Sylvia and I agreed to get married six months after the divorce was final, only out of respect for Dana. She took the news extremely hard, and allowing her time to heal was the least I could do. Sylvia felt the same way, and since she knew how much I loved her, she didn't have a worry in the world. Britney, though, drove her crazy with the boyfriend stuff. I told Sylvia as long as Britney brought home good grades, and she didn't bring home any babies, I was cool.

Trying to learn from my past mistakes, I took out quality time for my family. I scheduled no appointments on Fridays and left the office by noon. Before Britney got out of school, Sylvia and I had quiet time alone and we always planned a dinner or movie for later on that day.

Sylvia, being excellent with children, spent most of her time doing volunteer work during the week. She finally broke down and told me she couldn't have children, but that was all right with me. Britney was enough for us, and since I wasn't getting any younger, I really didn't trip.

On Monday, Courtney called the office and told me she caught a flat tire and was running late. I offered to help, since it was raining outside, and she told me where to find her.

When I arrived, she was in the car, as the rain heavily poured down. I got out of my car to help, and she held the umbrella over both of our heads as I squatted down to change her tire.

When the umbrella blew up, the rain poured and drenched both of us. After I finished, my clothes were soaked and so were hers. I told her to go home and change, then come back to work, but she implied that she lived too far away. Knowing that my house was closer, and I had to go home and change anyway, I told her she could use my dryer to dry her clothes. She followed me home, and on the way there, I called Sylvia to let her know we were on our way. She didn't answer so I hung up, and then called her cell phone and left a message.

When we got to my house, I gave Courtney a towel to dry off and walked her downstairs to the dryer so she could use it. I went to the closet to find another suit to put on and stepped out of my wet one.

As I put my suit on a hanger, so I could take it to the cleaner's later, Courtney came upstairs with the towel wrapped around her. Not even hearing her, I stood naked, as I was about to shower and change into my clean clothes.

"I'm sorry," she said, turning her head and shielding her eyes. "I didn't know you—"

"It's okay," I said, reaching for the towel on the bed and wrapping it around my waist.

"I couldn't get the dryer to start. I . . . I don't know, but maybe I'm doing something wrong."

I headed downstairs to see what was up with the dryer. Courtney followed me. It was one of those digital dryers, and after I figured out how to work it, Courtney and I went back upstairs. By the time we reached the kitchen, Sylvia came through the door. She looked at us wrapped in towels and tossed her keys on the table.

"Well, I'll be damned," she said.

I hurried to clear things up. "Did you get the message I left you?"

"What message?" she said, raising her voice. "I didn't get no damn message. What in the hell is going on here?"

Courtney looked over at me, and I quickly responded to Sylvia. "Courtney had a flat tire. I fixed it in the rain and we both got drenched. Since the house was close by, we came here so she could dry her clothes and I could change mine. I left you a message and told you exactly that."

"Well, I didn't get no message from you saying all that. Besides, she could have gone home or to the Laundromat to dry her clothes. I'm not too thrilled about seeing another woman in my house with no clothes on."

Courtney, being the passive, young twenty-seven-year-old woman she was, didn't say one word. She took a seat in the living room and waited on her clothes to dry. After taking a quick shower, I changed into another suit and grabbed my keys to go. Sylvia still had an attitude, but having a lot of work to do, Courtney and I headed back to the office.

I was at my desk in deep thought when Courtney knocked on my door and apologized for what had happened.

"What are you apologizing for? You didn't do anything wrong."

"Well, maybe I shouldn't have been walking around your house with a towel wrapped around me," she said in a soft voice. "If it were me, I would have been a little perturbed too."

"Perturbed, even if your husband or boyfriend was kind enough to call and tell you what was going down?"

"Hmmm, I don't know. But I already know Miss Sylvia doesn't play that. She doesn't like me, does she?"

"Yeah, she likes you. She just wants to make sure her replacement is good enough."

"I surely hope I am. The other day, I told my mother how much I enjoy working here. It's so peaceful and you're not difficult at all to work for. At the last law firm I worked for, those brothas were arrogant, bossy, and rude. They had no respect for anyone, especially their secretaries."

"That's a shame. Sometimes we forget where we come from and lose focus. They'll come down; trust me, they always do."

We stayed in my office for a while talking. When Sylvia barged in, I was surprised to see her. Courtney quickly got up from her seat and headed for the door to leave.

"Wait a minute, Courtney. I wasn't finished talking to you yet." Frustrated, I looked at Sylvia. "What's up, baby?"

"Nothing, I just stopped by to see you."

"You could have called and told me you were coming. There's no need for any pop-up visits."

"I don't have to call and tell you when I'm on my way. I was close by so I stopped in."

I looked at Courtney. "Courtney, would you please excuse me for a minute? We'll finish our conversation later."

Courtney spoke to Sylvia, but she didn't say a word. When Courtney walked out, Sylvia slammed the door after her. "I don't like that sneaky bitch. I don't like how she looks at me, and I do not like the way she looks at you. She is trouble, Jonathan, I'm warning you."

"You are out of your mind. You don't like her because she's young, she's attractive, and because she's capable of doing your job. I don't have time for this mess, Sylvia. She's a good employee and you are not about to scare her away because of your jealousy and insecurities."

"Please. I am not jealous of that teeny bop–ass bitch. It's just something about her that I don't like."

"Well, when you figure it out, let me know. In the meantime, I got work to do. I'll talk to you about this when I get home."

Sylvia stormed out of my office, and embarrassed by her ignorance, I called Courtney back into my office and apologized. She laughed it off and tried to convince me that that was just how some women are.

I didn't leave the office until nine o'clock that night. Courtney stayed and helped me get prepared for a $25 million lawsuit case I was working on. It was scheduled for next week, and I had put in overtime to prepare myself for it.

After I walked Courtney to her car, I headed home to face an angry woman. Sylvia wasn't one to forgive me so easily, so I was sure she was still mad at me. I was so right. As soon as I entered the bedroom, I saw her looking straight ahead at the TV, ignoring me. I showered, changed clothes, and went downstairs to tell Britney and her girlfriends to turn down the music. I then returned to our bedroom, climbed in bed, and pulled the covers over me. Sylvia snatched the covers off, and playfully hit me in the head with the newspaper.

"You'd better not be fucking her," she said, smiling. "If you even think about it, I am going to cut off your dick."

"Damn, I can't even think about it?"

"Hell, no."

"Not even a little bit?"

"I said no."

"But I'm a man, baby. Sex always crosses our minds."

"That's what you have me for."

"I'm tired of thinking about you," I said, pulling the cover back over me.

She snatched it back off. "You better not be tired. One thing I can't stand is a tired-ass, lazy man who's too tired to come home and make love to his woman. If you're too tired for that, then something's got to give."

"I'm never, ever, ever too tired for my woman. She just better find a way to trust me a little better and soon."

"I know, baby, but I don't know what is wrong with me. More so, I think I don't trust the women who surround you."

"There's no way for me to keep women from being around me. You're going to have to find a way to let go of whatever it is that's bothering you. That's all."

Sylvia and I talked so much that we didn't have time to even get down like we planned to. By morning, she was knocked out and I was almost too tired to go to work. Knowing what was ahead of me, I got dressed and headed to the office.

Courtney stood at my door with my coffee mug in her hand. She was full of energy and was ready to get started. She had pepped me up for the day, and we worked so hard that when lunchtime came, I invited her to go to lunch with me at CJ's.

We stayed at CJ's for about an hour or so and talked. Throughout lunch, I noticed her not being able to look at me, so I questioned her about it.

"You know, as a lawyer, I read a lot into people when I'm speaking to them. Is there something about me that bothers you?"

She smiled. "No," she said softly. "I just enjoy working for you, that's all."

"Are you sure? I think you're awesome, and I couldn't have found a better replacement for Sylvia."

"Are you aware that you compare me to her a lot? It doesn't bother me, but I am my own woman, you know."

"No, I wasn't aware of that, and nobody likes to be compared to anybody, good or bad. So I promise you, I'll watch it."

She smiled again and played around with the food on her plate. When I asked the waiter to bring me the check, Courtney laid down her fork and reached into her purse. She pulled out an envelope and slid it over to me. "I . . . I picked that up for you while I was at the store yesterday."

"Thank you," I said, opening the envelope and pulling out the card. It was a "thinking of you" card and the words that were written inside were so personal. She signed her first name, and after I finished reading the card I closed it.

"Was this your way of telling me you're feeling something for me?"

She let out a chuckle. "I don't know what I'm feeling, and I do not want my feelings to interfere with my job, but I wanted you to know how much I admire you."

I had been there and definitely done this before. Never in my wildest dream did I think I would be headed down the exact same path with another secretary. "Courtney, I'm flattered, but I have a woman whom I love dearly. We've been through a lot to get to this point, and if you think your personal feelings are going to interfere with your work here, let me know so I can make some other arrangements."

"I knew I shouldn't have told you, but I don't hide my feelings too well. I can tell how much you love Sylvia and I would never interfere with what you and she have."

"Thank you," I said, getting up from the table. I paid for lunch, and Courtney and I went back to work.

The following week was crazy, as I had expected it to be. I worked until nine, ten, and sometimes until eleven o'clock at night. Needing all the help I could get, some nights Courtney stayed with me and some nights she didn't. I wasn't trying to put her on overload, especially since she'd revealed her feelings for me, but it was strictly business for me and nothing else.

Sylvia kept me excited about our relationship, and she seemed pleased with me too. She complained a little about the late hours and still seemed jealous about Courtney staying late nights with me. I wanted to tell her about Courtney's feelings for me, but I didn't want to bring about more drama. Sylvia would definitely want me to find another secretary, but as good as Courtney was to me, I didn't want to let her go. Then maybe again, I should have.

19

SYLVIA

I sometimes knew another woman's motive even better than my own. Courtney wanted my man and she wanted him bad. Every time I confronted Jonathan about it, he insisted I was out of my mind. If not that, he'd change the subject and say, "She's just a young woman who's excited about moving forward with a rewarding career." That was bullshit and he knew it. I let it be known that I knew what the trick was up to. Earlier in the week, when I went to the office, I pulled her aside and told her I was keeping my eyes on her. I didn't care if she told Jonathan, but I made sure she heard me out.

He didn't know it, but I watched him leave the office with her several times. I had to make sure that nothing was going down. I remembered what we used to do on his late nights at the office and I feared he was doing the same thing with her.

As for trusting him, that bullshit went out the window months ago. I didn't trust no damn body—never had and never would. If the opportunity ever presented itself, and he and I were on bad terms, I knew Jonathan would fuck Courtney in a heartbeat.

Worried about all the long hours he put in at work, on Thursday, I called his office to see if he wanted to have lunch. His voicemail came on, and instead of leaving a message, I went to the office.

Courtney wasn't at her desk and Jonathan's door was locked. I had a key, so I let myself in. I closed the door and sat at his desk. Being nosy, I looked through his drawers and glanced at the phone numbers in his Rolodex. When I saw Crissy's number, I reached for the phone to call her, since we hadn't talked in a while. Underneath his phone were two envelopes. I picked them up, and when I pulled out the cards from inside, they were both from Courtney. In so many words, this bitch told him how much she thought about him. The words just ate at me:

You brighten my day and bring joy to my life. You're everything I imagined you would be.

What kind of shit was this? I thought. If he wasn't fucking her, he knew damn well that she wanted to fuck him. And then to play me like I was the fool and tell me I was out of my mind—no way.

I looked at his calendar and it showed he was at the courthouse. Room 325 to be exact. As furious as I was, I jotted down the room number and left to go confront him.

Before getting there, I tried to calm down, but when I looked in and saw Courtney sitting in the courtroom, I lost it. He never took me to court with him and had the nerve to flaunt her around like she was the shit.

When I barged in, he was standing and presenting his case. I interrupted him, as calmly as I could, and told him we needed to talk. Getting all bent out of shape, he raised his voice.

"Have a seat until I'm finished," he snapped. "I'm in the middle of something."

"Now, Jonathan," I said, raising my voice back at him.

He excused himself and stormed out into the lobby. I followed.

"This better be damn good, Sylvia! What in the hell is it now?" he yelled. I was sure everyone in the courtroom heard us because he spoke loudly and so did I.

I pulled the cards from my purse and shook them in my hand. "This is how you fucking play me! You're around here fucking this bitch, sporting her all over the place, and allowing her to give you cards! Did you think I wasn't going to find out?"

He snatched the cards and shoved me backward. "That's it! I can't do this with you anymore! I cannot do this anymore," he screamed. "You have lost your damn mind!"

He stormed back into the courtroom, and still not feeling satisfied, I charged in after him. "I've lost my mind and you're the motherfucker out here cheating on me? Really?"

He quickly swung around, and before I knew it, Jonathan smacked me so hard that my head snapped to the side, without me turning it. Shortly after, the police rushed to handcuff him. He tussled with them as they carried him away.

Mad as hell at him, I didn't even give a damn that he was going to jail. The people in the courtroom appeared shocked, and after the police took a statement from me, I left.

I waited outside until I saw his bitch, then I confronted her. When she saw me, she appeared nervous and walked abruptly to her car.

"Are you satisfied now? Was all of this worth it to you?" I said, walking behind her.

She stopped and turned around. "I barely even know you, Sylvia, but please tell me what you have against me?"

"Your cards, Miss Thing. Why in the hell are you giving my man 'thinking of you' cards? Is it that good to you where you gotta go out and buy him cards?"

She looked surprised that I had known about the cards. "Look, I'm not going to deny the cards, but Mr. Taylor made it clear to me that he loves you. You are so wrong accusing us of being together because we're not. I'm sorry for giving him those cards, but you should be ashamed of yourself for embarrassing him like that."

"Girl, who do you think you're talking to? You know damn well that you're having sex with him. Don't stand out here and try to protect him. Let's just get it all out in the open."

"If I were having sex with him, I would have the pleasure of telling you right now. For the last time, Mr. Taylor is not interested in me, nor has he ever been interested in me in such a way. Just face it, stupid-ass woman, that you are wrong." She turned and walked away.

"Who in the hell are you calling stupid, you nappy-head bitch!" I yelled. "If I didn't want to go to jail, I would kick your tail for starting this mess!"

Courtney just shook her head and continued to walk down the street. I got in my car, and by the time I pulled up in the driveway, I was a mess. Just what if Jonathan hadn't done anything? What a fool I'd made of myself? I couldn't believe how foolish I'd acted, and no matter what went down, I never imagined I could stoop so low.

Eager to get to the bottom of this, I called the police station around eight o'clock. The officer said Jonathan had already been released. I waited and waited for him to come home, but by one o'clock in the morning he was still a no-show.

Knowing exactly where he was when he needed to clear his head, I went straight to his office. When I pulled into the parking garage, Courtney's car was there and so was his. My heart raced fast, as I pushed the eleventh floor on the elevator. It wasn't moving fast enough, and I tapped my foot as I counted the floors on the way up. When I got off the elevator, I pushed the doors to the entryway but they were locked. I shook them, but when they wouldn't open, I ran to the other end of the building and used my swipe card to get in. I swiped it, and as soon as the light turned green, I pulled the door open.

Jonathan's office was on the other side of the building, so I hurried as fast as I could to get to it. Getting near, I could see his door was closed. I reached for my key to open it because I was sure it was locked from the inside. After I nervously fumbled around with the keys, I slid the key in the lock and turned the knob. Taking a deep breath, I pushed the door open and saw Courtney standing by Jonathan half dressed, with only her bra and skirt on. He was shirtless.

He jumped up from his chair, and having a loss for words, I ran out of the door. He yelled my name, but I just kept on running. By the time I got to the front doors, I remembered that they were locked. Jonathan rushed up behind me, so I kicked the door several times, trying to get out. A few pieces of the glass shattered, but the door wouldn't come open.

"Stop it!" he yelled, then held me tightly from behind. I screamed and kicked the doors harder.

"Let me go gotdamn it! Let me go!"

He squeezed me tighter until I could barely move. Exhausted from the bullshit, I broke down and fell to my knees. He still had a tight grip on me and fell to the ground with me. "Why?" I screamed out. "Why did you do this to me?"

"Because this is what you wanted," he said, calmly. "You were just not satisfied with me doing the right thing, so I was giving you the man you envisioned me to be."

Jonathan released his arms from around me and walked off. Feeling as if the whole world had caved down on me, I stayed on my knees by the door and hysterically cried.

Moments later, I heard a door shut and I figured Jonathan and Courtney must have left. Still numb, I couldn't move. When I did, I drove to the nearest hotel and got a room for the night. Seeing what a mess I was, the front desk clerk asked if I needed some help. I shook my head and walked to the room as if I were a zombie.

20

JONATHAN

Early Friday morning, Judge Mayfield broke the news to me. My $25 million case had been dismissed and he said I had been a disgrace to his courtroom. Never in all my life had I been referred to as a disgrace, and I was crushed to even have such a reputation.

Sylvia had ruined my life. Everybody I worked with knew about what had happened in the courtroom, and Britney wasn't even speaking to me. When I told her what happened last night, she had the nerve to tell me I was wrong. Now, how in the hell was I wrong? I had been nothing but good to Sylvia. Having sex with Courtney was never in my plans, but after the courtroom incident, I had to give Sylvia what she wanted. I felt like if I'd gotten blamed for something, then I might as well have done it. I hated to put Courtney in such a fucked-up situation, but I was so angry with Sylvia that I couldn't help myself.

I was glad that Sylvia interrupted us in the nick of time because it was wrong of me to use Courtney, knowing how she felt about me. And, still knowing that, I decided to let her go. She wasn't angry with me, and she even agreed it was for the best. I gave her six months' salary to help her out until she found another job.

Sylvia stayed away for the entire weekend. As furious as I still was, I didn't even care. I had no idea where she was, and when Britney inquired about her, all I did was shrug my shoulders.

"What's wrong with you?" she asked. "You act like you don't care."

"That's because I don't."

"So, it's like that? What if she's dead or something?"

"She's not dead, Britney. She just likes to play games sometimes."

"Well, I hope nothing has happened to her. It's not like her not to even call me."

"She'll call," I said, continuing to watch the football game and not really wanting to talk about it.

For almost two weeks, I didn't hear from Sylvia. On a Saturday morning, she strolled into the kitchen as if nothing had happened. She walked right past me as I sat at the kitchen table reading the newspaper.

I closed the newspaper, went into the bedroom, and watched as she pulled her clothes from the closet and laid them on the bed.

"Are you leaving?" I asked.

"What does it look like?"

"So, you don't even want to talk about this?"

"No, I really don't."

"Suit yourself."

I went into the living room and sat on the couch. Britney woke up, and when she saw Sylvia gathering her things to leave, she yelled and begged me to stop her.

"No. If she wants to leave then let her leave. I'm not going through this shit again, Britney, and if you want to leave with her, feel free."

Not wanting to be around, I put on my gray jogging suit and left the house. I went to the YMCA and ran around the indoor track until I couldn't run anymore. There were some fellas playing basketball so I started to hoop with them. I had so much fun that the time just got away from me. When I glanced at my watch, it was already four o'clock in the afternoon. I had dinner by myself at the Macaroni Grill then I went back home. Thinking that Sylvia and Britney were both gone, surprisingly, when I entered the bedroom, Britney lay across my bed and had fallen asleep. I nudged her shoulder and she woke up. She rubbed her eyes and slowly sat up. By the redness in them, I could tell she'd been crying.

"I've been calling you," she said. "Where have you been?"

"I didn't have my phone with me. It's on top of the refrigerator."

"Daddy, when is this going to stop? Everybody I care about always leaves me."

"Britney, that is not so. I have always been here for you, and I am always going to be here."

"But I begged Sylvia to stay. She didn't even listen to me."

"Don't take it personal. Sylvia did what she thought was best. Now, you and I got to work hard at restoring our own relationship and continue to be there for each other. I thought you were going to leave me today. That hurt me more than any woman walking out on me."

Britney wrapped her arms around me. "I'm sorry if you felt that way, but I never said I was going anywhere. You are stuck with me forever. That's until I go to law school. And I'm still going to be running back home to see you."

"I'm pleased to hear that," I said, hugging her back. "Now, go get in your bed so I can get some rest. I got a lot on my mind and I need to chill."

Britney go off my bed and headed for the door. Before she walked out, she turned to look at me. "Daddy, do you ever cry about anything? Don't sometimes you just want to break down and get it all off your chest? With all that you've been through with Mama, Dana, and now Sylvia, I don't understand how you stay so strong."

"I do cry, baby girl, but you never see me. Besides, it's not appropriate for a daughter to see her father cry."

"Says who?" Britney said, walking up and giving me a kiss on the cheek.

"Says me. Now, get your butt out of here so I can get some rest. I have a long week ahead of me."

Britney left, and before I went to bed, I took a long hot bath. I wanted to cry, but couldn't, as I thought about what happened between Sylvia and me. I still loved her so much, but if anything, I knew that things between us had moved too fast. Pushing forward without her was going to be difficult for me, but under the circumstances, I had to do what was necessary to stabilize my life.

21

SYLVIA

After Crissy told me Jonathan let Courtney go, she later brought me a letter that Courtney had given to her to pass on to me. In the letter, Courtney explained to me what a fool I'd been for not trusting Jonathan. She asked me what I'd asked Dana over and over again. That was, how in the hell did I let a good man get away? She confirmed her love for Jonathan and asked me why it was wrong for her to feel exactly the way I did when I was his secretary. In closure, she thanked me for interrupting them at the right time, and wished me well.

I ripped up the letter, and already feeling bad for messing up things between us, I couldn't keep my emotions intact. I at least had Crissy's shoulder to cry on, and for the time being, she let me stay in one of her rental apartments until I decided what to do.

Knowing that I was anxious to leave town and move elsewhere for a fresh new start, she arranged a job for me in Atlanta, working for her uncle at Duncan's Computers. She insisted that I would love it, and since the position paid more money than I'd ever made before, I knew it was in my best interest to go.

I made Crissy promise not to tell anyone about my plans to leave, and by Friday night, I was packed and ready to go. My plane wasn't leaving until Saturday morning, but I wanted to make sure everything was in order. I had so much shit that I had to put some things in storage. Crissy said she would have them sent to me as soon as I got settled.

Becoming one of the best friends I'd ever had, Crissy hooked up everything for me. And even though she hated to see me go, she knew it was best for Jonathan and me both that I did.

At Lambert Airport, I unloaded my bags and checked them in. I had about a two-hour wait, so I went to a tiny restaurant to grab some breakfast and chill. I thought about calling Jonathan and Britney to say good-bye, but I decided not to. I knew Britney would question me, and she would never understand why I needed to move away. And Jonathan, after all we'd been through, maybe, the least I could do was call him and say good-bye.

Thinking hard about it, I pulled out my cell phone and dialed his number. I quickly hung up only to dial it again. When I listened to it ring, I heard another cell phone behind me ringing. I hung up and dialed his number again. When I heard the cell phone behind me again, I quickly turned around. He was leaned against a pole behind me with a stern look on his face, looking awesome. Cleanly dressed in a navy blue suit and wearing a long trench coat, my heart melted. I turned back around and smiled so he wouldn't know how excited I was to see him. He came over and sat at the table with me.

"I was wondering when you were going to call. I knew you were, but I tried to be patient," he said. I looked at him and dropped my head, as my eyes started to water. "None of that," he said, raising my chin.

I swallowed. "I . . . I can't help it. Do you even know what it feels like when you know that you lost out on a good thing? I could kill myself, Jonathan, for what I put you through."

"Hurting from a loss is kind of like what I'm feeling right now. And don't go blaming yourself because I made some mistakes too. I should have told you about Courtney's feelings up front, but I didn't."

"Well, you didn't because I was always acting a damn fool. I should have just trusted you when you asked me to."

"Yeah, you should have, but, it . . . it's—"

"It's not worth it anymore, is it? As much as I want to throw away this plane ticket, and stay here in St. Louis to be with you, you won't let me, will you?"

Jonathan shook his head, and then placed his hand on top of mine. "You need to . . . we need to move on. I have not stopped loving you not one bit, but we could never be together after what we've been through."

I was hurt by his words and didn't even want to respond. I knew Jonathan was right, but I still had a tough time letting go. "So, will you and Britney come see me sometimes?"

"Of course. And only if you promise to come visit us as well."

"I will. I wish you would have brought Britney with you so I could have said good-bye to her."

"I wanted to, but I knew what a tough time she'd have seeing you leave."

"Yeah, you're right. But you be sure to tell her I love her and I'll call her every day so we can talk. And speaking of talking, have you heard from Dana?"

"Every once in a while, I do. She's got a new boyfriend and they're doing fine. Actually, I met him several weeks ago. I didn't tell you because I didn't know how—"

"How I would react, right?"

"Right."

"I really made a fool of myself, didn't I?"

Jonathan smiled, showing his pearly white teeth. "You don't want me to answer that, do you?"

I shook my head and laughed.

We talked for a while longer. He said he wasn't going to hire a new secretary, and if he did, he said it would be awhile. I asked him if he intended on dating again, and he said being in another relationship was the last thing on his mind. When I told him what a lucky woman she would be, he just smiled.

The announcement of my plane's departure came over loud and clear. I stood up and so did Jonathan.

"Do you have everything?" he asked.

"Just about," I said with so many regrets as I reached inside of my purse for my boarding pass. I pulled it out. "There it is."

"Let me walk you to your gate. I don't think they'll let me go that far, but I'll go with you as far as I can."

Jonathan took my hand, and when security stopped us and asked for our boarding passes, I showed him mine. Unfortunately, that was the farthest Jonathan could go. He kissed the back of my hand, and knowing that he was hurting just as much as I was, again, I asked him if he wanted me to stay.

"Baby, all you have to do is say the word," I said with tears in my eyes. "I will say to hell with Atlanta and spend the rest of my life with you. From now own, I promise I'll trust you."

I saw him swallow the lump in his throat, and even his eyes filled with water. He blinked them fast and shook his head. "Go, please. I promise you we'll keep in touch."

"But that's not good enough. I want to be with you." I reached up and grabbed the back of his head. When I pulled him forward to kiss me, he gave me a quick peck on the lips and backed away.

"Go ahead, baby, please. I don't want you to miss your flight."

I hurt all over as I departed from him and walked through the security gates. I didn't even bother to turn around because the tears poured so quickly down my face, I could barely see. I could feel Jonathan still watching me and silently prayed for a miracle to happen and happen fast. By the time I got on the plane, I looked around in hopes of seeing him, but that didn't happen either. When the plane lifted off the ground and headed for Atlanta, it finally sank in that our relationship was over.

I gazed out of the window, trying to figure out when, why, and where our relationship had gone so wrong. Trust was the key factor to having a successful marriage, but for whatever reason, I just didn't have it. I guessed knowing how he was sexually involved with Dana and me during the same time might have had something to do with it, but who knew? I also thought about how I damn near forced him to marry me. I should have known better, as forcing a man to do something he wasn't ready for was a big mistake.

Either way, there was no doubt that Jonathan's love for himself prevailed over his love for me. At any cost, he was determined to be happy, and as much drama as I brought about, he'd made his choice. I was in no way upset with him for deciding to move on; after all, it was my stupidity that cost me the man I still loved more than life itself. Whatever the reasons were for us being apart, I had to face it head-on and figure out a way to start a new

life without Jonathan Taylor. I had faith that I'd be able
to have a fulfilling life without him, and regardless of how
much I still loved him, I definitely had to make this move
and discover who or what I truly wanted going forward.
I smiled from the thought, knowing deep inside that I,
Sylvia McMillan, would be okay.

ORDER FORM
URBAN BOOKS, LLC
97 N18th Street
Wyandanch, NY 11798

Name (please print):_____

Address: _____

City/State: _____

Zip: _____

QTY	TITLES	PRICE

Shipping and handling: add $3.50 for 1st book, then $1.75 for each additional book.
Please send a check payable to:
  Urban Books, LLC
Please allow 4-6 weeks for delivery

ORDER FORM
URBAN BOOKS, LLC
97 N18th Street
Wyandanch, NY 11798

Name (please print):_____

Address: _____

City/State: _____

Zip: _____

QTY	TITLES	PRICE
	16 On The Block	$14.95
	A Girl From Flint	$14.95
	A Pimp's Life	$14.95
	Baby Momma	$14.95
	Baby Momma 2	$14.95
	Baby Momma 3	$14.95
	Bi-Curious	$14.95
	Bi-Curious 2: Life After Sadie	$14.95
	Bi-Curious 3: Trapped	$14.95
	Both Sides Of The Fence	$14.95
	Both Sides Of The Fence 2	$14.95
	California Connection	$14.95

Shipping and handling: add $3.50 for 1st book, then $1.75 for each additional book.
Please send a check payable to:
Urban Books, LLC
Please allow 4-6 weeks for delivery

ORDER FORM
URBAN BOOKS, LLC
97 N18th Street
Wyandanch, NY 11798

Name (please print):_____

Address: _____

City/State: _____

Zip: _____

QTY	TITLES	PRICE
	California Connection 2	$14.95
	Cheesecake And Teardrops	$14.95
	Congratulations	$14.95
	Crazy In Love	$14.95
	Cyber Case	$14.95
	Denim Diaries	$14.95
	Diary Of A Mad First Lady	$14.95
	Diary Of A Stalker	$14.95
	Diary Of A Street Diva	$14.95
	Diary Of A Young Girl	$14.95
	Dirty Money	$14.95
	Dirty To The Grave	$14.95

Shipping and handling: add $3.50 for 1st book, then $1.75 for each additional book.
Please send a check payable to:
Urban Books, LLC
Please allow 4-6 weeks for delivery

ORDER FORM
URBAN BOOKS, LLC
97 N18th Street
Wyandanch, NY 11798

Name (please print):_____

Address: _____

City/State: _____

Zip: _____

QTY	TITLES	PRICE
	Gunz And Roses	$14.95
	Happily Ever Now	$14.95
	Hell Has No Fury	$14.95
	Hush	$14.95
	If It Isn't love	$14.95
	Kiss Kiss Bang Bang	$14.95
	Last Breath	$14.95
	Little Black Girl Lost	$14.95
	Little Black Girl Lost 2	$14.95
	Little Black Girl Lost 3	$14.95
	Little Black Girl Lost 4	$14.95
	Little Black Girl Lost 5	$14.95

Shipping and handling: add $3.50 for 1st book, then $1.75 for each additional book.
Please send a check payable to:
Urban Books, LLC
Please allow 4-6 weeks for delivery

ORDER FORM
URBAN BOOKS, LLC
97 N18th Street
Wyandanch, NY 11798

Name (please print):_____

Address: _____

City/State: _____

Zip: _____

QTY	TITLES	PRICE
	Spoil Rotten	$14.95
	Supreme Clientele	$14.95
	The Cartel	$14.95
	The Cartel 2	$14.95
	The Cartel 3	$14.95
	The Dopefiend	$14.95
	The Dopeman Wife	$14.95
	The Prada Plan	$14.95
	The Prada Plan 2	$14.95
	Where There Is Smoke	$14.95
	Where There Is Smoke 2	$14.95

Shipping and handling: add $3.50 for 1st book, then $1.75 for each additional book.
Please send a check payable to:
   Urban Books, LLC
Please allow 4-6 weeks for delivery